LOST KINGS MC #7

WHITE
Knuckles

FAITH IS STRONGER THAN FEAR.

AUTUMN JONES LAKE

Faith is stronger than fear.

TWO TATTERED SOULS

After countless detours, Wrath and Trinity's wedding is only ten days away. Together they've battled their demons and are ready to declare their commitment to each other in front of their entire Lost Kings MC family.

ONE BITTER ENEMY

No one is prepared for the threat that crawls out of the shadows and issues an evil ultimatum. One that places Trinity's future in danger and jeopardizes the entire club. Trinity's more than ready to put her life on the line to save the club. For her it's not a question.

AN IMPOSSIBLE CHOICE

Wrath's role as protector of the club forces him to choose between the safety of his angel or the future of the Lost Kings MC and all they've built together. But Trinity won't relent. A queen always fights for her king. She'll risk everything to hold on to the love she shares with Wrath.

FAITH IS STRONGER THAN FEAR

When evil takes her for a ride, will Trinity's faith in Wrath and her faith in the Lost Kings MC be stronger than her fear?

White Knuckles is the seventh full-length novel in Autumn Jones Lake's popular Lost Kings MC series. It is suggested readers have at least read books four through six in the series before reading White Knuckles.

COPYRIGHT
WHITE KNUCKLES (LOST KINGS MC #7)
by Autumn Jones Lake

Copyright © 2017 – All Rights Reserved.
Print Edition

Digital ISBN: 978-1-943950-12-6
Paperback ISBN: 978-1-943950-13-3

Edited by: Vanessa Bridges, PREMA
Edited by: Tricia Harden and Jessica Descent
Proofread by: Sue Banner
Cover Design: Letitia Hasser, RBA Designs
Cover Photo: Wander Aguiar Photography
Cover Models: Jamie Walker & Tiffany Marie

ACKNOWLEDGMENTS

First, thank you to my readers. Your love of my characters, continued support, and eagerness for each new book continues to amaze, humble and inspire me. Thank you.

My critique partners, Cara Connelly, Kari W. Cole, and Virginia Frost, I don't think you were able to see a lot of White Knuckles—here it is! Be kind.

Thank you to Cara and K.A. Mitchell for helping me nail the blurb!

Clarisse, Elizabeth, Amanda, Tamra, Shelly, Angi J., Iveta, and Robin thank you for sticking with me for another Wrath and Trinity book!

Belinda, thank you for jumping on board and giving me your early assessment of White Knuckles!

Andrea De Palma Florkowski, thank you for looking over White Knuckles and letting me pester you with follow-up questions.

Sue, thank you for being so awesome.

Jezzie, thank you for taking one final look.

Vanessa Bridges, thank you for *everything*.

Becky, I'm so happy you finally know my deep, dark secret and I'm thrilled you love the Lost Kings too!

Iza, aka Mistress Ramsey, thank you for always cheering me on and being such a calming, positive force of nature.

My Lost Kings MC Ladies Facebook group, thank you so much for being there. There are now over 1,000 of you and it blows my mind. Thank you for loving the Lost Kings so much. Your questions and theories fuel me and your demand for the next book keeps me motivated. And of course the hot man pics Sammi provides every Wednesday are pretty awesome too! Thanks, ladies!

Mr. Lake—my own personal demon-slayer and biggest fan. I'd be lost without you.

Dedication

If you've found the one whose demons play nice with yours,
then this is for you.

GLOSSARY

I've only made a few changes to this glossary since publishing More Than Miles…but you may find some interesting information here.

The Lost Kings MC Organizational Structure

President: *Rochlan "Rock" North.* Leader of the Upstate NY charter of the Lost Kings MC. His word is law within the club. He takes advice from senior club members. He is the public "face" of the MC. Much to his annoyance, Rock is seen as the "father figure" in the club, especially by the younger members.

Sergeant-at-Arms: *Wyatt "Wrath" Ramsey.* Responsible for the security of the club. Keeps order at club events. Responsible for the safety and protection of the president, the club, its members and its women. Disciplines club members who violate the rules. Keeps track of club by-laws. In charge of the club's weapons and weapons training. Will challenge Rock when he deems it necessary. Outside of the MC, Wrath owns a gym, Furious Fitness. He is experienced in underground MMA-style fighting.

Vice President: *Angus "Zero" or "Z" Frazier.* In most clubs, I think the VP would be considered the second-in-command. In mine, I see the VP and SAA as being on equal footing within the club. Carries out the orders of the President. Communicates with other chapters of the club. Assumes the responsibilities of the President in his absence. Keeps records of club patches and colors issued. Z also co-manages the MC's strip club, Crystal Ball.

Treasurer: *Marcel "Teller" Whelan.* Keeps records of income, expenses and investments.

Road Captain: *Blake "Murphy" O'Callaghan.* Responsible for researching, planning and organizing club runs. Responsible for obtaining and maintaining club vehicles.

Prospect: A prospect is someone who has stated a clear intention of being a full patch member of the Lost Kings MC. The Lost Kings vet their prospects for two or more years. To vote a prospect in as a full patch member, the vote must be unanimous. Not all prospects will become full patch members. Some will realize the club is not for them. For others, the club will realize that the prospect is not a good fit for the club. Prospects are expected to show respect to all full patch members and do whatever is asked of them.

The Lost Kings MC currently has one prospect that we know of, Twitch, who was brought into the club by Wrath.

Other members

Cronin "Sparky" Petek: Sparky is the mad genius behind the Lost Kings MC's pot-growing business. He is rarely seen outside of the basement, as he prefers the company of his plants.

Elias "Bricks" Serrano: We saw Bricks and his girlfriend Winter in *Slow Burn, Corrupting Cinderella, and Tattered on my Sleeve.* One of the few members who does not live at the clubhouse, he performs a lot of general tasks for the club.

Dixon "Dex" Watts: We've also seen Dex throughout the series and gotten to know him better in *Strength From Loyalty (Lost Kings MC #3).* He co-manages Crystal Ball.

Sam "Stash" Black: Lives in the basement with Sparky and helps with the plants. We got to know him a little bit in *Tattered on My Sleeve (Lost Kings MC #4).* Otherwise, we're not really sure what he's up to downstairs.

Thomas "Ravage" Kane: We got to know him a little better in *Tattered on My Sleeve.* Ravage is a general member who helps out wherever he is needed.

The Lost Kings MC Ladies

Hope Kendall, Esq.: Nick-named *First Lady* by Murphy in *Corrupting Cinderella (Lost Kings MC #2)*, Hope is the object of Rock's love and obsession. Their epic love story spans four books: *Slow Burn, Corrupting Cinderella, Strength From Loyalty*, and *White Heat*.

Trinity Hurst: Caretaker of the Lost Kings MC clubhouse and the brothers. She and Wrath have a long, tattered love story full of lust, fury, and forgiveness in *Tattered on My Sleeve (Lost Kings MC #4)*. She and Wrath are also featured in *White Heat (Lost Kings MC #5)*.

Heidi Whelan: Teller's little sister. You have seen glimpses of Heidi through *Corrupting Cinderella, Strength From Loyalty, Tattered on My Sleeve*, and *White Heat*. She is also featured in a short story in *Three Kings, One Night (Lost Kings MC #2.5)* and *Between Embers (Lost Kings MC #5.5)*.

Lilly Volkov: One of Hope's best friends and frequent "booty call" of Z. You've met her in *Slow Burn, Corrupting Cinderella, Strength From Loyalty, Tattered on My Sleeve, White Heat* and two short stories, "Z and Lilly" in *Three Kings, One Night*. We last "saw" her in *Between Embers (Lost Kings MC #5.5)*

Mara Oak: Friend of Hope. Also an attorney. She's appeared in *Slow Burn, Corrupting Cinderella, Strength From Loyalty, Tattered on My Sleeve*, and *White Heat*. She's married to Empire city court judge, Damon Oak. Their story, *Objection*, will be available one day.

Lost Kings MC Terminology

Crystal Ball – The strip club owned by the Lost Kings MC and one of their legitimate businesses. They often refer to it as "CB."

"Conference Center" – The clubhouse of the Lost Kings MC. It was previously used as a high-end religious retreat and is sometimes still jokingly referred to as the "Conference Center" or "Hippie Compound."

Empire – The fictional city in Upstate NY, run by the Lost Kings.

Furious Fitness – The gym Wrath owns. Often just referred to as "Furious."

Green Street Crew – Street gang the Lost Kings do business with. Often referred to as "GSC." "Loco" is their leader and frequent nuisance to Rock.

LOKI – Short for Lost Kings.

Vipers MC – Rival and frequent enemy MC. Run Ironworks which borders the Lost Kings' territory. Their president, Ransom, and his SAA, Killa, appeared in *Tattered on My Sleeve* and *White Heat*.

Wolf Knights MC – Rival and sometimes ally of the Lost Kings. Their president, Ulfric, appeared in *Slow Burn*. Their SAA, Whisper, is a partner in Wrath's gym and appeared in *Tattered on My Sleeve* as well as *Slow Burn*. Actions taken by the Wolf Knights have had a serious impact on the Lost Kings in recent times.

Other MC Terminology

Most terminology was obtained through research. However, I have also used some artistic license in applying these terms to my romanticized, fictional version of an Outlaw Motorcycle Club.

Cage – A car, truck, van, basically anything other than a motorcycle.

Church – Club meetings all full patch members must attend. Led by the president of the club, but officers will update the members on the areas they oversee.

Citizen – Anyone not a hardcore biker or belonging to an outlaw club. "Citizen Wife" would refer to a spouse kept entirely separate from the club.

Cut – Leather vest worn by outlaw bikers. Adorned with patches and artwork displaying the club's unique colors. The Lost Kings' colors are blue and gray. Their logo is a skull with a crown.

Colors – The "uniform" of an outlaw motorcycle gang. A leather vest, with the three-piece club patch on the back, and various other patches relating to their role in the club. Colors belong to the club and are held sacred by all members.

Dressers – Slang for a motorcycle "dressed up" with hard saddle bags and other accessories. It's designed for long-distance riding.

Fly Colors – To ride on a motorcycle wearing colors.

Mother Chapter – First chapter of the club.

Muffler Bunny – Club girl, who hangs around to provide sexual favors to members.

Nomad – A club member who does not belong to any specific charter, yet has privileges in all charters. Nomads go anywhere to take care of business, usually at the request of the club president.

Old Lady/Ol' Lady – Wife or steady girlfriend of a club member. Has nothing to do with her age.

Out Bad – The shorthand way of saying a club member has been kicked out of the club for some kind of betrayal. Someone who is "out bad" might be in hiding from the club.

Patched In – When a new member is approved for full membership.

Patch Holder – A member who has been vetted through performing duties for the club as a prospect or probate and has earned his three-piece patch.

Property Patch – When a member takes a woman as his Old Lady (wife status), he gives her a vest with a property patch. In my series, the vest has a "Property of Lost Kings MC" patch and the member's road name on the back. The officers also place their patches on the ol' lady's vest as a sign they have agreed to always have her back. Her man's patch or club symbol is placed over the heart.

Road Name – Nickname. Usually given by the other members.

RUB – Slang for Rich Urban Biker. A term generally used by real bikers to describe a person who rides an expensive motorcycle on weekends and never very far. A poser.

Run – A club sanctioned outing sometimes with other chapters and/or clubs. Can also refer to a club business run.

CHAPTER ONE

Ten days before the wedding...

WRATH

"**S**INCE I CAN'T see the wedding dress, show me the wedding underwear."

Trinity flashes a wicked smile at me, not at all fooled by my effort to get her naked. "Who says I'm planning to wear underwear?"

As always, her husky voice goes straight to my groin. "Get over here."

She knows damn well as soon as she's within grabbing distance I'm yanking her on top of me, so she takes her time crossing the room. "Honestly, what I'm planning to wear isn't all that sexy."

"Babe, you could wrap some duct tape around your tits and still be the hottest fucking woman I've ever seen."

"You're such a sweet-talker this morning."

"Just trying to be helpful. You need to know if it fits, right?"

This time she levels a sterner look my way. "Are you saying I'm fat?"

She's fucking with me. Trinity doesn't waste energy worrying about stuff like that. "No. Now get over here. Don't make me ask again."

Instead of getting the fuck over here, she teases me by pawing through the bag she claims has all sorts of lacy goods in it.

"Hmmm…this? Or this?" she asks, holding up two tiny scraps in the air.

"You pick."

"Close your eyes. It's not as exciting if you watch me wriggle into it."

"Oh, trust me, it is." I don't even pretend to close my eyes, so she turns around. "Even better, you have the most perfect ass."

She heaves out a dramatic sigh and bends over, giving me an eyeful. I'm not even sure what the hell she's putting on. Some sort of bra top. White lace cups barely hide her breasts. The rest of the material is completely see-through. A bunch of sexy strings wrap around her ribcage down to a tiny thong made up of more sheer material and thin straps. She turns and raises an eyebrow, seeking my approval.

"Hot. Now get over here."

Her hands fiddle with the laces around her midsection. "You're the one who's hot. All half-naked and sexy first thing in the morning."

I stretch out, tucking my hands under my head to give her a better view. The way she runs her gaze over my body—fuck, I can't even explain what it does to me. What *she* does to me.

When she's close enough, I grab her arm and pull her down onto the bed. "Stop messing with it. It's hot just like that."

"But my boobs are spilling out of it."

I raise an eyebrow, making it clear that's my favorite part. "I know."

She laughs and tucks one leg under her butt, turning to face me. A small smile plays at the corners of her mouth as she reaches out and runs her hand over the scruff I've been growing. "I like the beard. Are you keeping it for the wedding?"

"You want me to?"

"Whatever makes you happy."

"You make me happy."

My words don't make her smile the way they should. She hesitates and a spike of unease pokes into me. "These are your last few days to back out, Wyatt," she says. The smile dies on her lips and her gaze shifts to the floor.

"Hey." I reach out and grab her hand. "What're you talking about?

2

I'm not going anywhere."

"You sure you want to be hitched to me forever?"

"Fuck yes. Who else would put up with me? I'm hard to love, angel."

She glances up. "You're easy to love."

"Yeah? You sure about that? Up in your business all the time? Demanding all your attention? Trying to fuck you every chance I get?"

A soft giggle works out of her. "I love all of it. All of you."

"Good. I love all of you, too." I sit up and pull her closer. "What's bothering you?"

"Nothing. I…this…us…feels too good to be true sometimes. That's all."

"Well, it's true." I fall back against the pillows, placing an arm behind my head. "I think I know what you mean. I feel the same way. You make me happy, Trinity."

"You make me happy, too," she whispers. "So happy."

"Good. Now prove it."

That earns me a smile. She leans over me, kissing her way up my chest. I jerk back when she tickles my neck with her tongue, then hold her still for a kiss. Her warm body against mine has me rock hard in seconds. I groan when she stretches out half on top of me and half on the bed.

Pulling away, I grab her hand and place it over my dick. "See what you do to me. Full mast in five seconds."

"Impressive."

We keep kissing, and she continues to stroke me through my shorts. Soft, lazy touches that keep me on the edge. I groan into her mouth, and she slips her hand under my shorts, freeing my cock.

"Get on me."

"Patience," she teases.

"I've got none when it comes to you."

Still playful, she kneels up and works my shorts off until I'm left wearing nothing but a cocky grin. "Happy now?"

"Ohhh, yes." I nod at the white lacy scraps she's still wearing. "Take it off."

She slips the straps over her shoulders, slowly, teasing the hell out of me. I never tire of how perfect she is, but like the greedy bastard she's turned me into, I need more. "Your tits belong in my hands." I reach out, opening and closing my hands to demonstrate.

She laughs and slides back a few inches, keeping her hand wrapped around my dick. I could easily sit up and grab her, but this is much more fun. Especially when she squeezes a little harder.

"Fuck, Trin. That's good," I murmur, giving myself over to the sensation.

Her phone rudely interrupts us.

"Oh, shit. That's the park." Before I even realize what's happening— *she's answering a call, when we're about to fuck?*—she elbows my damn dick diving for her phone on the nightstand.

"Ow!"

"Hello?" she says, answering the call.

"Um?" I ask, tapping her arm and pointing to my angry cock.

"Sorry," she mouths.

My next question's a little louder. "Are you kidding?" I really don't care if whoever's on the other end hears me.

She shakes her head and shushes me. I'm about to make a louder protest when she wraps her fingers around me and starts jerking me off again. "That's better," I grumble.

"Oh my God, really?" Her hand stops moving and my eyes open. "We can come up this afternoon if you—oh, tomorrow?" She raises an eyebrow at me.

"What?" I ask, not that it does me any good.

"I think we can make tomorrow morning work. Okay. Thank you."

"You owe me," I say as soon as she ends the call.

A sly expression slides over her face and she leans over, kissing the tip

4

of my dick. "Did I hurt you?"

"Yes. But I know how you can make me feel better."

"Oh, I bet I know, too."

"Getting naked's a good start."

Her breathing deepens, a sign she's more into this than she's letting on. She kneels up, strips off the white lacy outfit—I might help by ripping it off—then throws a leg over me, lines herself up and sinks down my cock. My hands grip her hips. "You're going to tell me what all that was about—right after you fuck me."

She gasps as she bottoms out. Her eyes pop open, and she stares at me as she slides up and down. "Good, angel?"

"Yes."

"You gonna come for me?"

"Fuck, yes."

"Good girl. Get to it."

She chuckles and grabs one of my hands, bringing it to her mouth to kiss my fingers. I cup her cheek, my thumb rubbing over her bottom lip as she grinds down on me harder and faster. "Good. Fuck. Like that, Trinity."

It doesn't take long for an orgasm to whip through her, leaving her quivering and shaking.

Before she's aware of what's happening, I tighten my hold on her hips and flip us. Her eyes open and she stares up at me, soft and sweet. "Get ready, Angel Face."

I HAVEN'T EVEN caught my breath before Wyatt flips me on my back. "I'm ready." Not that he was waiting for a response. His mouth lingers near mine, and I raise my head to kiss him. His blue eyes glimmer with a pure, possessive heat. Maybe I'm nuts, but his intensity thrills me every time.

He holds me a little tighter, kisses me deeper, hammers into me harder. I'm coming apart, and he's the only thing holding me together. I need more but I'm not sure I can take it. I arch my hips, and he slides his hands beneath my ass, lifting me higher.

"Come for me again." His harsh whisper lights me up, and I shatter with bliss. He lets out a fierce groan, driving into me one last time before shuddering through his own release. He barely finishes before his lips find mine, kissing me deeply, then sweeter, softer. He touches his sweaty forehead to mine, staring into my eyes. "Don't ever doubt how much I want you," he says.

He kisses my forehead before pulling away. "I'm the one who should be worried you won't show up."

"Crazy talk."

He holds out his hand, lifting me off the bed. "Let's clean up. I'm starving."

"Is that your way of asking for a sandwich after sex?"

I'm rewarded with a deep, rumbling laugh from him. "No." His mouth quirks into a devilish smile. "Maybe some eggs."

We keep teasing each other like that as he pushes me into the shower to clean us up.

While we're getting dressed, my phone buzzes with a text.

"Hey, you never told me who called before."

"Huh? Oh, I'll tell you in a minute." I glance down, reading Hope's plea to meet her in the dining room in ten minutes.

"Who is it?"

"Hope. She wants to know if we're coming down to the dining room. She says she has news." When he doesn't say anything, I glance up. "Oooh, maybe she's pregnant."

"Just what we need, more kids around here," he says.

"Come on, Alexa needs some buddies, otherwise she's going to be a spoiled little princess."

"Don't look at me."

"I—" Not sure what to say, I shake my head and finish getting dressed.

CHAPTER TWO
WRATH

O N OUR WAY to the dining room, I take Trinity's hand. "So tell me now, why'd you almost snap my dick off before?"

"Exaggerate much?" she teases, reaching down to rub me through my shorts. I suck in a quick breath. "Careful, or I'll drag you back to our room and fuck you again."

The corner of her mouth quirks up, but she must figure I'm serious because she pulls me down the hallway. "It was the park ranger who called."

"Yeah. Got that."

Sparky's already at the table when we arrive—unusual for him. Hope turns and waves. As we approach, Rock nods at the chair next to Teller, indicating he wants me to take it. He's got an arm slung over Teller's shoulder. The gesture appears casual, but I doubt Teller can move an inch or two in any direction.

"What's with the seating arrangements, prez?" I ask, because hell, I'm genuinely curious *and* I enjoy being an asshole.

"Nothing, just miss spending time with knucklehead here." He rubs his hand over Teller's hair, leaving it fluffed in spots. Teller scowls and pats his hair back into place.

Not buying that for a second, I assume Teller's been acting like a dick—yet again.

Trinity's big, pink wedding binder hits the table with a thunk as she slides into the chair next to me.

Ignoring the weirdness going on at the table, I nudge her arm. "Finish your story."

"Oh, so we can't get married at the area with the big pavilion…"

Blood thunders through my ears, drowning out the rest of her words. We're going on a much longer engagement than I ever planned on here. At first, it was fine, she has my property patch and that's way more important to me. We're determined to be married at Fletcher Park, but it's been one red-tape bullshit issue after another. If it wasn't so important to both of us to have the ceremony at the park—who ever thought I'd end up being so sentimental—we could have gotten married on the clubhouse property like Rock and Hope did. One more delay and I'm dragging Trin's ass down to Empire City Court and having Damon marry us.

"Wyatt?" she says, setting her hand on my arm. Her touch pushes my rage-y-ness back.

"What do we do?" I ask.

"Wait, what's wrong with the pavilion?" Hope asks.

"Some freaky storm—lightning hit and it burned down."

Before anyone else opens their mouth, Sparky waves his arms in the air to get our attention—even though he's about two feet away. "Bad omen. Bad omen. You gotta get married somewhere else, guys."

"Simmer down, Sparky," Rock says. Turning to us, he asks, "What are you going to do?"

Trinity's brow wrinkles. I don't think she expected to have this conversation in front of so many people. "The ranger said there's another area where they just finished construction. It's on the overlook side, which will be nicer anyway. He's giving us first dibs and waving the additional fee."

"He better," I grumble. "We don't have to move the date?" I ask.

"Nope. We do have to have the ceremony earlier though."

"How early?" Stash asks as he pulls out a chair and sits next to Sparky.

"What are you doing above-ground at this hour?" I ask.

Stash flips me off, and Trinity squeezes my arm to get my attention. "Eleven."

Sparky whistles and pretends to think about it. "For you two, I'll get up at the fuckin' crack-o-dawn."

Trinity chuckles. "Thanks."

"Do we get to take a look at the place first?" I ask.

"Yes. Tomorrow morning is the only time he can do it. Is that okay with you?"

I nod and her gaze skips to Hope. "Can you come, too?"

"Absolutely." She claps her hands together. "I'm so excited. This spot sounds a lot nicer, Trin." She gives Sparky a pointed look. "Sounds like *good* luck."

Sparky's cheeks redden and he mumbles, "Sorry."

"So, why'd you want us down here?" Trinity asks, taking the heat off Sparky.

I'd never say it out loud, but his bad omen comment bugged me, so I appreciate Hope's effort to spin this change into a positive.

"Nothing." Hope's eyes stray to Teller.

Trinity shrugs and flips her binder open. She's so damn cute, biting her lip and making notes, I lean in and kiss her cheek.

Sparky gags. "Guys, seriously. You're as disgusting as those two." He wags a finger in Rock and Hope's direction.

"Thanks a lot, Sparky," Hope says. There's a hint of a smile, so I don't think she's as annoyed as she wants him to think.

"Sparky! Are you in trouble?" Z calls out. He and Dex join us at the table. Ravage follows a few minutes later.

"Are we eating today or just sitting around?" I ask.

Alexa's happy baby-babbles reach us, and a few seconds later, Murphy strolls in—Alexa in one arm and Heidi on his other side. Brother looks like he has the world by the balls this morning. My gaze strays to Rock, who's watching Teller closely.

Suddenly I know *exactly* what's about to happen. I cross my arms over my chest. Teller's been a dick lately, sure, but I don't think he's going to flip out.

Trinity picks up her head and narrows her eyes at the happy little family. "What's up with you two?"

Heidi practically jumps up and down, throwing her hand out for everyone to see. "We're engaged!"

Her gaze lands on her brother.

Under his breath, Rock asks. "We good?"

Teller gives a slight nod and jumps out of his chair. "About time, fuckface," he says to Murphy, shaking his hand and pulling him in for a hug. Rock lets out a breath and rolls his eyes to the ceiling, muttering, "thank fuck."

Trinity runs over to see the ring and hug Heidi. She throws an accusatory look at Hope. "You already knew, didn't you?" Trinity asks.

"Well, they *are* living in our house."

Ravage grins and I shake my head, knowing he's got something snarky he's dying to share. He's been a little shit-stirrer lately.

"Are you serious? It's like a fucking epidemic around here." He points at Rock, then me. "First you two." His gaze finally lands on Hope. "I blame you for this, you know. This is all your fault."

Rock sits forward, probably about to choke Ravage. But Hope knows Rav's fucking with her. She smiles and sets her hand on his shoulder. "I'm sorry. I promise to keep my commitment cooties away from you."

He cracks up at that.

Teller takes his niece and reclaims his chair next to me. Alexa's a cute little shit, and I can't help wiggling a finger at her in hello. She grabs on tight and tries to use my finger as a pacifier.

"So, how was it?" Sparky asks.

I glance up and see he's asking Murphy.

"Perfect. Thanks, bro."

"Care to share?" Z asks.

Murphy shakes his head, so Heidi answers, "Sparky set up a whole camping thing out at the site for our house. Thank you, Sparky. It was really beautiful."

"Holy shit, Sparky left the basement?" Rav asks with wide eyes.

"Fuck you," Sparky grumbles.

"That how you proposed?" Z asks.

"Jesus Christ, are you really asking for the proposal story before the girls?" Dex says, gesturing at Trinity and Hope.

"Fuck off," Z grumbles. "It's a big deal."

Heidi turns her big brown eyes my way, then to Trinity. "I wanted to wait and announce it after your wedding." She tilts her had toward Murphy. "But..."

She's so cute and looks so worried we're going to be mad, I can't even tease her.

"It's all good. Congratulations."

Rock raises an eyebrow. What? I can be civil. I'm happy for both of them.

Happy for Alexa, too, because I know Murphy will take damn good care of her.

After we settle down, Swan brings out breakfast. Heidi jumps up to help her. Before Swan disappears back into the kitchen, Trinity pulls her down into the chair next to her. "I need your help with some makeup decisions," she says as an excuse. Trinity's been trying to include Swan in more stuff lately. I'm not clear whether she's trying to play matchmaker or if she feels bad that she dumped all her household chores on Swan.

Under the table, I take Trinity's hand.

"You're not in charge of makeup, best bridesmaid?" Sparky asks Hope, interrupting Trinity and Swan's intense discussion on the best foundation for outdoor photographs.

"Not unless she wants to look like a crack-smoking clown." Hope shakes her head. "Not my skillset."

"You're always saying you're not good at girly stuff. What *are* you good at?" Ravage teases.

Hope flashes a sweet smile. "Putting up with you guys."

Rock wraps an arm around her, whispering something in her ear.

"I think Prez has something else in mind," Dex says.

Trinity shakes her head. "She helped me figure out my dress and found the most perfect shoes."

"Hope's dress was pretty," Sparky says, making all of us glance his way.

"What? It was green. Of course I liked it," he answers with a shrug. "What color is yours, Trin?"

Trin gives me a sly look. "I'm not telling."

This has been an on-going joke with us since we got engaged.

"Wait, he can't *see* you in it." Sparky flails his arms around. "Why can't you *tell* us what color it is?"

"Do you have some secret dress fetish you need to tell us about?" Z asks.

Sparky flips him off without even looking in Z's direction.

Trinity pokes my side. "He keeps threatening to wear shorts."

"What? I have nice legs."

Heidi rolls her eyes. "You can't wear shorts to your wedding, Uncle Wrath."

"Sure he can," Murphy says, grinning. "Sounds like a good idea to me."

"We should elope," she mutters.

"Don't even think about it," Teller grumbles without looking up.

"You two leaving tomorrow?" Murphy asks, putting an end to the wedding outfit talk.

"Not until the afternoon."

"You all right with Teller helping me out?" Murphy asks. "I know

13

Dylan's gonna be there, but he doesn't have a ton of experience."

Murphy glances at Teller. While he might have taken the engagement news well this morning, Teller's still a grumpy dick from his accident. It also hasn't escaped my notice that he tensed up as soon as our wedding was mentioned. While part of me was relieved Teller had something other than fuck-buddy feelings for Trinity, after all this time, the longing looks and puppy eyes are getting on my fucking nerves. Since he still hasn't fully recovered from the accident that killed Mariella and fucked his legs up, I can't exactly kick his ass.

I think Murphy senses my irritation with his best friend, because he's been trying to defuse things for a while—like every time Teller opens his mouth.

By the slow turn of his head and the *what the fuck* face he sends Murphy's way, I don't think Teller knew Murphy planned to put him to work for the next few days. "I can barely walk. How the fuck you think I'm gonna train anyone at the gym, dickhead?"

"I could use help at the counter," Murphy answers calmly. Thank fuck for Murphy. He's the only one with enough patience to put up with Teller some days.

"You want me to play *receptionist*?"

Alexa lets out a screech, waving her little fists in the air to let Teller know she doesn't care for his angry tone.

By now everyone's silent. Teller flicks his gaze around the table before glancing down at Alexa, then up at me. "You sure you want me there?"

What a stupid question. Teller's worked in my gym before. Fuck, I had him on my payroll when he fought for custody of Heidi and needed to show the court that he had legit income. "Sure," I answer slowly. "If Murphy says we need the extra help, we need it. You know your way around the place."

"Guess I'm the only one without a job," Heidi jokes. I think she's worried I'm about to murder her brother.

Trinity surprises me by piping up. "Actually, Heidi, I wanted to talk to you about doing some work for me, if you're interested. The pay isn't great, but"—she nods at Alexa—"the location is family friendly."

Heidi perks up. "Sure. Doing what?"

"I need someone to sort all my photos, catalog them, and put them into galleries online. I'll show you how to do everything. I just don't have the time to do it myself."

"Wait a second," Murphy interrupts. "I don't think I want my fiancée looking at your man-porn all day long, Trin," he jokes.

It seems to finally dawn on Heidi what she's being asked to do. "Oh, hell yes. That sounds like fun."

Trinity grins. "We'll talk more after breakfast," she says, glancing around the table. I give everyone a hard stare, daring them to make one smart-ass comment about Trin's photography.

No one opens their mouth. Although judging from the smirk on Z's face, he's considering it.

"Did you miss what I said?" Murphy asks Heidi. He's grinning like a fool, so I doubt he cares one way or another.

"Don't be jealous. It's just a job."

That right there is karma biting Murphy's ass, because I'm sure he uses that exact same excuse when he has to pull a shift at our strip club.

"I need both of you to come by and help me figure out what to do with all those trees," Rock reminds us.

"I'll help, too," Z volunteers. Sparky mumbles something about his plants and takes off. As if we were going to ask him to help with the manual labor.

I slide my hand up Trinity's leg, squeezing her thigh until she turns. "When I'm done with that, will you come to the gym with me?" I ask.

"I have my doctor's appointment. After that, I'll stop by."

"No. I'll take you."

"You don't have to do that."

"I want to," I say in a tone that leaves no room for discussion.

We've probably reached some weird, co-dependent territory in our relationship, but I can't find a fuck to give. I like being with my woman. Love having her with me at work.

There's no place I *don't* like having Trinity next to me.

AFTER BREAKFAST, MOST of the guys leave. Wyatt pulls me onto his lap and settles his chin on my shoulder.

"Can you really go to the gym after chopping all that firewood?"

An insulted snort erupts from him, jostling me around. "Please, it's barely a workout. Besides, I don't think we're cutting anything today." He pulls me a little closer and runs his cheek against mine until I laugh.

"Your scruff tickles."

"Oh." He runs his hand over his cheek and chin. "You sure you don't want me to shave it off for the wedding?"

Placing my palms against his cheeks, I turn his head to face me. "No way. You're my very own lumberjack."

Heidi bounces back into the dining room, stopping in front of us. "I'm ready to start my new job."

Wyatt chuckles and nudges me off of his lap. "Where's your man?"

She turns and points toward the hallway. "Waiting for you with Uncle Rock."

After he leaves, Heidi fidgets for a few seconds, then takes the chair next to me. "Are you sure you want me to do this?" she asks.

"I wouldn't have asked if I didn't. Come on, I'll show you what I need." Our house isn't quite finished to Wyatt's specifications, so most of our stuff is still at the clubhouse. Heidi follows me down the hallway and into my room.

She listens intently and asks careful questions while I explain what I need her to do.

"I think I can handle it." She sits and studies the website where I want her to upload the photos a little longer. While she's checking things out, I name the hourly rate I plan to pay her and she hesitates.

"You really don't have to pay me, Trinity. I'll do it for nothing—"

"No, it's a lot of work."

"Thank you." She pauses and glances at the door. "This would be my first *real* job, so I appreciate it. My brother's always been so good to me, but he never wanted me to work when I was going to school. Rock and Hope have basically been supporting me since I...since I came home. It's time to pull my own weight, you know?"

I highly doubt anyone's worried about it, but I respect her need to make her own money. Plus, even if Heidi and I haven't always gotten along in the past, she's smart and meticulous. "You did your internship. That was a much harder job."

"Yeah, but that was an *internship*. They had to hire me because of school."

"With all the wedding stuff, I've been letting these pile up, so I need the help."

She glances at the equipment and straightens up. "I'll get it all sorted for you."

"You don't have to start right away. Work on it in your free time."

She cocks her head. "Are you excited about the wedding?"

"Yes. There's still some last minute stuff up at the park I need to take care of, but I'm so happy we're almost there."

"Me too."

"What about you? You excited to plan—"

"Yes and no. I feel...weird." She glances at the open door and in a lower voice asks, "It's a little soon. Do you think I'm horrible?"

A year or two ago I would have said, "Yes, you're a spoiled brat." But Heidi's been through hell and grown up a lot in the last year. Her decision to have Alexa at her young age has made me think...about a lot of things.

"No. Not at all. You've had a rough time." I don't know a lot about what her marriage to Axel was like, but from things Teller and Murphy have said, I've gathered it wasn't all sunshine and rainbow-farting unicorns. "You deserve to be happy."

My answer doesn't seem to satisfy her, but we're interrupted by Murphy knocking on my door. "Hey, we're heading out to the building site. Alexa's with your brother," he says to Heidi.

I pack up my laptop, SD cards and a notebook with a bunch of written instructions for Heidi, and she takes it almost reverently. "I'll be careful with everything, Trinity."

After a quick kiss from Murphy, she darts out the door.

Murphy hangs back. "Thank you for doing that."

"Hey, it's time for me to hire an assistant." My tone is light, hoping he'll ease up on the seriousness.

He nods and stuffs his hands in his pockets. "It's still…nice of you."

"You sure you don't mind her looking at hot, half-naked guys all day?" I tease.

Finally, he cracks a smile and waves his hand in the air. "Please. I got nothing to worry about." He runs his hand over the front of his body in an overly-cocky way. "None of your photos can compete with *this*."

I snort. "Actually, I could use a beefy, bearded ginger in my catalog if you're interested."

Is Murphy blushing? I think he is and barely contain my laughter.

"I don't know about that."

When he still doesn't leave, I take a few steps closer. "Congratulations."

He shrugs. "Think it's too soon?"

Somehow I manage not to snort. The two of them are an awful lot alike. In the back of my head, a voice says it's *weird* either of them give a damn about my opinion. Hope's the one who dispenses advice around here, not me. "For you two? No."

"We probably won't tie the knot for a while, but—"

"You wanted to nail her down?"

He finally cracks a small smile. "Something like that."

"You've been really good to her…and Alexa." Something about the way Murphy stepped up to take care of Heidi's daughter after Axel died always chokes me up. Maybe it's because before I found the Lost Kings, I never knew that kind of love. Or maybe I'm just an emotional mess because I'm getting married in a week and a half?

"I can't help it."

"Well, a lot of guys wouldn't want to be bothered. She's a lucky girl. They both are."

"Thanks." He glances over his shoulder. "I better get out there before your almost-husband kicks my ass."

WRATH

"THIS IS A fuck-ton of wood to split," I say, staring at the mountain of logs in front of us.

Murphy runs his hand over his chest. "Z needs to get a log-splitter. One of us should look into a wood furnace."

Rock eyes the logs, a slow smirk forming at the corners of his mouth. "I'll do some of it the old-fashioned way." He takes a swing with an imaginary ax.

This one's too good to resist. "Why? Hope got a lumberjack fetish?"

He grins at the obnoxious question. "Maybe. It'll be a good workout either way."

"If you say so. I don't need props to get my woman excited. I just need to look at her."

Rock snorts at the same time Murphy opens his mouth. "I—"

"No. Uh-uh. You don't get to share stories of whatever dirty stuff you do to Heidi. She's still the club's kid sister as far as we're concerned," I say pointing to Rock and myself.

"That's *not* what I was going to say." He shifts his gaze to Rock. "And please, warn us whenever this lumberjack thing goes down. Heidi's already halfway to sleeping with earplugs as it is."

"Us too," Rock says, shaking with laughter.

"Uh—"

Murphy cuts me off. "Alexa's teething."

I'm not a total asshole. "She okay?"

"Yeah, just cranky and screaming a lot."

"What a mood-killer."

A sheepish smile twists his mouth, and he ducks his head. "I don't know. I kinda want another one."

"Are you out of your mind? Why?" Taking one of these logs and whacking it over my head would make more sense than those two spitting out another kid.

His shoulders lift. "I want Alexa to have some brothers and sisters."

"Some? She's not a fucking cat, bro."

"Fuck you."

"Hey," I slap Rock's arm. "Sounds like Murphy plans to repopulate the club with the next generation of Lost Kings all by himself."

Rock snorts. "Someone should."

"Stop being a dick," Murphy snaps. "I don't want her to be lonely. That's all."

The smile slides off Rock's face, and he nods at Murphy. "Yeah, I get it."

I get it, too, but still enjoy hassling my brothers. "Aw, prez. You gettin' choked up because the good son's turned into such a responsible husband and father?"

Rock punches my arm. "Yeah, 'cause he sure had some shitty role models."

"True story."

Rustling leaves and snapping twigs turn our attention toward the woods where Z emerges from the trees with his two dogs. "We pickin' on Murphy?" he asks. "I'm down for that."

"No, they were having a father-son moment," I answer, leaning over to rub Ziggy and Zipper behind their ears. "Good son was sharing his plans for putting more buns in Heidi's oven."

Z lights up with a devious smile. "If he's 'good son' who's the bad one?" he asks, totally skipping any discussion of Heidi's oven.

"Who do you think?"

Murphy shifts, leaves crinkling under his feet. "Go easy on Teller. He still ain't right—"

"No shit," Z says. "I keep waitin' for him to realize you're nailing his sister and go Rambo on your ass."

Z and I have a good laugh.

Apparently Rock's had enough of our nonsense. "Can we get back to the wood? Maybe continue the family counseling or whatever the fuck we're doing later?"

"Sounded more like family *planning*," Z cracks.

"Jesus Christ," Rock mutters.

We really don't get much more accomplished than trading insults and planning how to split the wood. So, time well spent with my brothers.

On the way back to the clubhouse, Rock, Z, and the dogs walk ahead, while Murphy sticks to my side. "Are you really okay having Teller down at the gym?" he asks.

"Yeah, why you being so weird about it?"

He stops, which forces me to stop.

"You two coming?" Rock asks.

"In a minute," Murphy calls out. He waits until they're out of sight before answering my question. "I'm worried about him. He needs to get out of the clubhouse. The only person he ever wants to see is Alexa."

"Makes sense. She doesn't talk back and she needs him to do everything for her."

Murphy cocks his head but seems to consider my words. "I guess."

"As long as he keeps that attitude locked down and doesn't scare any of my customers away, he's more than welcome to work there."

"Thank you."

"You're gonna be a partner. Some of these decisions are yours now, too."

That finally lightens him up. "You're still the boss."

"Don't forget it."

He laughs.

"Should I be jealous?" Trinity calls out as she skips down the front steps of the clubhouse to meet us.

"Nope, just reminding him he's the boss," Murphy says.

I stop and Trinity leans up, wrapping her arms around my neck so I can lift her up. "You're the boss of me, too," she whispers against my ear.

"You fucking know it," I growl, squeezing her ass.

"Where are my girls?" Murphy asks.

I set Trinity down, and she points at the house without looking away from me. "Living room. With Hope."

"Later."

"Ready to go?" I ask after he leaves.

She answers me with a kiss that turns into more of my grabby hands on her ass.

"What time's your appointment?" I mumble against her lips.

"Too soon for what you're thinking."

CHAPTER THREE

I'M A LITTLE giddy as I walk out of my therapist's office. For a long time, the things we discussed would cling to me like sludge for days afterward. Sometimes it caused nightmares. Other times it made me tense and listless until Wyatt, demanding as he is, pulled me out of it.

Today he's waiting for me outside. Casually leaning against his bike. A few women in the parking lot keep sneaking sly glances at him, so I hurry over. To stake my claim? Damn right.

Sneaking up on him isn't possible. He lifts his head, a big smile forming on his lips. For me. He doesn't seem to notice anyone else is even in the area.

I can't believe he's going to be *my* husband.

"Everything okay?" he asks before handing over my helmet.

A little of my giddiness returns. "Great. She says I'm done for now."

Wyatt raises an eyebrow.

"I mean…I can call her if I need to, but she thinks I'm in a good place."

Now, in all the time I've been coming here, Wyatt hasn't asked me a lot of questions about it. He holds me when I can't sleep. Listens if I want to talk about something that comes up in therapy. But otherwise, I'm not sure if he thinks it makes me weak or if he's bothered by the twice-a-month visits.

"I'm proud of you, baby," he says, sweeping me up in a hug.

"Really?"

"Fuck, yeah."

"I couldn't have done it without you." I gesture lamely at the building behind us, suddenly unsure of what the hell I mean.

He sets me down gently. "Yes, you could, Trinity." His voice takes on a low, no-bullshit tone. "You're a fighter, like me. We just happen to be better together."

"I think so, too," I whisper.

"Good." He presses a kiss to my forehead and gives me another one of his serious looks. "You ready to be my wife now?"

Maybe Wyatt's more perceptive than I give him credit for. No, he's not a let's-get-in-touch-with-our-inner-wounded-child type of guy. But he seems to understand *me*. Sometimes better than I understand myself. While *I* hadn't caused any of the delays with our wedding, I hadn't been upset about them, either.

I feel good. Solid. Whole. Connected.

"Yes. I can't wait to be Mrs. Ramsey."

"I like the sound of that. In fact, maybe we should have it tattooed across your ass."

I roll my eyes. "No more ink for me."

His hand brushes against my side, where my "Wrath's Girl" tattoo decorates my hip. "Let's go deal with stuff at the gym. Then tomorrow we'll go to the mountains." He leans down and whispers in my ear. "After that, your ass is mine."

My body melts against him. "I wish we were going right now."

"Patience, Angel Face."

I groan and strap on my helmet.

It's a short ride to the gym. I recognize most of the cars in the parking lot since it's too early to be very busy.

I dismount first and Wyatt grabs my hand. "Hey, before we go inside, let me take you next door."

The space has been empty for months. Wyatt's told me he's in negotiations to buy the property next to his gym to expand Furious Fitness.
I'm excited he finally wants to show me around the buildings that used
to house, among other things, a spa and tanning salon.

"I think we could offer more classes back here," he says, pointing to
the spot in question. "We'll have one or two more offices. Bigger locker
rooms." He rattles off a bunch more improvements he has planned. I'm
overwhelmed and full of pride.

"What do you think?" he finally asks.

The enormity of how far we've traveled together and apart over-
whelms me. "You've come a long way since the surly, cocky guy who
walked into my bar all those years ago."

The look he gives me is full of affection and heat. "Yeah?"

"This is going to be huge," I say, spinning in a circle in the back
parking lot.

He flashes one of those panty-melting grins he's so good at. "I know
no other way, babe."

"There's my cocky Wrath." I run over, slamming into his body,
wrapping my arms around him.

He tips his head down. "You like it?"

"I love it. It's amazing. I'm so excited for you."

"This will be good for *us*, babe. A lot of improvements. I'm hiring
two more professional trainers to attract more clients. Murphy's buying
in as a partner."

"Really?" I hesitate for a second, my teeth nipping into my lower lip.
I'm not quite sure how to express my feelings in a way that won't be
offensive. "Don't be mad."

He raises an eyebrow. "Mad about what? What's going on in your
nutty little head?" he teases. A little more serious, he adds, "There's
nothing that would ever make me mad at you."

I push the words out quickly. "I'm really proud of you."

His lips turn up. "Why would that make me mad?"

"I don't know."

"Trinity, there are very few people in the world whose opinions I give a shit about. Yours is definitely one of them."

He hugs me a little closer. "We'll have the widest variety of trainers. I'm thinking of even adding yoga to keep the housewives happy."

"Talk to Swan. She's looking for more classes to teach."

"You're already a big help." He wraps one of his arms around my shoulders. "Now, I want to show you my favorite part."

Curious, I let him lead me to the empty space that used to be a nail salon.

"Are you planning to add mani/pedis, too?" I ask.

His lips slide into a sneaky grin. "No."

He unlocks the door and pushes it open, revealing an all-empty, white space.

"What are you using this for?"

"Not me. You."

"Me?"

His hands settle on my shoulders, gently pushing me farther into the store. "I think this space would make a perfect studio."

"For what?"

"For your business. So you don't always have to do photo shoots outdoors. You can have the right lighting and"—he waves a hand at the empty space—"whatever stuff you need."

"Wyatt, you think I'm ready for that?" It takes a second to process what he's saying. "I don't know."

His fingers settle under my chin, tilting my head back. "*I* know. You have more and more people who want your photos. More people who want you to photograph them. It's time you have the right space for it. It's not a hobby anymore, Trinity."

I stand there trying to absorb his words. Maybe because I don't have a whole lot of faith in myself, but I still think of my photography and design business as a hobby. Wyatt's taken me seriously since the day I told him how I spent my spare time. Went so far as to buy me all the equipment I needed. Now he's offering me a workspace, too.

It's huge. To me, it's huge. In actions and words, Wyatt supports my hobby-turned-business. It doesn't even seem to bother him that most of my time is spent photographing half-naked guys.

But buying me a building? That's long-term, looking ahead to the future, faith in me. The realization makes my words stick in my throat. "You don't have to do this," I finally whisper.

"Hey." His face is calm, but there's mischief shimmering in his eyes. "I'm going to be your husband. And as your husband, my responsibilities are more than all those crazy orgasms I give you."

Underneath my nervous laughter, my heart flutters. "God, you're arrogant."

He nods, agreeing with me, then turns serious. "You're really good at what you do. I want you to have everything you deserve. Want to be the one who gives it to you."

My eyes water, and I'm thankful for the dark sunglasses perched on my nose.

"Thank you."

"It's not finalized yet. Won't be until the sale goes through. But I want to make sure you like it and you'll be comfortable here."

"I love it."

"Good. You'll be right next door, so I can make sure you're safe. I still don't want you meeting with anyone alone."

Wyatt supports this new career path of mine, but he has one hard rule he won't bend on. I can't meet any of my models alone. Guys he trusts, like Jake, are fine. Anyone else, he insists on escorting me or scheduling the session at the gym. "I won't."

His body tenses up and he stares at me, searching every angle of my face as if he's trying to memorize my features. "I can't...I couldn't be without you, Trinity." He tilts his head. "All of this stuff is meaningless without you." While Wyatt and I enjoy teasing each other, the roughness in his voice tells me how sincere he is.

There's nothing to say or do, except slide my arms around his waist and squeeze him tight. I rest my cheek against his chest, absorbing his warmth, and listen to his heart thump. "I love you so much," I murmur.

He wraps me up in his arms, and we stand there together for a few minutes. At some point, my hand slips down and I might take advantage and squeeze his butt a little.

"The front door's still open." He rumbles with laughter. "Have some self-control, woman."

"I don't have any around you."

I get a similar ass-squeeze, then he pulls away. "Time to get to work."

He closes the door and takes my hand, walking us back to the gym. My mind's so busy trying to process everything, I don't notice Gina, one of his regular customers, until she's running toward us.

As our wedding day approaches, I find it difficult not to slap most of the women who fawn all over my man. Gina is no exception.

"Mr. Ramsey! Wait up, please."

He pauses, grumbling under his breath something I can't catch.

She rambles on about an after-school karate program she wants him to consider, never once taking a breath or looking at me.

Wyatt finally interrupts her. "Gina, this is my wife, Trinity. You've met, right?"

"You're married?" she gasps, instead of oh, I don't know, saying *hello*.

"Ten more days." I hug him a little tighter and pat his chest. Her eyes rake down my body, then back to my face.

"You're a stunning couple," she says. "You'll make beautiful babies." Her lips curve into a quick smile.

"Uh, thanks," I answer.

She twists toward Wyatt again and bats her heavily-slicked lashes. Who wears that much mascara to the gym for fuck's sake?

Wyatt tightens his hold on me and steers us toward the gym. "I need to check in with my guys, Gina. Jake's brother, Sully, will be taking over some of my classes. You can give the details to him."

She huffs but follows us inside.

A few more of his regular admirers are clustered around the counter. Today, they're busy gawking at Teller, which I'm sure he's not loving at the moment. They turn and stare at us when we walk in. This particular group of women are lucky I'm not a typical biker's ol' lady, or each one would be getting a punch to the throat right about now for eye-fucking my man when I'm standing right next to him. I never call them out on their shameless flirting, because I know for Wyatt it's only business and no matter how much they annoy me, I'd never do anything to embarrass him.

Doesn't stop me from wanting to lick him and declare him mine in front of each and every one.

Hell, he'd probably like it if I did.

WRATH

TELLER'S ALREADY EARNED his keep today by entertaining a few of my regular female clients. Fuck, do I get tired of their yammering and not-so-subtle hints. The more persistent ones stick around trying to capture the attention of the new guy.

All the female attention has replaced Teller's usual sour expression with a slight smirk. I can't say it's an improvement.

"Where's your buddy?" I ask after the ladies go away.

He points toward a gang of teenage girls who seem to gather here every other afternoon. "I don't think my sister's going to appreciate his fan club."

I know for a fact Murphy can't stand those girls, and the only reason he hasn't tossed them out is that I told him he can't. It's bad for business.

Finally, Twitch walks over to help. Murphy gives him a fist-bump and ducks away.

"Bro, seriously, how are they good for business?" Murphy bitches as soon as he sees me.

"*They* aren't. Their parents who pay their fees are."

Next to me, Trinity laughs. "My husband, the hustler."

I don't miss the way Teller shifts his gaze to the window.

"They're harmless," I say, "and the guys appreciate them." I jerk a thumb toward Dylan, who's moved in like a fucking shark to offer his personal trainer services to one of the girls.

"You running a gym or a hookup site?" Teller asks with a bit of snap in his tone.

"Watch yourself, welterweight."

He scowls at the nickname but shuts his mouth.

Trinity raises on tiptoes and presses a kiss to my cheek. "I'll be out back. Behave, boys," she says, throwing up her hand in a quick wave on the way out. I keep my eyes on her, watching as she stops to talk to Jake and his brother Sully.

"You trust Jake around her?" Teller asks.

I almost say "More than I trust you at the moment." But it's overly harsh and not even true, so I keep it to myself.

Doesn't matter what I was about to say anyway. Our attention's drawn to Heidi, carrying her daughter as she struggles to open the front door.

"What're you doing here, beautiful?" Murphy asks, opening the door and plucking Alexa out of her arms. He tucks Heidi against his side and shoots a look at Teller, as if daring him to say something.

Heidi's gaze darts between her brother and me, and I raise an eyebrow. "You realize we actually *work* here sometimes, right?" I joke.

She wriggles out of Murphy's hold. "I know. Sorry. I...was driving—"

"I'm messing with you, Heidi." At least when Heidi stops by, she usually helps out, so I don't mind having her here. Free labor and all that. Although I doubt she'll be able to do much since the baby's with her.

"Why'd you bring Alexa?" Teller snaps.

She glances at Murphy before answering. "I took her to look for a dress for the wedding. The one I had doesn't fit now."

Twitch pops up, beaming at Heidi like an idiot. "Hey, Heidi."

Both Teller and Murphy glare at Twitch. The tension between the four of them, while funny as fuck, is nothing I want to deal with, so I leave them to work it out.

I'm not even in my office for five seconds before Teller hobbles in.

"What's wrong?" I ask, scowling at his lack of knocking.

"Nothing. They're irritating me."

"Everything irritates you."

"You should have kicked her out. She shouldn't have the baby here, and they don't need to be all over each other all day long."

"Bro, settle the fuck down." I can't believe this even needs to be said or that *I'm* the one who has to say it. "Let them be happy for five seconds. They just got engaged."

He shakes his head and opens his mouth, probably to say something else stupid. I cut him off by pointing to the open door. "Close it."

That's right, I sit there and watch him struggle to get up and slam the door shut.

"Sit the fuck down."

His eyes widen, but he takes his seat.

"I thought you were cool with their engagement?"

"You don't understand. I want her to—"

"Teller. I love you, brother. It's time to worry about yourself, though."

He opens his mouth to interrupt me, and I hold up a hand before he spits out a single word. "I respect the hell out of you for making Heidi a priority pretty much your entire life—"

"Not enough of one apparently."

"Don't interrupt me." I stare him down until I'm sure he's going to keep his mouth shut. "She's an adult. And she's Murphy's problem now." He glares at me. "Time to let go. Focus on yourself." Thinking about my own sister, I realize I'm the worst kind of hypocrite. Had Faith made it to Heidi's age, I probably would have been ten times worse than Teller. Even so, I hate seeing him make himself so miserable.

"I—whatever."

"Don't *whatever* me, fucker."

He finally cracks a smile. "I feel like shit that I couldn't be there for her when she needed me." The smile slips off his face. "I wish I'd fought her harder about marrying Axel, pushed her and Murphy together...done something so she didn't—"

"Seriously? Christ, you really are Rock's mini-me. Quit blaming yourself for stuff you had nothing to do with"

He glances down at his feet. "It's hard."

There's a tap at the door before either of us says another word. Trinity pokes her head in and glances at the two of us. "I'm going to run out and grab lunch for everyone. You two want anything?"

She writes down our lunch orders, I give her some cash, and she turns to leave.

"Take someone with you," I say.

I don't miss her exasperated sigh. "It's right across the road—"

One hard look from me, and she rolls her eyes. "Heidi's coming with me. Everyone else is busy."

"Take Sully or Dylan. They can't be that fuckin' busy. Sully doesn't have any classes yet."

"Fine." She huffs but leans over to kiss my cheek. "You're lucky I love you so much, 'cause you're a pain in my ass."

Before I can grab her for a deeper kiss, she darts away. She pats

Teller's shoulder as she walks out, leaving the door open.

I watch Teller's eyes follow her into the gym for a solid minute, then clear my throat.

"That's the other thing we need to talk about."

Slowly—*too slowly for my taste*—he turns my way. "What?"

"You." I point at the door Trinity just walked through. "She's my ol' lady. About to be my *wife*. I don't share. The puppy dog eyes need to fucking stop."

For a second, I think he stops breathing. His jaw drops. But not in a guilty, I-got-caught way.

"I-I didn't... No disrespect. I wouldn't—" he stammers.

Yeah, just as I thought—he didn't even realize he was doing it. "I know."

"I'm sorry, brother." He takes a second to meet my eyes. "You gonna kick my ass now?"

"No." The answer comes out easily. No competitive fire gets stirred up inside me. I don't have a shred of insecurity about my relationship with Trinity. "I'm glad you...cared about her in the past. But you need to move on."

He maintains the eye contact. "I thought I had. I'm sorry." His apology is brief but sincere. It's all I need from him.

The silence that fills the room isn't even awkward.

"It's not an excuse, but I'm still so fucked up over what happened." He runs his hand over his legs. "Not this—"

"Keeping up with your physical therapy?"

His head snaps up and the fierce glare returns. "Yes."

He's in a bad place. That's what stops me from knocking him the fuck out for his disrespect. Instead, I try to be patient and share my own experience. "When I was recovering from my accident—"

"Yeah, you didn't *kill* anyone in your accident," he mumbles.

Shit. I want to help him, but everything that comes out of my mouth seems to make it worse.

"Brother, that's not your fault." The whole club knows *something* was going on with Teller and Mariella, and I really do understand how awful he must feel. "What was up with you two? Were you—"

"It wasn't like that."

I wait for him to add some detail, and he sighs. "You really want to hear this?"

"I wouldn't ask if I didn't."

He slides his gaze away from me and drops his chin to his chest. "She still wasn't right from her time with the Vipers. Lot of nightmares. When it got real bad, she liked to come stay in my room." He swallows hard and glances at the door. "I told her I'd keep her safe."

A heavy sigh eases out of me. "That's not on you."

He opens his mouth to argue with me, and I hold up my hand. "No. Listen, none of us were as close to her as you were. I know we don't bring it up a lot, but we all feel bad about what happened. She was a sweet girl who did *not* deserve that. You can't blame yourself."

"You don't understand," he says with a fire in his voice that's been missing for way too long. "*I'm* the one who kept pushing to take her out on the bike. I thought it would be fun for her. It was too cold to be on the bike. But *no*, I had to have my way. Never considered I would make us an easy target. That's on me. That's my fuck-up." His voice rises with each word, and I feel even worse about being so wrapped up in my own stuff that I hadn't realized how much he's been struggling.

Christ, I don't know what to say. This touchy-feely stuff is Rock's domain. Not mine. I'm supposed to be the one the guys come to for an ass-kicking.

"I get it, Teller. I do. But you need to keep pushing yourself, so when we find that fuck you're the one who ends him."

Some of his attitude evaporates. "I'm tryin'."

"You got Alexa. She needs you."

Finally, something I said cheers him up. He forces a quick smile. "Yeah. Don't know what I'd do without her."

"Maybe you should try spending time with someone else?"

He rolls his eyes at me. "Are you suggesting I fuck my troubles away?"

My smirk answers that question. What the hell else am I going to suggest?

"I'm not only fucked up in the head." He taps his fist against his thigh. "I'm a fuckin' mess down here."

The tilt of my head makes him snort. "My dick's fine. I'm still scarred as fuck though."

"Don't let that stop you. Chicks dig scars. Just makes them want to take care of you and shit."

I get another eye-roll for that one. "I've had enough let-me-heal-you pussy thrown at me since I got out of the hospital to make me swear off sex forever."

"There's something I never thought I'd hear you say."

"Don't worry about me," he continues, ignoring my comment. "I ain't interested in turning into some mild, suburban house-husband like you and Rock." He glances into the gym and screws his face into a scowl. "Or dad of the year like Murphy's apparently turned into."

When I finish laughing over the "house-husband" dig, I lean in closer. "You still got so much to learn, welterweight. Think acting like you don't need a woman makes you a real man?"

"I don't *want* any old chick—" He snaps his mouth shut, but no way am I letting that go.

"You sound like you have someone specific in mind."

His eyes widen. "Not Trinity. Not anyone. Someone—not involved in the club."

I definitely need to dig into that again at some point. "Find the woman whose demons play nice with yours. That's what it's all about, brother."

He cocks his head and hesitates before asking, "That what happened with you and Trinity?"

"Yes," I answer without taking my eyes off him.

He nods and stares off into space for a few seconds. "If I...if *we* get justice for Mariella..."

Jesus, if that doesn't stab me right in the chest. "I understand. We nailed Killa. We'll find Ransom."

His hands open and close a few times, and he stares at them as if he's picturing snuffing Ransom's useless life out. "No one's seen that fucker in months."

"I know."

"He's probably dead."

"Doubt it. Ransom's sturdier than a cockroach."

Murphy taps on my door and wiggles his eyebrows at Teller. "One of the ladies wants to know if you're available."

Teller doesn't smile. Only his disgusted snort indicates he heard Murphy.

Twitch slides in behind Murphy, and I seriously consider nailing a "Do Not Enter" sign to my office door. "You need me to put those sandbags out?" Twitch asks.

It's a reasonable question, but Murphy scowls at him.

"Christ, let it go, brother." I laugh. "Heidi ain't interested in him."

"Thanks a lot." Twitch's gaze darts between Murphy and me. "Don't be mad at me, Murphy." He points a bony finger my way. "I'm only nice to Heidi because *he* told me I had to 'show the old ladies respect' or he'd gut me. You can't be mad at me for following orders."

Murphy glances at me with a barely-controlled smirk. He loves fuckin' with Twitch.

And because *I* take my role as shit-stirrer seriously, I lift my shoulders in a careless shrug. "Sounds like something I could've said."

"He did," Twitch insists.

"Get back to work, prospect," Murphy snaps.

Twitch swings his pleading eyes my way. "Can he really boss me around like that at the gym?"

I stroke my hand over my beard and pretend to think about it for a second. "Sure."

After Twitch stomps out of my office, Murphy snickers. "He's so easy to rile up."

"Getting even for all the shit we gave you when you were a prospect?" I joke.

"Fuck yeah, it's my right as a full-patch," he answers, tapping his chest where his Road Captain patch would be if he were in his cut. "He needs a thicker skin if he's ever gonna patch-in."

"Did my sister cause more trouble?" Teller asks.

"No," Murphy says, shutting Teller down quick before lifting his chin my way. "Just warning you now, Rock called and mentioned having a quick meeting tonight."

Teller shoots a hopeful look my way. "Think it's about Ransom?"

The eagerness in Teller's voice makes it hard to form an answer. "Could be."

Heidi and Trinity return with lunch, ending our conversation. Talking about the former president of the Vipers MC leaves me tense. Rock and I need to have a one-on-one before Trinity and I leave.

"Here, let me have her," Teller says, grabbing Alexa. All the grumpy bastard seems to flow out of him once he has his niece in his arms.

Murphy takes the lunch bags from Trinity. "You coming?" he asks Heidi.

"I'll meet you in the lunch room," she mumbles as she carefully watches her brother leave my office.

Curious why Heidi's staying behind, I focus on her.

"Oh, geez, I think about a dozen ovaries just exploded out there," Trinity says, snickering while she watches Teller and Alexa out on the gym floor.

Heidi chuckles, then turns my way. "I hope you're not mad at me for stopping by, Uncle Wrath." She glances out the door and in a softer voice adds, "I really came to check up on my brother. I'm worried about him."

"We all are, sweetheart. I had a talk with him." Mostly about club business and butting out of her life, but of course I don't share that with her.

"Good. He'll listen to you."

I'm not sure about that, but I nod and smile to reassure her. "He'll be okay."

"I hope so. Thank you for letting him work here for a few days."

After she leaves, I pull Trinity into my lap and bury my face against her neck. "When did I turn into a fucking life coach? That's Rock's job. Not mine."

"Aww." She shifts against me, wrapping her arms around my neck and holding on tight.

"This is better," I mumble against her hair. Inhaling her sweet scent, listening to her breathe, the weight of her in my lap—everything about her pushes my doubts and irritation away.

"Better?" she asks.

"Yes. I love holding you."

She runs the back of her hand over my cheek. "Hungry?" Leaning back, she snags the bag of food off my desk.

The answer to that is yes, but not for food. "Yeah. I wanna lay you out on my desk and eat *you*."

"You think that's a good idea with a full house?"

"No," I grumble.

"Tomorrow." Her voice lowers. "Tomorrow, I'm all yours. You can do whatever you want to me for three whole days." Her words, the wicked grin, her husky voice—none of it helps what's going on in my shorts, so I nudge her off my lap.

"Go sit over there." I prod her toward the chair on the other side of my desk. "Otherwise, I'm going to fuck you no matter who's out there."

"Patience. It will be so much better if you wait for it."

"You're going to regret those words, Angel Face."

Trinity

WYATT'S DEEP, SEXY voice should be outlawed.

I'm this close to jumping up on his desk and letting him have his way with me. But I take a seat across from him instead.

I can be patient.

He takes a few papers out of his desk and hands them to me.

For once, I'm feeling useful. Every bit of him radiated tension when I came in here. Now, he's more relaxed as we talk about the next steps for the gym expansion.

"Am I interrupting?" Jake asks, pushing Wyatt's door wide open.

"You know you are," I tease.

"What do you want?" Wyatt snaps.

Jake ignores Wyatt's tone—I suppose he's gotten used to it over the years.

"I wanted to ask Trinity if any of her hot friends will be at the wedding."

"All my hot friends are taken."

"Okay, your ugly friends, then."

"Jerk." I wad up my napkin and throw it at him. He catches it and grins.

Whisper stops by and glares at Jake. "Kissing her ass again?" he asks, nodding at me. His gaze skips to Wyatt as if I'm not even in the room, which isn't unusual and doesn't bother me one bit.

Jake rolls his eyes but doesn't have a chance to respond before Whisper starts badgering Wyatt. "You got *another* one of your brothers here?" he asks.

"Yeah, just for a couple days." Wyatt's face remains passive, but I sense his annoyance at being questioned.

Fiancée or not, Furious Fitness is Wrath's business and not something I'd stick my nose in—no matter what he said earlier. But I've always wondered how long his partnership with the Wolf Knights MC's Sergeant-at-Arms would last. Especially since Ulfric was dethroned and Merlin took over as president. From the little I know of their club, Ulfric was the only thing keeping them on the right side of civil.

As an ol' lady, I may not butt into MC business, but I damn sure pay attention to what's going on in my man's world.

"Fucker can barely walk. What's he supposed to do here?"

Wyatt's eyes narrow at Whisper's tone. "Whatever the fuck I need him to do. What's your problem?"

"Nothing. Just feelin' outnumbered. Maybe I oughta bring some of my crew in."

They stare at each other for a few seconds, Jake shifts uncomfortably and stuffs his hands in his pockets. I decide to intervene. "Are you bringing Melanie to the wedding, Whisper?"

He slowly drags his gaze to me, as if it annoys the shit out of him to acknowledge my presence. I paste a sweet smile on my face, while mentally, I'm flipping him off.

"You still gonna be hanging around here so much after you wrap your ball and chain 'round his neck?"

I'd love to answer, "Yes, asshole, I'll be right next door in the studio my ol' man bought me." But I'm not sure if anyone else knows about Wrath's plan for me.

"Wrath showed me around next door. Looks like it'll be great, Whisper," I say instead. My cheeks ache from the fake-ass smile I keep in place.

Like the jackass Whisper is, he pretends I didn't say a word and walks out.

"Shit, I'm sorry. I shouldn't have said anything," I mumble.

Wyatt reaches across the table and rubs his fingers over the back of my hand. "It's fine."

"What the fuck's his issue lately?" Jake asks, closing the door behind him.

"He's not really on board with the expansion." Wyatt sits back in his chair, keeping his eye on Jake. "You know this."

"Yeah, well, it's gettin' old."

"You sure you're okay with me leaving for a few days?" Wyatt asks. My heart stops. I've been looking forward to this brief trip ever since Wyatt set it up.

Jake's face smooths into a mask of seriousness. "Bro, how long have I known you?"

Wyatt gestures toward the door. "Come on, you know this place is my baby."

Jake snorts. "I'll guard it with my life."

"Bullshit. You're cheating on me with Sully's gym."

"Fuck you. You know I'm just helping him out. Same as he's doing here." Jake turns serious again. "We got this. Known you a long time and can't remember you taking a real vacation that wasn't "club business." He smirks. "Even when you broke your fuckin' leg you were in here every day." He glances at me and smiles. "Take your girl away. She's certainly earned it for putting up with your grumpy ass."

I cover my mouth with my hand to muffle the laughter spilling out.

Wrath chuckles, then lifts his chin at the door. "Having Teller help out wasn't because I don't trust you—"

"Didn't think it was. I'll catch you two later."

"He's a good friend." I say after Jake leaves. "What's up with Whisper, though?"

"Don't know. I keep hoping he'll ask me to buy him out."

"Can you do it? I mean with everything else going on? Our house has been way over-budget, the expansion—"

The corner of his mouth turns up. "You worried I can't take care of you, angel?"

"No. Not at all. That's not what I meant."

His grin widens. "I'm not worried. You're gonna be a famous pho-

41

tographer and take care of *me* pretty soon."

Once again, his faith in me leaves me speechless for a second. "Somehow, I don't see you playing house-husband."

He throws his head back and laughs. "Not according to Teller. He thinks Rock and I have been de-balled by our women."

Now I'm the one laughing. "He's probably jealous of you two." I cock my head. "What were you talking about for so long, anyway?"

"He needed a few life lessons."

"That doesn't sound ominous or anything," I tease. The smile dies on my lips. "He's still having a hard time about Mariella, isn't he?"

"That's part of it."

My eyes water and I glance down at my hands. "I think about her all the time. I hope he doesn't blame himself."

"Of course he does. He's an overprotective meathead like the rest of us."

I let out a soft snort and swipe at my damp cheeks.

"We can't bring her back, but we'll get justice for her, Trin," he says in a low, earnest voice.

Finally, I'm able to glance up and meet his ocean-blue eyes. "I believe you."

CHAPTER FOUR
WRATH

IT ENDS UP being a long day at the gym. Thank fuck Trinity stuck around. She was the only one holding me back from punching someone.

As Murphy predicted, Rock's determined to annoy me further tonight, insisting we sit down at the table for an informal church.

"What?"

His expression says a bunch of things, including "I'm not in the mood for your bullshit."

Z's already in his seat and holds out his fist. "Shocked you're still around," I say. "You've been a ghost lately."

He lifts his shoulders but doesn't give me an answer. Not even a joke or a middle finger. So unlike Z.

Teller looks downright exhausted as he drops into his chair. I should've told him to go home earlier. I get that Murphy wants to keep Teller occupied, but Murphy should know better than anyone that Teller won't ever admit he's tired or needs to rest.

After our usual bullshitting and catching up with each other, Rock silences us and points at Sparky who requests help for packaging up some weed.

"Who's making the delivery to Loco tomorrow?" Rock asks.

Dex holds up his hand. "I gotta be over that way tomorrow anyway.

Can I drop it at the house?"

"Aw, you in need of some lovin', bro?" Ravage asks.

Dex's face screws into a scowl, making it obvious the last thing he's interested in is getting serviced by one of Loco's working girls. "You offering?"

"Loco's girls are gonna get a complex if you keep sending Dex," Ravage says to Rock. "Waste of free pussy."

Rock sits back and pins Ravage with a stare that wipes the smile off his face. "The last thing I need is you getting lost in Loco's whorehouse." He nods at Dex again. "Loco has some intel on the MC pushing in from Vermont, so I need you to meet up with him at some point," Rock says.

"You sure he'll be okay meetin' with me?" Dex asks. Smart question. Loco loves dragging Rock to meet-ups, just for the hell of it.

"Yeah. Already spoke to the fucker twenty fuckin' times today." He turns my way next. "How's Dylan doing?"

Not the question I'd been expecting. "Fine. Why?"

"Chaser was lookin' for an update."

"Chaser and Stump are coming for the wedding, right? We still sending them home with a package?" Murphy asks.

"Yeah."

Rock picks up a bunch of papers in front of him and shuffles through them without seeming to read them. Silence falls over the table while we wait for whatever's next on his agenda. "Grinder's getting moved to Pine Correctional at the end of the week."

"No shit," Z and I end up saying at the same time.

"You think he might have a chance of gettin' released some day?" Teller asks.

"Maybe."

"Yeah, since he hasn't had anyone asking him to shank other inmates for the last ten years, maybe he's finally earned some goodwill," Murphy points out.

"Let me know when he's transferred. I'd like to go see him," I tell

Rock.

He raises an eyebrow.

"I'll tell him I'm gettin' married. Make him happy knowing he won that bet."

Finally, Rock's mouth twitches into a smile. "Yeah, okay."

We run through some more minor business, and Rock finally dismisses everyone.

Everyone except me. He doesn't even have to say anything. By the way Rock keeps his eyes on me, it's clear I shouldn't bother gettin' out of my chair. Z sticks around, too.

"What's on your mind?" I ask as soon as everyone's gone.

As usual, Rock gets right to the point. "How'd Teller do today?"

There's no sense in lying to Rock. "Rough start, but he held it together."

"I figured."

"I had a talk with him. The only thing he needs is justice for Mariella."

He blows out a frustrated breath. "I'm trying. Sway's been pressuring the Viper's New Jersey charter, but they claim Ransom's out bad. They swear they have no plans to re-establish a charter up here and don't know where the fuck Ransom's hiding."

"Bullshit," Z snaps. "Someone down there has to know."

"It's a precarious situation," Rock reminds us.

No shit. Even though it's not *us* doing the asking. Any Lost King poking around in Viper business, when we're responsible for taking their local charter down, is hazardous.

"I'm thinking maybe now isn't the time for me to take off."

He leans back and watches me for a minute before speaking. "Go. You two need it. We should back off. Otherwise we'll push Ransom so deep underground we'll never find him."

I know Rock's right, but it still feels like a shitty excuse to leave when I should be here helping.

"I can make some—"

"No," he says, cutting me off. "Loco's crew is on it. Sway…our guys. We'll find that coward."

"Teller needs to be the one to finish him."

"I'll do everything I can to make that happen." Rock's gaze swings to Z. "How about you? Find what you needed on the road?"

"Not really."

"You stickin' around?"

"Yeah. You know I can't stay away from you long, prez." He smirks and Rock leans over to punch his arm.

"Dex does a good job at Crystal Ball, but he keeps bitching that things run smoother when you're there."

"Aw, prez, he's like the stripper whisperer." I fall back against my chair, laughing at my own joke.

Z chuckles, too, not annoyed at my joke or embarrassed by his special skill set. "I know how to keep the ladies in line."

After we finish mocking Z, he pins Rock with a serious stare. "Where we at with the land here?"

"Got plenty. Why?"

"Was thinkin' of building a small cabin. Maybe out past the stone theater."

Now, *this* is news. "Why? You're like the frat party director 'round here."

He cuts a more serious glance my way. "Gettin' old. You should understand."

"Whatever you want, Z. We'll work it out," Rock assures him.

"Thanks." He nods at the door. "Better go out there and see what's going down."

After Z leaves, Rock turns my way.

I raise an eyebrow.

"What?" Rock asks, reading the question on my face. "He doesn't need a wife to wanna build a place of his own."

"Didn't say he did. Just seemed to come out of nowhere."

"Really? He's been fucked for a while."

I shrug. Not because I don't care about whatever Z's going through, but because I figure if he wants to share, he will. Until then it's useless to sit around guessing.

"Anything else, prez?"

"No."

We finally leave the table and step into the living room. There's a party tonight, but it hasn't quite gotten started.

Hope's on the couch, waiting for Rock I assume. She jumps up when she sees us and hurries over.

"I was starting to wonder if Wrath was in trouble," she teases.

Rock flashes a smile but doesn't explain what took us so long. Something Hope seems to accept without a thought.

A warm body I recognize by feel alone molds to my back and a soft arm wraps around my middle. I reach behind me, curling my arm around my girl, and pull her forward. "Hey, handsome," Trinity says in a low voice.

Before I answer, I notice the catalogue in her hand. More wedding tuxes. "No," I grumble.

Her mouth pulls down into her adorable pout.

"It's too late anyway. They'll never be able to find something in my size."

"Even Rock wore a suit to his wedding," she protests.

Rock takes a step back, holding his hands up. "Don't drag me into this."

"But—" Trinity starts.

"Tell me what color dress you're wearing, and I'll make sure my shorts match."

Her mouth twists. "No."

My hand slips and I give her ass a slight squeeze. "You've talked me into everything else. Have some mercy on me. I can't do the tux."

"Fine." She leans up and kisses my cheek. "I need to check something in the kitchen. Be right back."

After she clears the room, I turn to Hope. "You goin' with us tomorrow?"

"Of course."

I lower my voice. "If I tell you something, promise not to tell Trin?"

"Maybe."

I stare at her until she huffs. "Okay."

"I'm not wearing shorts."

"Ew. You better not go pant-less."

"You wish."

Next to her, Rock chuckles. I don't have a chance to explain my plan, because Trinity returns to the living room. Her eyes narrow as she takes the three of us in. "What?"

Hope easily launches into pesky bridesmaid role, reaching up and tugging on my beard.

"Is this staying?" she asks Trinity who laughs.

"I like it," Trinity says, patting the side of my face.

Hope gives me a critical look. "Really? It doesn't give you beard burn?" She turns and runs her hand over Rock's cheek. "It's always scratchy when he grows one."

I lean down and rub my cheek against Trinity's until she laughs. "If you use it *right*, it's a sensation enhancer during *certain* activities." I raise an eyebrow at Hope until my meaning sinks in.

"Oh." She tilts her head at Rock. "Maybe you should try again."

"Whatever gets my face between your legs, baby doll."

Shock colors Hope's cheeks pink but she shakes with laughter, while next to me, Trinity moans in disgust.

A little silliness with the girls is a good way to purge the seriousness that followed us out of church. Even Rock lightens up and says they're planning to stick around for the party, something I don't think the two of them have done since they moved out of the clubhouse.

"I told Murphy they could have the house for a few hours," Hope explains.

"Is *that* why we're over here?" Rock asks.

"Well—"

"Doesn't seem like they can have much fun with a teething baby at home," I point out.

Hope chuckles. "She's not that bad."

"Uh—" Rock starts and Hope smacks his chest.

"She's not."

Trinity holds up her hands. "I have no intention of finding out."

"A-fuckin-men," I agree.

Hope chuckles but doesn't question either of us, which I appreciate. Every other woman I come into contact with lately has asked when Trin and I plan to have kids. As if getting married isn't enough, now we have to spit out babies to be legit or something.

Fuck that.

"What's wrong?" Trin asks.

I squeeze her a little tighter. "Nothing."

CHAPTER FIVE

Nine days before the wedding...

"HOLY HELL, YOU weren't kidding about the place burning to the ground." Hope gasps and cranes her neck to stare at the site where Wyatt and I were supposed to be married.

"Right? Wow. Wyatt, did you see it?"

"I saw," he answers without taking his eyes off the road.

"Pull into Painter's Pavilion. That's where we're supposed to meet him."

Hope jumps out of the truck first. The big wedding binder stayed home, but she's clutching her blue bridesmaid notebook tight—I've taught her well.

"Hi, I'm Trinity." I hold out my hand for the park ranger. He takes it while staring at me, like he's waiting for me to bite.

He walks us around the site, and I don't want to say it out loud, but this is so much better than where we were going to get married.

"Most importantly, your party has to be cleaned up and out of here by four p.m."

"Four?" Wyatt asks, shooting me a look.

"I thought we could be here until sunset?" I ask.

"Nope. I need this place picked up, and I mean spotless, by four. No rice-throwing, confetti-throwing or—"

"No throwing of any material, sir, we get it," Hope assures him.

I cough-snicker into my hand.

"Music has to be at a reasonable level that does not interfere with other park activities."

"No problem there," Hope says, scribbling in her notebook.

"No alcohol allowed in the park, either. Anyone who gets caught with alcohol will be tossed out."

Wrath gives me a look, like maybe we should have paid more attention to the fine print when we decided to have the wedding here. I lift my shoulders. Too late now.

After a few more warnings, he steps back to let the three of us wander over the grounds. "This is so much better, Trin," Hope gushes. "You can either get married down here, with that gorgeous view behind you..." She throws her arms out wide, indicating the concrete deck overlooking the mountains and valley, "or, if heaven forbid"—she crosses her fingers and stares up at the sky, making Wrath chuckle—"it rains, we can do it in the gazebo."

"We can have the prospects set up a tent," Wyatt suggests. He glances around for the park manager. "Is a fuckin' tent allowed?"

The guy doesn't even bristle at Wyatt's coarse language. "A tent will require an additional deposit. And it—"

"Must be removed by four, got it," Hope says. "Oh, wow. The bathroom building is brand new, Trin. That's good. The old ones were worse than outhouses."

The park manager glares at her, but Hope either doesn't care or is oblivious. I'm guessing the second one.

WRATH

"HOW LONG IS the actual wedding part going to be?" I ask Hope while

Trinity wanders around snapping pictures.

She has the nerve to roll her eyes. "As long as it needs to be."

"You're frustrating, you know that?"

"It's why I'm so much fun." She all but sticks her tongue out at me.

"Maybe for Rock." I turn, pretending to look around the place. "Where is he, anyway?"

"Home. He didn't need to be here for this. His only job is getting you here on time."

"Oh, I'll be here on time."

She tilts her head to the side. "You're really looking forward to this, aren't you?"

"Yeah. Why?"

Her shoulders lift. "I don't know. When I met you...I never would have...you know—"

"Pictured me settling down?"

"I guess."

"I didn't want to back then."

"And now?"

"Now what?"

She huffs out an annoyed breath. "I love Trinity. Like a sister."

"Oh. Is this your version of a 'hurt my friend and I'll kill you' speech?"

"Well, now you took all the fun out of it."

I can't hold in my laughter any longer. "You're a brave little spitfire." I slip an arm around her shoulders. "All I want to do is take care of Trinity and have her take care of me."

"Boy, is she getting the raw end of *that* deal."

When I finish laughing, she says a little quieter, "She told me about the photography studio you're planning to buy her. That's really thoughtful."

Knowing Trinity was so excited about the studio, she already gushed to Hope about it is a nice reassurance. "Thanks."

"Oh, God," Trinity shouts. "What are you two conspiring about?" Her voice lowers as she reaches us. "He's not wearing a kilt to the wedding, is he, Hope?"

Hope bursts out laughing and pulls away from me. "God, I hope not." She makes a skirt-lifting motion. "They don't wear underwear under those things. No one needs a peek of that."

"Hey." My protest is muffled by my own laughter. "You'd be lucky to see the good stuff."

She snort-laughs even harder.

Shaking her head, Trinity wraps her hand around Hope's arm and drags her away. "Let's get some measurements," she says, gesturing to a patch of concrete.

I'd help, but I have no idea what they're trying to accomplish, so I watch them instead. When Trinity seems satisfied, she rolls up her tape measure and flips me a thumbs up.

Finally.

CHAPTER SIX

"WE'RE LEAVING IN ten."

Turning, I find Wrath filling the doorway with an eager expression in place. He looks so happy, I can't even tease him for *telling* me instead of asking. "Eager much?"

"Yup. Our cabin in the woods is waiting."

"Isn't that a horror movie?"

His mouth curls into a smirk as he moves across the room and pulls me out of my chair, tucking me tight against the front of his body. He palms my ass then gives it a smack. "Don't be a wiseass."

It feels so good to be pressed up against him, I won't even complain that he interrupted some work I was trying to finish before we leave.

Instead, my arms loop around his neck. Knowing what I'm after, he lifts me up and I wrap my legs around his hips.

"What do you say?" he asks.

"I go where you go, fiancé."

"Fuck, I love hearing you call me that. Husband's gonna be even better."

My lips find their way to his forehead, pressing a soft kiss there before traveling to his mouth, where I enjoy a smooth, sensual slide of our lips meeting.

"I love you, Wyatt," I murmur before opening my eyes.

"Love you, too, angel," he says, setting me down. He cocks his head. "You good with the park situation now?"

Excitement hums through my veins. "*Ohmygod*, yes. I love the new space even more. It's so much nicer. The view's better on that side of the park—"

His lips cover mine, cutting me off before I get carried away. When he pulls back, he's studying me with seriousness. "I love how excited you are about our wedding."

Not for the first time, I'm struck by Wyatt's sweetness. Even if he doesn't show much enthusiasm about little wedding details—like the tiny cobalt-blue glass vases I found on sale and plan to use as centerpieces—he's never made me feel silly about any of it. "Thank you for going up there with me."

"I wouldn't have missed it." His lips twitch. "Especially the part where Hope threatened to kill me if I don't treat you right."

Hope can be reckless or ballsy—depending on your point of view—but even *I* have a hard time picturing her saying that to Wyatt. "She did not."

"Nah, but that's what she meant."

"So that's what you two were talking about?" Their evolving friendship—for lack of a better word—never stops amusing me.

He leans down and presses another kiss against my lips. "Yes. And that you told her about the studio."

"Oh. Was that okay?"

"Yes. I'm happy you like it." Laced with his words is a hint of relief.

"I love it." I lean in, rubbing my body against him. "I guess I should have done a better job of showing you how much."

I get a crisp smack on my ass. "You'll thank me by putting it to good use." He looks over my shoulder. "And getting your ass in gear. We still have to stop for groceries and stuff. Are you ready?"

"Almost."

"Good. I don't want you worrying about anything except all the dirty things I'm going to do to you." He nods at my computer. "You all set for a few days?"

"Let me finish sending a few emails. Then yes. Heidi has all my other stuff, so she'll be working on that while we're gone."

He glances around the room, spying my bag on the bed. "Don't bother bringing clothes, you won't need them."

"Oh really?"

"Well, maybe something to wear in the kitchen so you don't burn any important bits."

I laugh so hard, I end up falling back on the bed. "So this is really more of a vacation for *you*? Sex and being waited on hand and foot?"

"I told you no other woman would put up with me." He snatches my hand and yanks me closer. "I'll take you out to dinner. Not sure what's up there, but we'll find something. We can go hiking, too. Bring your camera."

"I was only kidding. Sex and food work for me."

He buries his face against my neck, playfully growling, biting, and licking my skin until I laugh and push him away. "That's why you're the perfect woman."

We spend a few more minutes kissing, but before we get carried away, Wyatt pulls back. All business again.

"It's too chilly to take the bike that far." He gestures to my bag again. "Bring whatever you want, we have room in the truck."

When my man said *ten minutes*, he meant it. I rush through my last-minute emails. My bags are ready to go. I even remembered to pack extra pillows—just in case. Wyatt, on the other hand, seems to have a lot more stuff than a simple three-day trip requires.

"What's all that?"

His mouth quirks into a sensually-devilish smile. "Supplies."

"This place has heat and running water, right? I'm not into outhouses and candles."

"Not those kind of supplies."

I have no idea what to make of that. But my skin tingles, imagining all the possibilities.

While we're outside packing up the truck, Murphy stops over. "Heading out?"

Instead of answering the question, Wyatt has one of his own. "Why aren't you down at Furious?"

"I'm on my way now."

Wyatt narrows his eyes. "You got this, right?"

Normally, Murphy would bristle at being questioned like that, but he seems to take his new role at the gym seriously. "Yes, don't worry about anything. I'll be there until closing tonight. Twitch called out, but Dylan said he'd stay."

"Make sure pretty boy gets the cleaning done. Little fucker doesn't like gettin' his hands dirty."

Murphy bursts out laughing. "Right? You noticed that, too?"

"Fuck yeah, I did."

"He's been real good at gettin' people to sign up for classes and stuff, so don't be too hard on him," Murphy says.

They wrap up their conversation, and Murphy gives me a quick hug before heading into the garage.

"Ready?" Wyatt asks, boosting me up into the truck.

I'm actually really excited about our trip. "Does the cabin have a fireplace?" I ask when he slides into his seat.

He turns, his handsome face dipping into a frown. "I think so, why?"

"It'll be romantic."

A teasing smile tugs the corners of his mouth up. "You wanna sit in front of the fire and stare into each other's eyes or something?"

"Not if you're going to make fun of me."

He leans in closer and rubs his thumb over my cheek. "Hopefully there's a bearskin rug I can screw you on in front of this fire," he says in a low voice that conjures up a precise picture of us doing exactly that.

Now, if some other woman overheard him, they might be offended at Wyatt's bluntness with me. But I find it amusing, because he doesn't say shit like that to be disrespectful. No, he says it to tease me. And turn me on. Which, it totally does.

After leaving the clubhouse, it's a long drive up the Northway. We never run out of things to talk about though. The farther we go, the more Wyatt seems to loosen up. More than once, he said he wanted to take this trip to give *me* a break from all the wedding planning stuff, but *he's* the one who needed a break. I'm looking forward to keeping his mind off of work and club business for a few days.

When our GPS shows we're still a couple miles from the cabin, Wyatt slows the truck. "This might be the last grocery store we pass. Want to stop now or go back out later?" he asks.

"Now. Once we get there, I don't want to leave." I punctuate my words by running my hand along his inner thigh and *accidentally* brushing his crotch.

"Watch it," he growls.

"What?" I ask with wide eyes.

He grumbles as he puts the truck in park. "Let's make this fast."

I whip out my shopping list. "It's short."

"Nothing on me is short, babe," he deadpans.

"You're hilarious."

Inside the store, we end up grabbing more than what's on my list. We're in the dairy aisle and I'm bending down for a carton of eggs when Wyatt's suddenly pressed up against my side.

Slowly I stand and set the eggs in the cart. He leans down, placing his lips against my ear. "Why are you trying to give me a hard-on in the middle of the grocery store?" His voice isn't more than a husky whisper, but it sends shivers down my spine.

In case I need proof, he bands his arm around my waist and gently thrusts his hips into me.

I open my mouth—to tell him to stop or strip me naked, I'm not sure—when another late-night shopper rounds the corner. She's busy studying the shelves and doesn't notice us, but I still pull away.

I glance down, zeroing in on the bulge behind his zipper. "You're going to get us arrested."

He briefly closes his eyes. "You're killing me."

My hands close over the cart to get us moving, but he stops me. "You're kidding, right? Give me a second."

I barely contain my laughter as he closes his eyes and, I assume, counts backwards from one hundred or something.

We make it out of the store without any trouble. Well, except for the smoldering looks Wyatt keeps shooting my way. I'm a big bundle of anticipation as he steers us back on the road.

Wyatt's excitement seems to fill the truck the closer we get to the cabin. His hand slips from the steering wheel, settling on my knee for a few miles before gripping my inner thigh, then traveling up to graze my breast. "Take your shirt off."

"What?"

A car passes us and he growls. "Pull your pants down instead."

"Again, what?"

"I'm waiting."

Curious, I unbutton my jeans and wriggle them down. Wyatt's hand tickles my belly as he tries to force it down my pants. "More," he demands.

I work them all the way to my knees and glance over. "Happy?"

"Fuck, yes. You're fucking hot as fuck."

"That was a lot of fucks."

Wyatt's not in the mood for jokes. "Lean back and spread your legs for your man."

The low, sexy voice he uses has me following his every command.

He flips on the blinker and steers us onto a bumpy dirt road. "There. No cars." His hand returns, lodging between my legs. He brushes his fingers against my inner thigh, then traces up my slit.

"Sit back more. Scoot down. Spread your legs wider."

"So bossy," I whisper as I do everything he asked.

"You love it," he says, slicking one finger to my entrance and back up to circle my clit.

"Yes, I do." My words tumble out, soft and slurred. Concentrating on speech is too difficult with the way he's touching me.

"So soft and wet." He slides two fingers back and forth. Stroking and sinking deeper into me with each pass. My clit gets a little extra attention, but not as much as I need.

"Wy-Wyatt." I moan and arch my hips, inviting him to do more.

"Feel good?"

"Uh-huh."

He makes a sound somewhere between a growl and a grunt. "Can't get the right angle."

I'm so lost, I barely notice the truck stop. I do notice the loss of his hand. My eyes pop open. "What? Where?"

"One second. Don't move."

He opens his door and jumps down, hustling around the front of the truck. Before I have a chance to brace myself, he flings my door open. Reaching in, he unbuckles my seatbelt. "Lie back."

I don't even have time to do it before he's ripping my sneakers off and tossing them somewhere in the woods behind him. My pants get yanked down my legs and flung into the backseat of the truck.

"Wyatt!" I'm giggling and moaning, loving all of it as he slips his hands under my ass, lifting me. He leans in going straight for my clit, teasing at first. My hips move with his rhythm, and he holds on tight.

He switches to long, slow laps with the flat of his tongue, every now and then looking up to gauge my reaction. As always, he adjusts to what I need. Faster. Harder. Another hard swipe along my pussy. His hands move to my inner thighs, pressing my legs wide open, guiding them over his shoulders.

I can't help moaning and hope to God we're someplace remote because I have to be making enough noise to draw a crowd. I reach down, threading my fingers through his hair, and he groans.

All his attention focuses on my clit, and I tilt my hips to meet him. My heart thumps faster, my breathing ragged, heat racing over my skin.

"Wy-Wyatt. I'm—"

He makes a humming sound of encouragement but doesn't stop, and that's when I go off. Legs shaking, body twisting, nails digging into his scalp, holding him in place.

"Fuck, that was fucking beautiful," he says when I finally release him. He grabs my hand, backing up a step and pulling me with him. I barely have time to catch my breath before I'm flung over his shoulder. His hand smacks my ass a few times.

"Wyatt!" I'm laughing the whole time he carries me up the stairs, fumbles in his pocket for a key, kicks open the cabin door, and brings me inside.

Gently, he sets me down on something cold, flat, and hard under my butt cheeks. "Wyatt?"

"Stay," he orders. "Shirt off."

The way he's giving the short, clipped directions is so fucking hot, I can't get my shirt and bra off fast enough.

He flattens his palm against my chest, gently pushing me back. Next, he picks my feet up, placing my heels on the edge of the counter. His hands run over my legs. Delicious shivers of anticipation follow his fingertips.

"Spread wide," he says, nudging my knees apart. He grabs one of my hands, placing it over my pussy. "Play with yourself. I'm gonna bring our stuff in, and first thing I wanna see when I walk in the door is your fingers in your pussy."

"Okay," I whisper.

"Good girl."

He leans over and kisses my forehead before leaving, and I get to work.

WRATH

THIS TRIP'S ALREADY fucking awesome. Trin's scent clings to my skin. I can't wait to get back inside and fuck her senseless.

I turn before stepping outside and find her doing as I asked. Fucking unbelievably hot.

Hurrying down the stairs, I grab all of our bags and the cooler before heading back inside. Once I shut the door, the only things I plan on doing in the next seventy-two hours are fuck, feed, and talk to Trinity.

"You close, angel?" I ask as I approach the counter.

"Uh-uh," she mumbles.

"Here." Slipping my hands under her shoulders and knees, I spin her so her head's hanging off the counter. Perfect. She blinks up at me and smiles. "What're you doing?"

"Getting my dick out for you to suck."

"Oooh." She reaches up, and I bat her hands away.

"*No.* Fingers in your pussy."

The pout she puts on is fucking adorable. Even better when I slide my cock between her lips. Cradling the back of her head with one hand, I guide myself into her mouth and back out again. She seals her lips around my shaft, sucking like I'm the best thing she's ever tasted.

She gags a little when I go too far.

"Okay?" I ask.

She moans and hums, happy noises that I think mean *yes*, so I keep going. I've been worked up since she climbed into my truck earlier, so I'm not gonna last long. At the last second, I slip out of her mouth, shooting cum all over her tits.

"Fuck." I can't stop coming or groaning. The way her hands reach up to hold my thighs makes it even more intense.

When I finish, she picks her head up, staring at her chest, then up at me with a raised eyebrow.

"I was afraid you'd choke if I came down your throat, since you were upside down and all." I gesture to the edge of the counter, and she giggles.

"Give me a second." It takes more than a second to get my bearings and find some paper towels to clean her up with. My pants are somewhere around my ankles, so I stop to unlace my boots and kick them off.

"Mmmm...naked Wyatt. No clothes for you while we're here, mountain man."

I slip my shirt off, dropping it on top of my pants and shoes, then pick her up off the counter. "That so?"

"Yup."

"Fucking love you, Angel Face."

"You know how to start a vacation with a bang." She snickers at her joke, shaking in my arms.

I drop a kiss on her forehead and take in her flushed cheeks. "You didn't come, did you?"

"Just now? No."

"Can't have that."

She points at the cabin door. "I think you took care of me out there."

"Yeah, but I'm an over-achiever."

"Lucky me." She loops her arms around my neck and nuzzles her nose against my chest while I carry her around the cabin looking for the bedroom.

"Knock it off, that tickles."

"You smell good," she murmurs right before her teeth graze my nipple.

"Careful, angel."

We finally find the bedroom, but there are no sheets or anything on the bed.

"Fuck."

She wriggles in my arms and I set her down. "I brought sheets."

"You did?"

"Yes. You said cabin in the woods, I wasn't sure how rustic it would be."

"Didn't even occur to me."

"That's why you have me," she teases.

She scurries back out to the living room, and when she doesn't return right away, my dick leads me right to her. Don't care if there're sheets on the bed or not, I want her in it. *Now.*

"Trin?" I stop in my tracks. "Why are you dressed?"

"There's a bag missing. I wanted to run and grab it without giving the woodland creatures a thrill."

"I'll do it."

"No. No clothes for you, remember?"

I watch as she races out to the truck and pulls more than one bag out. Man, I was so focused on the goodies *I* packed and talking to Murphy before we left, I didn't pay any attention to what she stuffed in there. As I have that thought, my gaze lands on my bag of tricks for Trinity and scoop it up before heading into the bedroom.

She meets me in there and starts making the bed, asking for my help once or twice. When she's finished, she finally notices that I've emptied out my bag and lined it all up on the nightstand.

Her honey eyes widen. "I'm scared to ask what you're planning to do with your little anal arsenal over there."

"Who said anything about anal?"

She cocks her head and makes an adorable *are-you-kidding?* face at me. "Isn't that what this whole trip is about?"

I don't answer until I'm standing in front of her. "No. It's about us getting away and spending time together. Having you all to myself."

Her beautiful, angel face softens. "Wyatt." She lifts her chin and flashes a naughty smile before her gaze drops to my dick. "How can you be so hard and so sweet at the same time?"

As much as I love her being cute, I'm also impatient as fuck. "Strip for me."

Her eyes widen, but she gets busy shedding clothes. Doesn't even bother trying to be seductive or teasing about it—which is exactly what I need right now.

When she's beautifully naked, I guide her over to the side of the bed. I sit on the edge and make her watch while I pretend to consider each item. I already know what I want to use. But it's much more fun to keep her guessing.

"Wyatt, please. Why are you torturing me like this?"

Should I feel like a dick? Maybe. But Trinity whining for my dick in her ass is a big fucking turn-on.

My hand connects with her ass for a nice crisp smack. "What did I tell you?"

"When *you* think I'm ready."

"Right. And you're not ready. So calm the fuck down."

Her lips push into a pout, and she turns to face the wall. I barely hold in my laughter. It's killing me. My dick's calling me a thousand foul names. But I don't want to hurt her. Nope, I want to blow her fucking mind. I want to erase every single bad memory and give her a good one.

And I *love* a challenge.

CHAPTER SEVEN

Eight days before the wedding...

I WAKE UP the next morning with Wyatt's hand between my legs, gently stroking. It doesn't matter that we spent the rest of yesterday afternoon and evening in bed, my body's already responding to his touch.

"What're you doing?" I mumble, already burning with need for him.

He answers with soft kisses on my shoulder, traveling down to lick my nipples. Lower, he thrusts a finger in me, working my slippery flesh with gentle but firm strokes. Our eyes meet, and the hazy insanity of passion throbs through me. He sweeps a greedy stare over my body, exciting me even more.

"Close your eyes. Let me have my way with you," he demands.

All I can do is moan in response and do as he asks. My hips rock against him. His lips brush over my cheeks, and he leans away from me briefly. His fingers feel so fucking good, I don't think about what he's doing other than the pleasure he's giving me.

"Turn over." He nudges my hip, and for a second, his fingers slide out of me. A needy little whimper is all I get out before his hands grip me again.

Warm, slick liquid spills over my back. His big hands rub the oil into my skin with the perfect pressure. Firm, almost too much, but just right. He rubs, taking his time thoroughly kneading my back. Slowly, he travels down to my lower back, then my ass. He groans as his fingers knead into my butt. More oil drips onto my skin, sliding down my spine and ending between my butt cheeks.

"We're making a mess," I murmur into the sheets.

"We're about to make a much bigger mess," he answers.

His hands keep moving over me, fingers digging deep into my muscles, relaxing and turning me on at the same time.

"Your ass is perfect." He shifts, making the bed squeak. His teeth graze my skin, and he places a light kiss at the small of my back. A second later, I feel his finger slide down between my cheeks.

My body tenses up, but Wyatt is there, whispering soothing noises at me. I gasp as he pushes a well-lubed finger against me.

"Relax."

I take a deep breath, letting it out slowly.

His other hand grazes my inner thigh. Slick and warm. He taps my leg until I catch on and spread wide for him. He rubs soft circles around my clit. A gentle buzzing reaches me, and I suck in a quick breath when he places the small bullet vibrator against my pussy.

I need the distraction because what he's doing to my ass is more intense than I counted on. Not painful. Strange. I can't decide if I like it or not, but I don't want him to stop. I reach down and roll the little bullet, pressing it harder against me. "Wyatt," I gasp out.

"Come, angel."

It's a soft, fluttering orgasm and before I finish, something harder presses against my ass. I'm strangely excited. He'd kept me on edge all night, not knowing if he'd use one of the toys on me or not. After a few gentle pushes, whatever he has slips in, unyielding and uncomfortable. I squirm against his hand.

"Shh. You can handle it. Relax and take it for me."

Oh, he knows exactly what to say, because I'll do anything for him. Even accept the strange pressure of the toy he slowly pulls out, then pushes back inside me. Wyatt's arm slips around my waist, lifting me. His cock slides along my pussy, grazing me at first, then achingly slow he presses inside.

"Good?" he asks.

It is good. So good. Why do I like it so much? *"Mmmmhmm,"* is the only answer I give.

He chuckles at my wordless reply and drags his hips back.

"You want more?" Wyatt's voice comes out low and rough. Waiting for my answer must take a lot of self-control.

"Yes." I tip my ass up, inviting him to do whatever he wants, and he thrusts forward.

Each stroke comes harsher than the last. His hand slides across my ass, cupping it. Rough fingers dig in, gripping me tight and possessive.

"Oh. Oh." I'm so full. So overwhelmed. I can't decide if I like it or not. My body and mind can't keep up with all the different sensations.

He twists and pulls at the toy in my ass, teasing me until I realize I'm pressing back against him, desperately trying to get more of both sensations. His hands, his mouth, everything about him works to bring my overwhelmed body nothing but pleasure.

"Wyatt." My voice turns desperate as his thrusts speed up.

"You feel so good. So fucking tight." I hum with happiness at the praise. I want to return every bit of pleasure he gives me in whatever way he craves.

"Fucking come for me." He grits out each word.

As if my body had been waiting for those exact words, I come undone. There's nothing soft about *this* orgasm. I'm limp and tingling with satisfaction when Wyatt stills, making the sexiest groaning sound as he comes inside me. He lingers, kissing my back and shoulders. Soothing me with gentle touches before slowly pulling out.

I turn and try to push myself up.

"No, stay. Just like that," Wyatt orders in his sex-rough voice that makes me freeze in place.

I'm lost in my own thoughts, my body humming with happiness, when he returns to clean me up. He swivels the toy in my ass, and my body jerks away.

"I can't decide if I should make you wear this all day or take it out and give you a break."

"Um, I vote to take it out. It's weird."

He leans over and teasingly bites at my shoulder, making happy growly noises against my ear. "Yeah, but it's so much smaller than my dick."

"Good thing that's not going anywhere near my ass," I challenge, trying to get some sense of what he plans to do.

What I get instead is a soft smack on my ass, and then he slowly drags the toy out. "I'll be right back."

I roll over on my back and watch him walk away. Powerful legs, perfect butt that I want to get my hands on. Something must be wrong with me because I can't get enough of him.

"Did you drug me?" I call out.

He doesn't answer until he's back in the bedroom. "What?"

"Did you put something in my food? I can barely move, but I want you to fuck me again."

I don't have a chance to appreciate the wide grin on his face before he launches himself at me, playfully jumping on the bed and gathering me in his arms. He rolls us so I'm on top of him. "No drugs, you nut. I'm just that good."

I lean down and press a quick kiss against his lips. "Yeah, you are."

He pushes the hair out of my face and pins me with a serious stare. "Tell me the truth. Did you like that?"

"Umm. I like everything you do to me."

"That's not an answer."

"Sure it is."

The exasperated breath he blows out fluffs my hair out of my eyes. "Did it feel good? Be honest."

"Yes." My admission comes out easier than I expected.

He kisses the tip of my nose. "Thank you."

Playfully, I nip at him and he tickles my side. We tease each other like that for a few more minutes before he drags us out of bed and into the shower.

As we're drying off, I let out a big yawn. "It's barely morning, and I already need a nap."

Wyatt takes the towel out of my hands and briskly rubs it over my shoulders and back. "Well, I've ridden you hard since we got here."

"Yeah, you have." I wiggle my butt at him and am rewarded with a solid smack on one cheek.

"Get your hot little ass dressed so we can go for a walk. Get some fresh air before breakfast," he suggests.

"Sounds good."

While we're getting dressed, he tosses a pair of leggings at me. "Wear these."

I don't even blink at his bossy tone. Why bother when we both know it turns me on more than I'll ever admit. "They're really more for lounging around."

"Yeah, but your ass looks fantastic in them."

"My ass looks fantastic in everything."

He stalks closer, then pulls me in for a hug, squeezing my butt. "Fuck, yeah it does. Especially in my hands."

I laugh and duck out of his hold. "We're never going to go for that walk if you start groping me."

One corner of his mouth lifts in that sexy smirk I can't resist. Picking up the leggings, I wave them in his face. "They're not really carry-friendly."

He grumbles a bunch of unhappy noises. "Yeah, I'd rather have you armed in case we run into a bear or you know, an ax murderer."

"You're really selling this walk."

Eventually, we make it out of the house. Wyatt takes my hand, and we head into the woods behind the cabin. It seems like the last few months have been nothing but both of us working long hours. Whether it's me and my photography or Wyatt's gym and club duties keeping him busy, we haven't had much time to fool around and just *be* together.

"I love being with you," he says as if he'd read my thoughts.

I squeeze his hand. "I love being with you, too. We have fun together, right?"

"Always." He stops and glances down at me with a serious expression. "Not just the sex—although, that's fucking awesome."

"Fuck yeah, it is," I tease, jabbing my finger in his gut. That was stupid. His stomach's like a brick wall. "Ow. I think I broke a nail."

"Nutty girl." He tugs me along a faint path through the woods. The trail follows a small stream, and I keep stopping to see if there are any fish.

"We don't have any poles," Wyatt says, stopping to check the water with me.

"What, you can't play Tarzan and catch one with your bare hands for me?"

He busts up laughing. "I can, if that's what you want." Suddenly he stops and pulls me close. "What do you think about owning a cabin up here? Like this one?"

"We just built a house. You want to move *here*?" Is he suggesting leaving the club? I can't imagine Wyatt wanting to do that.

"No. A vacation place. To get away from everything when we need to."

"Oh. Sure," I say off the cuff, certain he's not serious, but his next words knock me sideways.

"It would make a nice wedding present for my girl."

"What? Did you...is it ours?"

"Not yet. I wanted to see if we liked it first. The owner's had it on the market for a while, so I think we can get it for a good price."

The way he keeps saying *we*, even though I haven't really done any-thing to contribute to our finances, I don't know, it does something to me. It's a silly thing to fixate on at the moment, but I can't help it.

"I love it here. But I love wherever we go as long as we're together."

He gives me a soft smile and kisses my forehead.

"Really, Wyatt. Whatever you want is fine by me."

"I've seen the pictures of your dream house on the beach," he teases.

"Mmm…a hut in Belize where you can run around in a loin cloth all day would be perfection," I joke back.

His mouth lifts into a sexy smirk. "That might be a *little* out of our price range right now."

"Cabin in the woods works for me, too. I'll follow you anywhere."

He takes my hand again. We traipse through the woods together, enjoying the quiet. My stomach growls and I'm about to tell Wyatt I want to head back, when he suddenly stops.

"What?" I giggle and he shushes me.

All the fun is sucked right out of our morning.

Wyatt points to a spot ahead.

"It looks like a Christmas tree farm," I whisper.

"Look closer."

It takes a second to see what has him on alert. Growing in between the wide evergreens are giant pot plants.

"Take your Ruger out," he says, so quietly I almost don't hear him.

I lift my sweatshirt and pull the revolver Wyatt insisted I bring on our vacation from the holster inside my waistband.

He slips up his shirt, drawing his Glock into his hand. He's com-pletely still as his eyes scan the surrounding area. Finally, he points to a pole at the edge of the property.

Security cameras.

"Let's get out of here," he says. "Go." He nudges my arm and I turn but abruptly stop.

"Wyatt, wait!" I hush-shout.

He crashes into my back and wraps his hands around my upper arms to steady me.

I point to the black metal in front of me. "Bear trap."

"Holy fuck. How the fuck did we miss that?" he whispers.

"I don't know. Good thing we stopped or one of us would be missing a foot."

He takes my hand again and carefully leads me back to the trail to our cabin. We don't encounter anything else out of the ordinary.

I don't question him, just keep moving. Even when he stops several times to make sure no one's following us.

It's a long walk. When our cabin's in sight, I break into a run.

WRATH

IN MY HEAD, I'm running through a thousand scenarios. The little Christmas tree-pot farm we found appears to be the innocent set-up of a hobby-farmer. The camera and bear traps suggest something more sinister.

"I'm going to change and then I'll fix breakfast," Trinity says as I open the cabin door for her. "Are you all right?" She frowns and runs the back of her hand over my cheek.

"All good. I'm gonna grab some firewood. Lock the door behind you. I have the key."

She doesn't question me, just gives me a quick kiss and goes inside.

I will grab firewood—because I haven't forgotten our plans to screw in front of a roaring fireplace, but I'm more interested in patrolling the perimeter of the property first. No one followed us back, I'm sure of that. It's possible the camera was fake, and bear traps had more to do with actual bears than the pot farm.

Possible, but unlikely.

I walk around the outside of the cabin double-checking doors and windows.

Once I'm satisfied everything's secure, I grab some logs and head inside.

After starting the fire, I follow Trinity's happy humming to the kitchen.

Where I stop and stare.

"So maybe we won't buy *this* cabin," Trinity says while she's busy chopping vegetables.

I can barely concentrate on her words though.

She's in the kitchen wearing an apron and nothing else.

Hottest sight ever.

"Uh, yeah. Could be more than some local hippie growing his own supply."

Not taking my eyes off her, I carefully place my Glock on the table and push one of the kitchen chairs against the wall so I can watch every move my little angel makes.

I end up sitting there with a dry mouth and a hard dick trying to play along.

She nods and turns to wash her hands, giving me a fantastic view of her naked ass.

"Isn't it strange to have an outdoor grow-op in New York?" she asks over her shoulder.

I'm so busy staring at her ass it takes a few seconds longer than normal to process her question. "Yeah. Brilliant though. Some Podunk, harmless looking Christmas tree farm. Far away from town, from civilization." I pause and think about the video camera and bear trap again. "Could've been dangerous if whoever's growing it thought we were trying to steal their crop."

"Or turn them in," she says softly. "Even if they saw us on the camera, the fact that we didn't get closer or take any pictures means they'll probably leave us alone."

Christ, she's fucking smart. Too bad all my blood has rushed south and I'm only able to grunt in agreement.

"Up here, so far away from everything—there's probably shady stuff going on all over the place," she adds.

"True."

She chuckles at my one word answer and tilts her head to the side, flashing a wink and smile my way. "At least it's not a meth lab."

"Positive thinking. Nice." The last word comes out strangled because her apron gapes as she moves, providing me with a glimpse of side boob and perky nipple. I'm losing control over the situation below my belt. Sitting back, I undo the button of my shorts and ease the zipper down to relieve some of the pressure. "Whatcha making me?"

"I'm making *us* frittatas," she answers without glancing over.

"Trin?"

"Yes?" She doesn't turn. Doesn't look at me. But there's a teasing smile playing over her lips.

"Shut the stove off and come here."

"But I'm right in the middle of making breakfast." Her mouth might be protesting, but I catch the flick of her wrist as she twists the knob, turning the flame off.

"Get over here." My voice comes out rough and demanding.

She runs her hands over the front of the apron a few times as she approaches. When she stops in front of me, her leg barely brushes up against mine. I tilt my head back, taking all of her in. Figuring out exactly what I want to do to her.

Slowly, I reach out and run my hands along the edge of the apron, the backs of my fingers barely graze her thighs. Her lips part, but she stays perfectly still.

I pat my thigh. "Sit."

The corner of her mouth pulls up, as if she's humoring me. She perches on my leg, keeping her toes on the floor.

My hand slips through a gap between the apron and her body, curling around her breast. "When'd you decide on this?"

Her eyes widen, as if she thinks I don't approve. Grabbing her hand, I place it over my dick, so she knows exactly how much I love it.

"At home."

"*Mmm*...I like it. You gonna do this for me all the time once we're moved into our house?"

I'm rewarded with a sly smile. "If you want me to."

Banding one arm around her waist, I shift her so her back's against my chest. She reaches out to cover her legs with the little bit of apron, and I catch her hands in one of mine, pressing them between her breasts. My other hand arranges her legs so they're draped over mine, leaving her wide open for whatever I want.

I trail my fingers up her thigh, stopping at her hip. "Are you wet, angel?" I ask against her ear.

She leans back even farther, resting her head against my shoulder, "Yes."

I slide my hand down lower and stroke her inner thigh, then her pussy. She groans deep in her throat and struggles to open her legs wider. "Good girl," I whisper as I slip one finger inside her. "When did you get wet?"

My thumb slides over her clit, and she jerks against me. I want to work her up until she's restless and aching for my cock, but I'm not sure how long I can hold out. "Answer me."

"Ah, when, what?"

"Do you want to come?"

She gasps and nods frantically. "I'm always wet around you," she blurts out, panting hard.

I turn, nuzzling her neck, kissing and nipping while she squirms in my arms. "I like that answer."

She lets out a soft snort. "Of course you..." the rest of her sentence is lost to the sweet sounds of her moaning as I add another finger and slowly pump them in and out of her.

"You want me to fuck you, Trin?"

She moans louder and my heart pounds.

Abruptly, I release her hands and untie the apron.

"Stand up." Since she's having trouble finding her balance, I guide her with my hands on her hips until she's facing me.

The apron falls to the floor, leaving her bare and beautiful in front of me. I reach out and tease my fingers over her hard, pink nipples.

"Wyatt," she whines.

"Love your whiny, begging voice."

She purses her lips into the pout she knows I also love. "Don't be mean."

I sit up, grabbing the back of my shirt to take it off. With the material over my head, I'm only able to catch the faintest movement of her legs shifting. Rubbing together. "Problem, angel?"

Her lips curve into a sly smile once I have the shirt off. "Better now."

"Come on." I struggle to free my cock and grab her hip, digging my fingers into her ass to pull her forward. "Giddy up."

Soft laughter falls from her lips as she straddles me. "Did you really just say that?"

"Yup." Her nipples brush against my chest, and I pull her closer. Skin to skin. Nothing between us. I guide her to my dick. A hiss of air eases out of me as she takes me in slowly. She leans forward, wrapping her arms around my neck. Her lips touch mine. It's that soft teasing kiss that finally flips me from lazily fucking around into beast mode. I wrap one arm around her hips, gripping her ass hard. My other hand cups the back of her neck, bringing her closer for another kiss.

She moans into my mouth while she circles her hips, riding me as much as she can while the tight hold I have on her ass restricts her movements. I give her one final kiss and help her sit up. "Look at you. So beautiful. How'd I get so lucky?"

"Uh...uh..." she stutters but never gets any words out. Instead, she struggles to grind into me harder.

I reach down and tap her leg. "Put your feet on the bars of the chair."

I bite back a curse as she wriggles and finds a foothold. The chair creaks as she moves up and down.

A lick of panic races over her face. "We're going to break the chair."

"I got you." My hands squeeze her ass. "Get to work."

A slight smile plays over her lips. Then she closes her eyes. Tucks her bottom lip between her teeth and lets herself go. Each breath comes in a short, sharp burst.

"Wy—"

"Right here, angel. Come for me."

Bracing her hands on my thighs, she leans back. So far the ends of her hair tickle my legs.

I place one of my big hands in the center of her chest, running it down her soft curves. "Come on, my dirty little angel."

A small answering cry. I thrust up and she gasps.

"Oh."

"That's it," I encourage. My situation's quickly becoming critical, but I need her to come first, so I hang on. Her pleasure *always* comes before mine. That won't change because we're getting married. "Come on." My hand slides down, my thumb finds her clit, rubbing and softly flicking until she jerks and cries out. I keep my fingers moving against her, drawing her orgasm out until she's limp and clinging to me. "You're not finished yet," I warn.

She gives me a sleepy, blissful smile. I can't wait for any other response. I grip her ass, holding her still so I can thrust up into her again and again. She rests her hands on my shoulders for balance and digs her fingers in. "That's right. Hold on."

The familiar tingle at the base of my spine makes me frantic. She seems to sense I'm close and tightens around me.

"Fuck." My body jolts and I groan through my release. Trinity tucks her face against my neck, kissing and licking my skin while I fill her up.

The blast of pleasure seems to go on forever.

I'm semi-conscious and Trin's totally out of it when I finish.

The chair creaks under us.

Time to move. If I can remember how.

Holding her tight, I lift us both off the chair.

She picks her head up and kisses my cheek. "Ready for more?" she asks.

"Not until you feed me."

MY BODY'S STILL humming as I watch Wyatt make breakfast. I was going to do it, but he wrapped me up in a blanket and sat me down at the table, saying he wanted to take care of me. Since my knees were still wobbly, I agreed. Well, that and he's shirtless. There's something about my half-naked man making breakfast I can't say no to.

He finally sets a plate of veggie scrambled eggs in front of me before taking the other chair. Reaching across the table, he places his hand over mine. "I wanted you in my lap, but we've probably abused the chairs enough."

I snort and squeeze his hand. "We've fucked in the kitchen more than the bedroom."

"Are you complaining?"

"Nope."

The corner of his mouth lifts. "Good. I'd be offended if you were."

I stab my fork into the eggs. "It's not my frittata, but it's good," I mumble around a mouthful. "You take such good care of me."

His thumb strokes the back of my hand for a few seconds. I glance up into his intense ocean-blue eyes. "This is what I was made for." His rough voice sends warm shivers down my spine.

"What?" I whisper.

The simmering look he gives me sends heat racing over my skin.

"Taking care of you."

CHAPTER EIGHT

Seven days before the wedding...

WRATH

EVEN THOUGH I had no plans to leave the cabin, I want Trinity to be able to walk when we go home. If we stay inside I'll end up fucking her raw, so the next morning I suggest a drive through the mountains.

She gives me a suspicious look as if she guessed the reason behind my change in plans. "I figured you would have packed plenty of lube."

I bark out a laugh and yank her closer. "Since this cabin is out, let's go see what else is around, smartass."

"I didn't realize I was marrying a real estate mogul."

I help her into my truck and give her a quick kiss. "Wanna make sure my girl's taken care of."

When I slide into the driver's side, she glances over. "You *do* take good care of me, Wyatt." She waves her hand at the house. "I don't need *stuff.* You know that, right?"

I grab her hand and set it on my leg. "Yeah, I know."

We don't have a particular place in mind, but I like that. It's a nice change. Getting lost on some mountain backroads with my girl. Only thing better would be if we'd brought the bike.

"Missing your Harley?" Trinity asks, glancing over.

"How'd you know?"

Before she has a chance to answer, her phone buzzes and she pulls it out.

"I thought we said no cell phones?"

"For *you*. I'm not as in-demand." She glances at the screen and snickers.

"What's so funny?"

"It's a text from Heidi. She says: "Wished you'd warned me about Uncle Wrath's photos. I could've done without.""

"Great. She'll probably run her mouth to Murphy about it." I shake my head, but I really couldn't care less.

"I'm sorry. I forgot those were on one of the cards I gave her."

"It's fine. I'm not worried about it."

"I'm surprised she's gotten so far already."

"You plannin' to hire her as an assistant on a regular basis?"

"Maybe." She leans over and squeezes my leg. "Now that I'm going to have an official studio."

My mouth turns up. Real fuckin' happy I can do that for Trinity. I can't wait for the sale to go through. I'm planning to get her set up in her studio first. It makes sense because it's a smaller space, not that anyone has big enough balls to question me about my plans.

"Oh, look, there's an open house down there."

I miss the sign she pointed out and have to turn around. "You want to have a look?"

"Sure. It says it has deeded waterfront."

"Nice. Think you'd like that better?"

"Yes. But it's probably crazy-expensive."

Houses up here seem to range from so-low-you-wonder-what's-wrong to I-could-buy-an-entire-island for that price. There's something like three thousand lakes and ponds up here, though. Maybe we can find something.

Something turns out to be fancier and way more than I had in mind. "Maybe we'll wait on this one for a few years," I whisper to Trinity after letting the real estate agent give us a quick tour.

At the truck, she leans against the door and puts her hands around my neck, drawing me down for a kiss. "I really like planning our future together," she says when we part.

"Me too."

Trinity

IF YOU'D TOLD me ten years ago I'd be looking for lakeside lodges with Wyatt, I would have laughed in your face. This laid back, casual Wyatt seems to completely contradict the biker-fighter-enforcer image he presents to everyone else. That I'm the only one he allows to see this side of him only strengthens the bond we have.

"You're my future, Trin," he says after shutting his door. "I can't think of tomorrow, or next year, or ten years from now without you next to me." My throat's tight with emotion, so I don't answer right away. Once we're on the road, he takes my hand. "I never thought about getting old, or even wanted to think about it. Now I do, because I want to do it with you."

"I feel the same way."

"Good."

We stop at a few smaller lakes, and I snap some gorgeous photos. As darkness falls, we pass a small bar and restaurant and my stomach rumbles.

"Want to stop here?" Wyatt asks.

"Looks like a busy place."

"Come on. You must be getting tired of cooking for me all the time," he says, slipping into a parking spot.

When he opens my door, I lean in and in a low voice explain, "All the kitchen sex makes it worth it."

He chuckles and takes my hand. "Don't worry, I'll still fuck you when we get home." He casts a glance around the darkened parking lot. "Maybe *before* we get home."

"You'll have to catch me first." Laughing, I pull out of his hold and race to the front door. He catches up to me, grabbing me around the waist and pulling me to his side.

"Can't escape me that easy, angel."

The place is packed, but it's a short wait before we're shown to a small, sticky table in the corner.

After glancing at the menu, Wyatt snorts. "Forty-five dollars for a venison strip loin. We need to make Teller take a few more deer off the property this fall."

"Are you going to hunt with him?"

"We'll see. I hate sitting still for that long."

I chuckle, because that's exactly the answer I expected from him.

The food actually turns out to be really good, and I jot down a few notes on my napkin so I can recreate one of the dishes at home. Wyatt watches me with a puzzled expression. "I want to try and make it when we get home," I explain.

Before he says anything, the waitress hands him our check. He passes her his credit card without glancing at the bill.

Reaching across the table, he takes one of my hands. "How are you feeling?"

Confused, by the change in the tone of his voice, I glance up. "Fine. Why?"

"Just checking."

CHAPTER NINE

E VERYTHING IS DARK and still when we return to the cabin. "This feels weird. Even though the clubhouse is out in the middle of the woods, there are always people around."

At first I wasn't sure Wyatt heard me. Then the outside security lights burst to life, bathing the area around the house with bright, white light and he seems to relax. "You're not getting tired of me, are you?" he asks.

"No. Not at all. This is nice. Just the two of us. I understand how important the club is, but once in a while—"

He flips up the middle console and reaches over, urging me closer. "Come here."

"Don't you want to go inside?"

"In a minute. Come here," he says again.

Curious, I slide over a few inches. "Keep coming." He slips his hand under my butt, urging me up. "Come sit in my lap."

We turn and twist and slide around the front seat until he has me where he wants me—straddling his lap. He leans back, staring in my eyes. "Is this what you wanted?" I whisper.

One of his hands cups the back of my head, pulling me closer. "Make out with me," he says against my lips.

I can't help it—I chuckle once before his kisses swallow my laughter.

I wrap my arms around his neck pressing myself tight against him while he takes the kiss deeper. He tastes like coffee and peppermint—two things that shouldn't go together but are perfect because it's Wyatt.

"Mmmm," I moan, and his lips curve up, breaking our kiss.

"Are you trying to relive your high school years?" I whisper, my voice shaky from desire.

He cocks his head as if my question made no sense.

"You know, making out in the front seat of your car."

He chuckles. "No. Never did that."

My mouth twists in a skeptical smile.

"I'm serious. I didn't have a car."

"Oh. Well, I'm honored to be your first."

His eyes soften and all teasing leaves his face. He lifts a hand, brushing the hair from my face. I can see the question he wants to ask.

I duck my head. "I never did that, either."

His hands drop to my waist, gently squeezing. "Guess we're each other's firsts."

It's a little absurd and a whole lot sweet.

"I don't think I said it before, but you look really pretty tonight." His finger traces the edge of my sweater. "I like this color blue on you."

"Thank you," I whisper. The simple compliment warms my skin.

We return to trading gentle kisses. Gentle turns a little more frantic. Wyatt's hand grazes the bottom of my sweater, slipping under to tickle my skin. As I arch my back, he slides both hands under my sweater, cupping my breasts—

A sharp blare startles us apart, and we both laugh when we realize I accidently leaned against the steering wheel, hitting the horn.

"Maybe it's time to take this inside," he says in a low voice that suggests exactly what he wants to do inside.

"Sounds good," I whisper.

He helps me off his lap. "Wait in the truck for a minute."

I nod and collect my purse but keep an eye on him as he carefully checks the area around the front porch. When he seems satisfied nothing's amiss, he returns to the truck, opening my door and helping me down.

He points to a section of grass in the front yard. "Looks like a coyote traveled through here. I don't want you outside by yourself."

"No problem."

When we step inside, he still seems preoccupied. "Want to join me in the shower?"

One corner of his mouth tips up. "Yes. Let me go grab some more firewood. You get the shower started."

"Deal."

I hurry into the bathroom, figuring I have enough time to quickly sweep a razor over my legs. Wyatt joins me sooner than I expected, flipping the shower curtain open and grinning at me.

"Whatcha doing?" he asks.

"Shit, you scared me." I flick some water and suds at him, which only makes his grin wider. "What does it look like I'm doing?" I ask, waving the razor in the air.

"Hmm." He strips down, keeping his eyes on me the entire time. "Need some help, angel?"

"Maybe." I step back so he can fit into the shower with me.

"Fuck, you're pretty," he says, running his gaze up and down the length of my body. His eyes stray to the razor still dangling from my fingers. "Whatcha shaving?"

I point down. "My legs. Maybe some other parts."

He breaks into a devilish smile and plucks the razor out of my hand. "I'll handle the *other parts*."

"Really?" Before I have much of a chance to protest, he's kneeling in front of me. "Spread your legs," he orders. Kneeling or not, Wyatt's definitely in charge.

He flattens one of his palms against me, cupping my pussy. Two thick fingers press inside me. I groan and grab his shoulder for balance.

"That's right. Hang on to me. Feel good?"

"Doesn't seem very professional." I gasp and nod at the razor in his hand.

His deep chuckle slides over my skin like warm honey. He reaches for a bottle of conditioner and spends some time rubbing it into my skin. "Just a quick touch-up," he murmurs as he slowly scrapes the razor over my sensitive parts. It's not the first time Wyatt's done this. It still makes me shiver with pleasure and vibrate with laughter at the same time. "That tickles!"

"Keep still."

When he's finished, he rinses me off but doesn't make a move to stand.

"What are you—"

He uses his thumb to expose my clit and smiles up at me when I gasp. Slowly, he licks, barely touching his tongue to me at first. Desperately, I try to roll my hips, shove my pussy against him, needing the friction he seems determined to withhold.

He dips his tongue lower and gives me long, slow licks. I'm so close to going off, I whine in frustration when he pulls away and stands.

"Wyatt." I pout and he leans down to kiss my cheek.

"The tub's killing my knees," he says with a teasing grin. Flipping the curtain aside, he gives me another evil smile. "Don't take too long."

"I'll finish myself—"

"Don't you dare," he growls, right outside the shower. "Mine, Trinity."

I'm shaking so hard, I'm not sure I can finish shaving my legs, but I do a quick swipe or two and flick the water off.

I pause long enough to rub some oil into my skin and slip on underwear, flannel sleep-shorts and a tank top.

Wyatt calls me over to him when I step out of the bathroom.

He eyes my shorts and top. Stretching my arms over my head, I let out a big, fake yawn. "I'm sleepy."

His eyes narrow, but the corner of his mouth twitches as if he's trying not to laugh. We both know I won't be able to sleep after he wound me up so tight.

"Put your hands on the wall and give me your ass." His *let's get down to business* tone dampens my panties instantly. He's turned so serious, it's hard to read him now. The uncertainty makes my heart race.

My body screams *finally!* as I turn around, hooking my thumbs in the waistband of my shorts and dragging them down my legs.

Each movement I make is precise and designed to tease him. He slaps my ass in response. "Don't be cute. Spread your legs."

My skin tingles. *That voice.* My body loves it. I'm humming with anticipation. Excited for whatever he has planned.

Even though I'm facing the wall, his gaze sears my skin. "Arch your back," he says, coming closer. I do and he slips one arm around my middle, arranging me to his liking. His fingers slide down the front of my panties, through my wetness, and he hums against my ear. "Excited about something, angel?"

"You know I am," I whine and get another swat on my butt.

"Quiet."

Slowly, he makes his way to my clit, circling but not touching until I can't help moaning.

His other hand slides over my back, down over each cheek. When my body tenses, he leans over me, pressing soft kisses along my spine. "Relax, you're all mine," he whispers.

God, he knows me so well. And I know him. He won't be happy with just my heart and body. He wants everything. I want him to have everything and I want all of him until we're completely intertwined.

When I'm relaxed and hovering on the edge of orgasm, he takes his fingers away. "Wy—"

"Shh."

He hooks his fingers in the sides of my underwear and drags them to my knees. I move to take them off, and he stops me with two gruff words. "Leave them."

Wyatt knows how to make me suffer and feel safe at the same time. Behind me, he kneels down, running his hands up and over my thighs and hips. He presses my legs even farther apart. The first touch of his tongue makes me jump and moan at the same time. Reaching behind me, I twist my fingers in his hair, and he abruptly stops.

"Hands on the wall."

Eager for more of his talented tongue, I comply. I don't think my body can take it if he leaves me on the edge again.

He waits a few seconds before sliding a finger through my wetness. "Nice," he whispers.

Soft kisses tickle the sensitive spot behind my knee, traveling up to my inner thigh. I so badly want to turn and shove his face against my pussy. Force his mouth exactly where I need it. Somehow, I hold back, waiting while I tremble with anticipation. His big hands grasp my ass, opening me as wide as the underwear around my knees will allow, so he can bury his face between my legs. He thrusts his tongue inside me, then slowly makes his way to my clit.

I gasp, fingers curling against the cold, unyielding wall. "God, Wyatt."

He squeezes my ass in response. "Quiet."

Facing the wall means I can't be sure of his plans. But from his tone I know he's wearing a wicked smile. He thrusts two fingers inside me, withdrawing them right before I come. Slowly, he works his way to my ass with one hand while gently stroking my clit with the other. My body ramps back up, legs shaking with an impending orgasm, and I let out a whimper. "That's it, angel," he whispers. "Go ahead. Come for me," he encourages.

I quiver and tremble through it, and when I'm limp he shifts. A click-pop sound fills the air and then his slippery fingers slide down the crease of my ass—gentle at first. There's a sharp bite of pain as he presses his thumb against my ass. I can't help it, I wriggle away. But he tightens the arm around my waist. "Shh, relax." It's the softest I've ever heard Wyatt be. Soft but so serious. So focused on every little thing he's doing to me.

This is why I trust Wyatt. He'd never hurt me, and that makes the twinge of pain easier to stand. As demanding as he can be, he's also protective and responsive—somehow always in tune with my feelings.

And let's not forget how much he loves making me come.

It seems like he spends hours working his fingers into me. I come at least two more times. Maybe I should be embarrassed about how slippery my thighs are, but I'm too focused on the sensations to care.

Finally, something different—*harder*—presses against me and I jump. "What is that?"

"Shh. It's slightly bigger than the one you took this morning. You can handle it."

He works the plug in slow and steady. When it's finally in place, I let out a deep sigh. He works my underwear all the way down my legs now and tosses them aside. He stands, sliding his body along my bare skin. I get a soft kiss on the cheek. "Stay put. I'll be right back."

He's only gone for a few minutes. I'm shaking with need when he returns.

"Time for bed," he announces.

"What?"

I turn and find him grinning like a big blond devil.

"You're going to make me sleep with something in my ass all night? Are you nuts?"

He runs his hand over the front of his shorts drawing my attention to his hard cock, straining the limits of the material. "I haven't decided," he says in a casual tone.

Spinning me around and holding me tight against his body, he leans over and drags his mouth along my shoulder. His warm lips press soft kisses against my neck until he reaches my ear. "I might take it out in the middle of the night and replace it with my cock." Uncontrollable shivers work over me, and I can't believe how much I want him to do exactly that *right fucking now.* "Or I might make you wait until morning."

I groan and sag in his arms. "You're loving this, aren't you?"

And that's how he leaves me. Burning with need. Need for something I can't believe he has me craving. Afraid—but the fun kind of fear that makes my heart race.

WRATH

I HAVE NO plans to make Trinity wait until morning. But I do love teasing her. Once we're in bed, she pushes her little ass into me. She's teasing me, trying to get me to fuck her. Instead, I wrap her up tight in my arms. She sighs—somewhere between content and needy. For a few minutes she's still, then more squirming.

"What's wrong?"

She actually makes a little growling sound. "You know what's wrong."

"Go to sleep."

I twist my hand so I can brush my thumb over her nipples, and she wiggles again but doesn't make a sound this time. After a few minutes, her body relaxes and her breathing evens out. That's when I slide one of my hands over her belly, shoving it between her thighs. She gasps and turns, rolling onto her back and spreading her legs to give me more room. "Wyatt."

"What, angel?"

Another needy moan fills the bedroom. "Don't make me beg. It's not nice."

Leaning over, I take one nipple between my lips and suck hard. "But I love the sound of you begging. It's the sexiest sound in the world."

"You're having fun, aren't you?"

"You have no idea, angel."

"Then fuck me already."

"Where?" I ask, drawing out the word. "Tell me how much you want it, Trin."

Her hair tickles my arm as she nods.

"I want the words."

"Please."

"No, try again. What do you want?"

"Make me come."

She groans and wiggles against my hand, and I stroke her a little harder. I want her to come over and over for me tonight. Want her to remember nothing but how good everything I did made her feel. How good I'm going to make her feel for the rest of her life.

"You were so good," I whisper against her ear. "So pretty while you took that plug in your ass for me." I reach down and grab the base, wiggling it. The tension returns to her body, and I soothe it away with a kiss. Rolling over, I reach out and flick on the bedside lamp.

"Wyatt?"

"I need to see you."

She watches as I return to her, closes her eyes when I kiss her softly on the lips. A brief touch before my mouth devours the rest of her. I suck, nuzzle, and lick my way to her belly button. Above me, she stretches her arms, her body shuddering violently. I grip her hips with both hands and use my tongue on her until she's on the brink.

When she's close, I pull away, returning to my position above her body, rubbing my dick over her slick skin. One of my hands moves to cup her face as I slowly push inside. She moans into my mouth as I set a slow, lazy pace. In no time she's panting, her inner muscles holding me tight.

"Come on. Your pussy's so fucking hot. Come for me."

"Wyatt." She spreads her legs wider as if she can't get enough.

"That's right. Take every inch of my cock."

"I…" Whatever she was going to say is lost to a series of moans and sighs.

Before she finishes, I pull out, easily flipping her over. I don't have to ask, she gets up on her knees and elbows, arching her back. Pure, raw power flows through my veins at the way she offers herself.

I work the plug out slowly and drop it on the nightstand. She sighs and tucks her arms underneath her body. "Good, angel?"

"Mmhmm."

"Scared?" I want some actual words from her.

"No," she whispers.

"That's what I want to hear." I run my hand over her back and reach over to pick up a bottle of lube and a small wand vibrator, dropping the lube on the bed next to us. I flick the vibrator on and tease it over the backs of her thighs. She jumps and then laughs softly. "That tickles." I shift it between her legs, slowly inching it up until it's pulsating right over her clit.

"Still tickle?" I'm glad she can't see the evil grin I'm wearing.

"Ah…Oh…No."

She's so fucking close. "Take this." I nudge the vibrator into the hand she thrusts back. "Hold it on your clit like a good girl."

She groans. A little quicker she adds, "Wyatt, can I come?"

"Fuck, yes."

When I think she's in the middle of her orgasm, I gently press my dick against her ass. Her body tenses up immediately.

"Easy."

My hands grip her hips tighter, and I push inside. The tight ring of muscles there resist and I stop. "Take a deep breath and let it out slow."

She releases a sharp hiss of air, and the head of my dick slips in. "Good?" I ask as I slowly keep pushing my well-lubed cock into her.

She gasps. "God *dammit*, you're big."

The laughter that rumbles out of me forces my dick in a bit more. Fortunately, she's laughing with me and it helps.

My body's screaming *go,* but I hold back, giving her time to adjust.

"Fuck, Trin." I barely groan out the words. "Relax." Instead of relaxing, her muscles tighten and I hang on by a thread.

She lets out a short whimper.

"Does it hurt?" I ask.

"Yes." She waits a second. A second where I barely move or breathe. "Not a bad hurt."

I drag my hips back and dribble more lube on my cock. My hands slide over her ass, squeezing, moving up to rub her lower back while I push my way inside again.

Another harsh breath leaves her lips. "You're so much bigger than that fucking toy."

I can't help laughing again, which makes her giggle, and I slide in a little deeper. "Good, angel. So good. Relax."

"Oh, God." Her entire body shudders. "It feels awful and awesome at the same time."

"Do you want me to stop?" I'm not sure it's even possible.

"No."

I pull back then push in even deeper. Underneath us, her toy keeps buzzing. "You got that on your clit?"

"Yes," she answers in a breathy little voice.

Another shudder works over her body. Her muscles tighten and I groan. "Fuck. Trin. You have no idea." This slow fucking is the best kind of torture.

She sighs and pushes back against me.

"Good girl. Better?"

She hums and makes more noises in the back of her throat. My hips finally press against her ass. All the way in.

I lower myself over her, kissing her shoulder, nipping her ear. I rest my palms against the mattress on either side of her, completely sheltering her with my body. "You feeling owned now, Trinity?" I whisper against her hair.

Her body shivers, and she curls one of her hands around mine. "God, yes."

"Tell me. Who owns you?"

"You. Fuck. Oh my God. You do. You own me, Wyatt."

I twist my hand in her hair, gently turning her head so I can see her face. "Is every beautiful inch of you mine?"

She meets my eyes, and a soft smile flickers over her lips. "Yes."

"Are you going to come for me while my cock's in your ass?" I ask, brushing a soft kiss on her cheek.

Her eyelids flutter shut. "How can you be so sweet and dirty at the same time?"

"It's a gift." I chuckle, then turn serious because I'm dying to pound into her. "Now, are you going to come for me?

"I…I don't know."

I thrust in harder and gauge her reaction. "You feel so good, Trinity." She moans and whines. Pushing against me at first, then trying to pull away. My hands clamp down over her hips, keeping her still. "You have to come for me, angel."

I increase my speed, and there's a moment where her quick, surprised noises turn into moans.

"Better?"

"Uh…Oh my…"

I reach for her hand, grasping the toy and rolling it firmly over her clit.

"Bad girl, you didn't have it in the right spot."

The soft buzzing when I position the vibrator just right sets her off. She goes nuts, bucking against me. "Too much." She swats me away, nothing more than butterfly wings beating against my hands. I only press it against her harder. More desperate little noises push past her lips. Her eyes roll back in her head. "There," she whispers. "Fuck. Right there."

Louder whimpers and moans fill the room as pleasure finally hits her. She comes hard, squeezing the fuck out of me. I thrust in deeper, never pulling all the way out. Colors swirl and burst behind my eyelids. Finally, I empty myself inside her as I reach what has to be the most intense orgasm of my life. The sensation goes on so long I lose track of everything.

My mind's absolutely blank as I pull away. I have to take a few seconds to slow my breathing. Regain control. Make sure I didn't hurt her.

She's quivering, and I push her hair off her face to check on her. Her cheeks are flushed and wet with sweat and...tears?

"Trin? You okay? Did I hurt you?"

A sort of sob-giggle works out of her, and she opens one eye. "No. So intense. Think I'm still coming." Her mouth curves into a lazy smile after she gives me her clipped answer.

"Oh." I'm still so sex-stupid, it takes a second for her words to sink in. "Excuse me while I go beat on my chest for a few minutes."

She flops one hand in the air, finally landing on my leg and squeezing. "Thank you. You were right. As always."

"Wow. Feels good to have you admit it."

"Don't be mean."

"Never. Come on. Let's get cleaned up."

It takes a lot to get Trinity out of bed and into the shower. She clings to me in the sweetest way, allowing me to wash her down and check her over.

"How do you feel?"

"Sleepy," she mumbles.

I shut the water off and help her out of the shower, drying her off while she braces herself against my shoulders. While I dry myself, she leans against the vanity staring at our reflections in the mirror.

"You all right?" I ask, standing behind her and placing my hands on her hips.

"I can't move."

She doesn't resist at all when I swing her into my arms. "Poor Trinity. All worn out from the big man-beast rutting all over you," I tease as I carry her into the bedroom. She bursts into giggles, finally settling down when we're under the covers.

I SWEAR OUR souls have actually twined together, and I have no idea where he ends and I begin. I might be high. Even after he gently cleaned me up in the shower and toweled me off, he still made me laugh. I think I love that the most about him. About us.

Tucked into bed next to him with the lights off, our deep connection still pulses between us.

"Wyatt, do you feel this, too?" I murmur.

"Yes," he answers, as if he knows exactly what I'm asking. It warms me even more, and I snuggle closer, resting my head on his chest.

I'm drifting between sleep and awake when he rumbles out a few words. "You own me, too."

"What?" I mumble.

"The only person I see. The only person I think about. Everything inside me belongs to Trinity."

He's quiet after that, and I wonder if he even realizes he said the words out loud.

"You've changed what everything means for me, angel," he says right before I fall asleep.

CHAPTER TEN

Six days before the wedding...

WRATH

TRINITY'S AWAKE AND staring at me early the next morning. Automatically, my hand reaches out and brushes over her cheek. "How do you feel this morning?"

"Happy," she whispers.

"Hurt anywhere?"

"Only in a good way."

I guess that's an acceptable answer. I sit up and turn her over, running my hands over her back and ass, both to make sure I didn't leave any marks and because I love touching her.

"Do we have to go home today?" she mumbles into the pillow.

"Yes, angel. In a couple weeks, we'll be on our honeymoon. We're gonna do this all over again." I lean over and nibble on her shoulder until she laughs.

"That sounds good," she murmurs.

I continue tracing her curves with my fingers, loving how soft she is everywhere.

"Are we nuts?" Trinity's voice breaks the quiet around us and stops my exploration.

I roll back to my side of the bed, sensing she has something she needs to get off her chest. "Probably, but what specifically are you worried about?"

She turns to her back. "Do you want children?" she asks, staring at the ceiling. I'm thrown. For me, the question came out of absolutely nowhere.

"I feel like we've already talked about this," I answer.

"Are you sure?" she persists. "You're so sweet with Alexa."

The mention of her name turns my mouth up. "Yeah, I love the kid. I also love giving her *back* to her parents when we're done watching her."

She snorts softly. "Yeah. That's how I feel, too."

My hand runs over her cheek. "What's wrong, angel?"

"Nothing. I don't...I don't want you to not have everything you want because of me."

"*You're* everything I want." I think over what she's saying. "What about you? You like spending time with Alexa, too." My hand tickles over her stomach. "No longings down here?"

"No longings." She rolls over on her side to face me, propping her head on her hand. "You can have them forever you know. I don't want you trading me in for a younger model one day."

That has to be one of the stupidest things Trinity's ever said. "Who the hell else would put up with my moody ass?"

She rolls her eyes. "Lots of women. You just keep getting sexier as you get older."

"Can you stop reminding me that I'm old?"

"I mean it."

There's determination shining in her honey eyes. I need to get this right so she understands she's the only thing that matters to me. "Serious talk, Trin. No bullshit?"

"Yes."

"I like our life the way it is. I like things being just the two of us. We can do stuff like *this*—disappear for a few days and do nothing but fuck."

She snorts and dips her head, brushing her cheek against my chest.

But this is too serious to ignore, so I press my fingers against her chin, tilting her head up to look at me. "Are you changing *your* mind? Be honest. I won't be mad."

"No." Her voice comes out clear and steady.

"Then trust what I'm telling you. You're the one person I'll never, ever lie to."

Her eyes widen, knowing I mean so much more than just club stuff I can't share with her.

I search for a way to make her believe what I'm telling her. "How about this? We'll check in with each other every now and then."

"Until what? I hit menopause?"

"Don't interrupt me." I trace my thumb over her plump lips. "This is me, promising you, if I change my mind, I'll tell you. But I need you to make me the same promise."

She stares at me for a few seconds before snuggling closer. "Okay," she whispers.

"There. Was that so hard?"

"No. Don't make fun of me. I'm trying to—"

"What? Have every last 'couple' talk before you're tied to me forever?"

"Well, yeah. I want you to be sure—"

I blow out a frustrated breath. How the fuck do I explain this so she *gets* it. "Trin, have you ever seen me do something I don't wanna do?"

She lets out a soft snort. "No."

"Then stop worrying so much. Your pussy may be magical, but if I didn't want to marry you, I wouldn't."

"Wow. I feel like I should be insulted."

"Why?" I lean forward and without touching her, press her back against the mattress. Looming over her, I cage her in with my hands on either side of her shoulders and lean down to kiss her. She wiggles under me, placing her palms on my chest.

"Damn, you're sexy," she says in that breathy voice that makes my dick perk right up. Not that he hadn't been on standby with her naked next to me and all.

"The real question, Trin, is are *you* sure you want to marry me?"

"Why? Because you've got a gym full of horny housewives after your hot ass?"

Her mouth turns down, so even though I think she meant to tease me, something about the situation bothers her.

"You know that's just business. I can barely stand *talking* to any of them. I definitely don't want to fuck any of them."

"It doesn't matter," she whispers.

I press a quick kiss to her lips. "Everything matters when we're talking about you. I mean, are you sure you can tolerate me being a grumpy bastard most of the time?"

"I love you the way you are."

"And that's why I love *you* so fucking much. You love *me*. You're not out to change me or fix me. You make me a better person by being you."

"Wyatt, that's the sweetest thing you've ever said."

"Good. Can I fuck you now?"

Her forehead wrinkles in a playful frown. "Well, now you ruined it." While her words sound scolding, her hips tilt and she spreads her legs. Even though I'm ready to pound her into the damn mattress, I want to finish this talk.

"Do I make you happy, Trinity?"

"God, yes."

"Tell me."

She bites her lip, but her eyes never leave mine. "Don't laugh, because this is how I really feel," she whispers.

Everything about her voice says how vulnerable she's feeling. "Go on," I encourage.

"I liked my life, before we…figured things out between us. But everything was in sepia tones. Nice to look at. Adequate. With you…with us together, everything is in vibrant, pulsing color, and I can't wait to open my eyes every morning and see what's around me."

My heart sputters, and I can't form any words. Worry creases her brow. "Does that sound stupid?"

"No." I cup her face between my hands and press a kiss to her fore-head. "No. Somehow you always say what I feel but can't put into words."

I'M RAW HAVING admitted the thoughts that had been in my head for a long time now. My silly, artistic interpretation of how he moves me. But Wyatt doesn't laugh. Not even a little teasing.

Last night. This morning. Everything about our trip has strength-ened how I feel about him. About us.

"I can't wait to marry you. Even if you won't tell me what you're wearing," I tease to lift some of the heaviness of our talk.

"It's nothing bad."

"No blue tux?"

"Nope. What color is your dress?"

"Well, after the way you've defiled my body the last couple days, I definitely can't wear white."

He throws his head back and laughs. "I've been a real animal, huh? Claiming you every possible way, day and night?"

"Whatever will we do on our honeymoon?" I tease.

"Don't worry, I can think of a thousand more ways I want to fuck you."

"Aw, that's the second sweetest thing you've said today."

"Get over here and kiss me, you nut." He reaches out, cupping the back of my head and rolling closer to seal his mouth over mine. We trade lazy kisses for a few minutes, but then his kisses grow deeper. More intense. He pulls me on top of him, holding me tight. Completely in control. His hand at the back of my head keeps me where he wants. The way he wants. My hips wiggle against him, and he groans into my mouth. I'm aware of spinning and then I'm underneath him, arms around his neck, pulling myself up for more of his demanding kisses.

He dips his head down, slicking his tongue over my collarbone, kissing my neck until I moan. "Wyatt. Please."

"Patience, angel."

I should be worn out. Exhausted from everything we've already done this weekend. "I can never get enough of you, Wyatt."

"Good."

"Do you think that will change one day?"

"I'll make sure it doesn't."

He says it with so much confidence that I believe in him one hundred percent.

His phone rings, and I shake my head. "No, no, no."

"Fuck." He cocks his head, listening to the ringtone. "It's gotta be Murphy. He promised he'd only call if it was an emergency."

"Okay." I untangle myself from his body, and he rolls to the edge of the bed, snatching up the phone.

"What?" he barks.

I chuckle as I stand and stretch, putting a little extra into the movement because I know my man's watching. All at once his demeanor changes. No more sexy, playful Wyatt who's annoyed about the interruption.

Something much darker passes over his face.

"I'll be there as soon as I can."

He disconnects and sets the phone down on the nightstand before looking at me.

"Get dressed. We need to leave. *Now*."

CHAPTER ELEVEN
WRATH

CAN'T SPEAK. There are no words to cover this. Everything I've spent the last fifteen years working for has been burned to the ground.

My gym. Furious Fitness is a pile of burning black ashes, melted plastic, and crime scene tape. I'm standing here staring at what's left, trying to process what happened but coming up blank.

Why?

Numbness spreads through my chest. Rage will come later. Right now, I'm full of icy dread. I seem to be watching everything from a distance. I understand what everyone's told me, but I can't make sense of it.

Someone burned down my gym.

The investigator hasn't ruled it arson *yet*. What the fuck else could it be?

Violent heat creeps up my spine. I try to swallow down all my fury so I can survive any questioning without turning myself into a suspect. My fists are clenched so tight—waiting for the right thing to take my anger out on—my knuckles are white. From a million miles away, I watch as I will myself to uncurl each finger.

It has to be related to the club. But whose club? Mine or Whisper's?

Worse, what if it's *not* MC related at all? Then there's some other unknown enemy out in the world. Some threat I haven't identified yet.

"Mr. Ramsey, can I speak to you?"

I shake myself out of my trance. "Yeah." The first step I take reminds me Trinity's still by my side. "I'll be right back, babe."

"Okay," she whispers. She hasn't said much since we got here. The fire seems to have hit her as hard as it hit me. Christ, a couple days ago I stood here and told her about all my big plans, and she was so fucking excited. Proud of me.

My gaze lands on the building next door. Completely intact. Maybe all hope isn't lost after all.

If I don't wind up in jail.

Trinity's lips tremble into a shaky smile. "I'll be right here."

I'm halfway between numb and rage. Probably not the best time for me to talk to the police. Asking if we can do this later doesn't seem like a smart move, though.

Get it together.

"Are you the sole owner?" the officer asks me.

"No, I have two partners." Whisper is nowhere to be found, but I point Jake out in the crowd.

"Does anyone else have access to the building at night?"

"Not really. My girlfriend has a key. My brother, who's been working here, has one. That's it."

"We found the body of a young male. Late teens. Anyone like that work for you?"

Grief slugs me in the stomach.

Twitch.

There's a roaring in my ears, drowning everything else out. Twitch is the only person on my staff who fits that description.

I've seen some sick shit in my life. Hell, I've committed a few horrors myself. But knowing there's a body in that charred mess, and it might be a kid I've known for years, hurts. "We've got lots of teenage members. But one kid who went through my after-school program has been working here for a while now."

"Got a name?"

I give him the information he needs. Not that it will do much good. Twitch's parents checked out of his life a long time ago. I don't mention the kid was also a prospect for the MC. Leaving LOKI out of this as long as possible will be best for everyone.

"You think that's who—" I stop and choke on my disbelief. "Set the fire? Or was he caught in the blaze and couldn't get out?"

"We can't say for sure yet." He hesitates and in a lower voice adds, "Given the position of the body, I'd say it's likely he started the fire."

I shake my head. Twitch's vice was cracking safes. Picking locks. Breaking into places for the thrill of it. This level of destruction? No, the kid never pinged my pyro radar.

"I really don't see him doin' this. I've known him for a couple years now. He's straightened out." *Straightened out* is probably a stretch. *Lived in fear I'd kick his ass if he stepped out of line* is closer to the truth.

The cop gives me a weary smile. "Sure. He have a record?"

"Juvie."

He scribbles that down. "You know the dates?"

I give him my best guess. "It was bullshit B&E, nothing close to this."

The cop pins me with an almost sympathetic stare. "You know, I've heard a lot of good things about the after-school program you run here. Helped lots of kids. Gave 'em a safe space. But something I've learned on the job—some people can't change. You can't help everyone."

I'm not sure what's worse. A cop feeding me a bunch of bullshit to cheer me up? Or that he—a stranger—thinks he knew Twitch better than I did?

I'm all out of fight so I let it slide, giving him a quick nod to acknowledge his shit advice.

Rock and Hope join me after the officer leaves. "I'm so sorry, Wrath," Hope says gently, brushing her hand over my arm. "Is there anything I can do to help out?"

"Not yet." I glance at Rock. "There's a body."

Rock curses under his breath and glances around. "Not good, brother. That's gonna bring a lot of unwanted attention. They know who it is yet?"

"No." I hesitate because I hate admitting to my president…my best friend, that I might have brought someone into the club who betrayed us. Burning the gym down isn't just about me, it will have an effect on the entire club for a long time. "It could be Twitch."

Hope gasps. "Oh, no." She shakes her head, tears already wetting her lashes.

Rock drills me with a questioning look, while slipping his arm around Hope's shoulders.

"You know I wouldn't have…brought him in, if I didn't trust him. I don't think he's responsible."

"Don't get ahead of yourself. Let's wait for more information. For what it's worth, I don't see him doing it, either."

That's a relief. "Look, I know he hadn't…been with us long, but if it *is* him, we need to take care of him. He doesn't have anyone else who'll do it."

"Yeah. Of course we will." He reaches out and squeezes my shoulder. Even though he doesn't speak a word, I know it's his way of saying "focus."

My chest tightens. Prickles move over my skin, and I glance around. I'm off. Unsettled. Something besides the blackened mess in front of me makes it hard to breathe. "Where's Trin?" I ask.

Hope points to the back parking lot where Trin's talking to Jake and helping him move stuff away from what's left of the building. I leave Hope and Rock without another word and stalk over to my girl. "What are you doing?"

"Just moving the picnic benches out of the way." She points to the cop who just questioned me. "He said it was okay."

I'm boiling-pissed the cop spoke to my girl without me noticing.

Even if it was something simple. Not that Trin's stupid. She knows not to volunteer information to people outside the club. It still pisses me off.

"Mr. Ramsey?" A deep voice intrudes on the anger building inside me.

"What?" I snap, turning around.

I find a guy almost as big as me staring back with an impassive expression. He thrusts a hand in my direction. "Keegan Brand. Senior Investigator with the Empire County Sheriff Department. I need to speak with you."

As if having the Empire Police picking through everything isn't bad enough, they called in an arson investigator from the Sheriff's department. *Fan-fucking-tastic.*

"No problem. Can you give me a few minutes?"

"Sure. I'm going to walk the site with one of my guys."

"*Jesusfuckingchrist*," Jake mumbles as the guy walks away. "Watch yourself with him," he advises in a low voice.

"Where the fuck is Whisper?" I ask.

"Don't know. Called him a bunch of times." He steps away. "I'll try him again."

"Thanks." My mind's already going to the worst case. Whisper's been real fuckin' unhappy with me lately. Would the fucker really burn our business down, though?

"Wyatt?" Trinity's soft voice reaches me.

"What?" I answer, a little harsher than I meant to. Fuck, she's the only good thing in my world. No way should I be snapping at her.

"Do you think we should postpone the wedding?" she asks.

Blood thunders through my veins, and for a second, no sounds reach me. That's the *last* goddamn thing I want to do. Especially now.

I need her more than ever.

"No, I don't want to postpone the wedding." I snarl the words at her, and she backs up a few steps.

"Everything all right?" Rock asks.

Perfect timing as usual. *Godfuckingdammit, Rock.*

"No, it's not all right. She shouldn't be here." At least there's one thing I can control in this situation—Trinity's safety. I need her home where she's safe.

"What? Wyatt, no. I was just—"

Ignoring her, I turn to Rock. "Please get her out of here. It's not safe. Take her home."

He nods and calls Z over. Hope follows him to join our miserable little group.

"Hey, you don't look happy, brother," Z says.

"Ya think?"

"Can you take the girls home, Z?" Rock asks. "I want to stay here while he's dealing with the arson investigator." He tips his head toward Investigator Brand. As usual, Rock's aware of everything going on.

Hope taps his shoulder. "Um, I'm sticking around for that, too. In case he needs a lawyer."

"Jesus Christ. I wasn't even *here*," I grumble.

Hope grabs my hand. "I know. I want to cover all of our bases." She casts a dirty look at the Empire PD's detective poking through the rubble. "I don't trust them."

I can tell Rock's not happy about it, but he agrees Hope should stay.

"Wyatt, can we—" Trinity starts to say.

"No." I pull her to the side, but it doesn't matter. I'm sure everyone hears us anyway. "Go home. I can't deal with this and worry about you right now."

Her mouth turns down. "I want to help. I wasn't—"

"No. Go home and do wedding shit. We're getting married in a couple days."

She drops her gaze to the ground, and I feel like a fucking asshole for yelling at her.

"Come on, Trin," Z says, wrapping an arm around her shoulder. He shoots me a *you're-an-asshole* glare but finally does what I need and gets her out of here.

I'm unreasonably pissed watching Z's truck exit the parking lot. I turn and find Hope glaring at me. "Yes, Cinderella?" I ask with exaggerated patience.

"She just wanted to help."

"Not your business," I growl at her.

She keeps glaring at me until Rock touches her arm, his way of calling her off. She shoots him a dirty look before stalking away.

"Asshole," Rock grumbles at me.

This feeling of being split in two spears me. I drag my hands through my hair, looking anywhere but at Rock. "Fuck, I shouldn't have been so harsh with Trinity." I finally meet his eyes. "Or Hope."

He grips my shoulder, offering some brotherly reassurance. "At least you admit it. Let's handle this, then you can go home and make it up to Trinity."

"Thanks."

Investigator Brand has a no-bullshit way about him that normally I'd respect. I also have the impression he hasn't always been on the right side of the law. While normally I don't have a lot of respect for cops' intelligence, there's something about the way this guy takes everything in that makes me proceed with caution.

"Who are you?" he asks Rock.

"Friend."

"You one of the partners?"

"No."

"Then you're not needed for this conversation."

He turns away, dismissing Rock.

If we were anywhere else, Investigator Brand would probably be rolling around on the ground with a few bullet holes. But Rock's practical and knows when to pick his battles. He steps away without another word.

Hope, God love her, fills his void. If she's still miffed with me, she doesn't show it. She stands so close her arm brushes against mine.

"And who are you?" Brand asks with a raised eyebrow, as if he's humoring the little lady. Yeah, that'll work out well for him.

"I'm a friend."

He flicks his hand in a dismissive gesture. "You're not needed, either." Poor bastard doesn't realize what a little pit bull Hope can be in these situations.

She whips out a business card and slaps it on top of the clipboard he's holding. "While obviously I came down here in a friend capacity"— she waves her hand over her casual outfit of jeans and a sweater—"I'm *also* an attorney. If you don't mind," she says, making it clear she doesn't give a fuck what he thinks, "I'd like to stay with my *friend* while you question him."

Investigator Brand stares at her for a few minutes, noticeably annoyed. She crosses her arms over her chest and scowls right back.

Their standoff almost makes me want to laugh.

"Fine." He stuffs her card in his pocket and whips out a notepad. "Right now, incendiarism is suspected," he says, not even bothering to fuck around.

"Do you have any factual basis to support that theory?" Hope asks right away.

"We're still determining the origin and cause of the fire." He points to a darkened path that used to be the hallway leading to the back door. "Traces of an accelerant. Probably gasoline. We still need to run tests."

"Jesus Christ," I mutter.

"So, I need to ask you, Mr. Ramsey, who has access to the building at night?"

"Me, my partner, Darnell Hall," I say, using Whisper's real name. "Jake Wallace, my other partner. My fiancée. A friend's been helping me out. He was closing up while I was away the last few days."

"Who's that?"

"Blake O'Callaghan." He hesitates over spelling out the last name, which if I were in a different mood would make me laugh. That's how I tagged Murphy with his road name.

"Mr. Wallace says you're the managing partner?"

I'm not surprised he's already spoken to Jake. "That's right."

"Is the business insured?"

The change in questions doesn't throw me. I'm surprised it took him this long to ask. His way of trying to trip me up, I'm sure.

"Of course it is."

He nods. "You mentioned you were away. Where?"

"My fiancée and I went up to the Adirondacks for a few days."

"Why?"

So I could finally fuck her ass. That's crude, even for me. "Vacation."

"Can you give me the name of the hotel?"

"We rented a cabin. I can give you the name of the owner."

"Later. Can anyone else verify where you were?"

Sure. My big ass is probably on some pot-farmer's security camera footage up in the Adirondacks.

Thank fuck I took Trinity out. "I have receipts from a few places we went up there."

He nods, but it doesn't seem to change his opinion of me. Why should it? As far as he's concerned, even if I didn't personally destroy my gym, it doesn't mean I wasn't in on it.

"How are your personal finances?"

"Fine."

"Have any credit card debt?"

"Doesn't everyone?"

"That's not an answer."

My shoulders lift. Eventually, he might probe into my background and find out about my club affiliation. I'd rather say as little as possible now so he can't accuse me of lying later. Still feels like I'm volunteering way too much information. I glance at Hope, but she's impossible to read at the moment.

"What's the financial condition of the gym?"

"Good." I point to the buildings next door. "We're planning to expand. I'm in negotiations to buy that property."

He seems surprised. He can fuck right off. I worked hard to make this place what it is…what it *was*.

"Got financials or a profit and loss statement to back that up?"

"My accountant does." Meaning Teller, because he does the books for not only the MC, but Crystal Ball and Furious.

Hope finally speaks up. "You understand he's not obligated to turn those over to you?"

"No. But if he doesn't cooperate, I'll get a subpoena."

She makes a *good-luck-with-that* face.

"Ever filed an insurance claim before?"

"For the business? No. Never had a reason to."

Investigator Brand looks less and less thrilled as we go through his lengthy checklist of questions. I'm sure he took in my ink, surly face, and bad attitude and assumed I'd lit the match.

"No alarms went off, and it looks like the security system was tampered with. Did you have the video back-up off-site?"

Fuck me. Z had been bugging me for a while to upgrade the system so the video would be stored somewhere else. I didn't see the point.

Actually, that's not true. Whisper insisted it wasn't necessary. At the time, I thought it was because he didn't want me to know how many of our female clients he nailed after hours. Now, I wonder if he was motivated by something else.

"No. My security guy suggested it, but we hadn't gotten around to upgrading yet. The hard drive was in my office."

Brand glances at the rubble. "We'll see if we can salvage something." He doesn't sound convinced it's possible. Maybe that's for my benefit—his way of tricking me into doing something to implicate myself. This fucker's hard to read. Not the average donut-muncher the Empire Sheriff's department usually produces.

"Who informed you of the fire?"

"Blake. He called me this morning. My fiancée and I left right away."

"Who closed last night?"

"I assume it was Blake, but I haven't had a chance to talk to him yet."

He pins me with a stern look. "You just said he called you about the fire."

"Yes," I answer with exaggerated patience. "But it was a quick call. We didn't discuss anything else."

Hope clears her throat. "Are you planning to jump on every little thing, Investigator Brand? Clearly my friend is trying to cooperate."

He shuffles through his notes, ignoring Hope, then glances around the parking lot. "He here now?"

I scan the area and wave Murphy over. His gaze darts between Hope and me as he approaches. "What's up?"

Investigator Brand introduces himself and gets right down to business. "Who closed last night?"

Murphy glances at Hope before answering, something Brand doesn't miss. "She your lawyer, too?" Each word comes out laced with sarcasm.

"Blake's also a friend of mine," she says.

Brand rolls his eyes. Hope nods at Murphy.

Murphy sighs before answering. Only because I know him so well do I sense something's off with him. "I was supposed to be here until closing."

"And?" Brand prompts.

"Things were slow. Not unusual for a Saturday night. Place was clean. Twitch said he'd finish mopping and set the alarm on his way out." He drops his head, staring at his feet. "I left at eight forty-five."

Obviously Murphy thinks I'm gonna be pissed or something. But I can't figure how another fifteen minutes would have made much of a difference. Even worse, *he* might be the body on the floor if he had stuck around.

"You try to reach this Twitch yet?" Brand asks.

Murphy waves his cell phone at him. "Yeah. First call I made after I called him," he says tilting his head my way. "Been calling Twitch all morning but just keep getting his voicemail."

Brand glances back at the building briefly before he asks for more information from Murphy. Once he's satisfied, he dismisses him and focuses on me again. "Mr. Wallace is the one who was on the scene first after the fire department got things under control. Does that sound right?"

"Makes sense. Jake would have been the one to open today."

"911 call came in around five a.m."

I glance around at the busy road. "Do you know who called it in?"

"Unidentified male."

"Great. Big help," I grumble.

He cocks his head. "Do you have any enemies, Mr. Ramsey?"

"Probably."

"Care to name any?"

Hope touches my arm briefly. "What's the point? He can't make wild guesses."

Brand answers without taking his eyes off me. "Sure he can, counselor."

"Take your pick." My shoulders lift. "Lotta other gyms in the area."

I leave it at that.

He tilts his head. "Are any in the business of burning down the competition?"

The question sounds sarcastic, but his stern expression doesn't change.

"Not that I know of," I answer with my own caustic tone.

We stand there staring each other down for a few minutes. Hope must be concerned we're about to throw some punches.

"Is that all, Mr. Brand?" she asks.

"Yeah," he answers slowly. "That's it for now. When we ID the body, I'll have more questions for you. Stay local."

"Trust me, I ain't going anywhere."

I'm marrying Trinity in six days no matter what.

I WANT TO do the only thing I know how to do in this sort of situation—care for Wyatt. I want to be by his side. Help him sort through the rubble. Make the phone calls I know need to be made. Smother him with affection to counteract the devastation of losing something so important.

But he won't let me.

A few years ago, being shut out this way would have driven me to some sort of behavior I'd regret later. Now, I understand Wyatt—and myself—so much more. Even though I'm hurt, I understand why he needed me to leave.

"Don't take it personally, Trin," Z says, starting up his truck.

"I'm not."

He glances over with a skeptical twist to his mouth.

"Fine. Yes, my feelings are…hurt. But this isn't about me."

Once we're on the highway headed home, he glances over. "You're a good girl, Trin. When I go back, I'm gonna kick his ass for snapping at you."

"Don't you dare. He's got enough to worry about."

"He's probably already pissed he let you go."

"Maybe." I glance down and brush dust of my jeans. "I'll take care of him later."

"I'm sure you will," he says with a suggestive smirk.

"Not like that, you perv." I smack his arm and he laughs, which lightens my mood a lot. "Thanks for making me laugh, Z," I say quietly after we both settle down.

"That's what I'm here for."

We don't talk a lot more. What's there to say?

When we get to the clubhouse, I do a good job of avoiding everyone and head straight to our room.

A few hours later, there's a tap at the door that takes my attention away from what I'm working on. I don't have a chance to ask who it is before Wyatt pushes the door open and steps in.

"Hey," he says.

"Why're you knocking on your own door?"

He lifts his shoulders, keeping his gaze on the floor.

"Are you okay?" I ask, hurrying over to him.

He gives the barest shake of his head before I slip my arms around him and squeeze. It takes a few seconds before he returns the embrace, burrowing his face against my neck. "I missed you all day. I shouldn't have snapped at you."

There's nothing to say, so instead I hold him tighter.

"You still gonna marry me?" he asks after a few minutes of silence.

"What?" I pull back, searching his face for something I can't quite name. When he meets my eyes, all I see is love and a rare glimpse of vulnerability. "Are you serious?"

We've known each other a long time. It's not as if I don't know how gruff my man can be when pushed to his limits. "A few harsh words when something horrible has happened won't make me give up on you. Sorry, you can't shake me off that easily, wrecking ball."

He lets out a dark chuckle, so I continue. "We're going to have so many ups and downs in our life, Wyatt. I'll be right by your side for every single one."

"This is more than a *down*, Trin. I had a fuck-lot tied up in the gym. It's going to take months to sort out. Not to mention I now have an arson investigator breathing down my neck."

"We'll get through it."

"I'm sorry I was a dick."

A smile tugs at the corners of my mouth. My man's just lost the business it took him years to build. He won't come out and say it, but he's worried I'm mad at him over a few sharp words.

I run the back of my hand over his cheek, and he leans into my touch. "I love you. We're fine." I don't offer any ridiculous platitudes like "We'll rebuild bigger and better than ever!" because I honestly don't know what he wants to do yet.

One thought keeps repeating in my head. I need him to know what was in my heart earlier. "All I wanted to do was help you today."

"I know, angel."

"You're always there for me. You do so much for me, I—"

"Hey," he says, grabbing my hands. "You do more for me than you realize." He hesitates and glances away. "I needed you someplace safe. That's all."

"Are you hungry? Do you want me to make you something?"

"No. I'm exhausted. I wanna grab a shower and get some sleep. Rock wants us all to have a sit-down in the morning." He shakes his head. "I need to be back early in the morning to meet with the insurance adjuster."

"Do you want me to go with you?" I ask quietly.

"No."

I reel back, willing myself not to be hurt. He hurries up to finish his answer. "Not because I don't *want* you there. Or because I don't *need* you." He pulls me to him and rests his chin on my head. "I'm fuckin' worried, Trin."

I stop and consider his words. "I have some wedding errands to run."

"I don't want you going out alone."

"Hope's going with me."

He shakes his head. "No. I'll have one of the guys take you."

"Oh, great. They'll love that."

"You know every single brother would take a bullet for you two. They're not going to mind. Anything else?"

"Probably, but I can't think of it right now." We stand there in the middle of our room holding each other for a few quiet minutes. "I'm here, Wyatt. Let me help. What can I do for you?"

He kisses the top of my head. "Tell me we'll look back on this years from now and laugh."

I don't see that happening any time soon. "I'm sure we will. Maybe not tomorrow…"

His rumbling laughter eases the worry from my chest.

"No, probably not."

I pat his chest and force a smile. "Go take your shower."

After giving him a few minutes alone, I wander into the bathroom to set a towel and a pair of shorts down for him. A few seconds later, he sticks his head out, glancing at the things I laid out.

"Thanks," he says.

Edgy and restless, I drift back into our room. Instinct says Wyatt needs something more from me.

While he loves me in sexy, lacy stuff, my man's usually more turned on by the simple things. With that in mind, I slip into a white tank top that's so thin, it's basically see through and a pair of tiny shorts I like to sleep in—when he doesn't rip them off me.

Kneeling in the center of the bed, I face the bathroom door and wait.

A few seconds later, my patience pays off. Wyatt emerges from the bathroom, a towel around his hips and water dripping from his hair.

"Wyatt?"

He tips his head up, his gaze traveling over my body before locking on my eyes. He raises an eyebrow, waiting for me to continue.

"Will you take care of me?"

The tension in his shoulders melts. One corner of his mouth lifts, and the hard lines on his forehead soften. "What do you need?"

I hold my hands out to him. "You."

In a few steps, he's in front of me. He takes my hands, pulling me up against his body. "I'm here."

WRATH

I RUN MY hands down her sides, stopping to cup her hips. "You're all mine."

She tucks her bottom lip under her teeth and stares up at me. "Yes."

For the first time since I got the call about the gym, the roaring in my ears fades. It's just us.

I cup her neck and lean down to press my mouth against hers, kissing her like a starving man. I groan at the taste of her. *So good.*

My hands move to her waist, brushing against the hem of her tank top. I slide it up, exposing her breasts to my hungry eyes. Her nipples are hard points against my palms, and her head falls back as my thumb circles them.

"So pretty."

Her breath rushes out when I suck one into my mouth and push her back against the bed. "I want to lick you, then fuck you."

She shudders. "Wyatt."

"Love when you wear this," I mumble as I strip off her top. "Can see your nipples through it. So fucking hot." I kiss my way down her body and tease my fingers against the waistband of her shorts. "Love these, too. How they barely fit your sweet little ass."

I slide those down her legs and toss them on the floor. "You won't be needing them tonight."

My hands are everywhere. Touching and exploring all my favorite spots. I hook my arms under her knees and hold her open the way I want. I take a long, slow lick from her pussy to her clit. Teasing her with my tongue until her eyes roll back in her head and her toes curl.

"Wyatt." She gasps and scrapes her fingernails through my hair.

"No. Hands up. Touch the headboard." She doesn't even hesitate to stretch out the way I like. "Mine," I growl the word against her pussy, but I know she hears me because she answers.

"Yes."

Her body twists as I hold her open to lick and suck her slick flesh.

I glance up at her. "You knew this is what I needed, didn't you, angel?"

After one final lick, I make my way up her body. Stop to kiss her stomach and right between her breasts. I kiss her mouth and she groans, brushing her tongue against mine. My lips travel over her jaw, to her neck, and then suck on her earlobe. "You knew I needed to bury my face in your sweet cunt and forget about everything, didn't you?"

She lifts her hips and her eyes pop open. "Yes."

I kneel up and stroke my cock a few times so she can see what she does to me. "You want this?"

As if she can't wait another second, she wraps her legs around my hips, undoing my towel with her feet and kicking it away. "Want my cock bad, huh?"

The corners of her mouth twitch up. "Fuck me."

I press my dick against her pussy. She gasps as I push into her and reaches for me. "I'm here, baby," I say, taking her hands.

"Wyatt."

I pull back and thrust in deeper this time. Her body twists and arches to meet me. "Hold on to me, Trinity."

Her arms wrap around my neck and my hands grip her hips, holding her in place while my body strains to get as close to her as possible. We're nowhere near finished. I pump into her faster, changing the angles up to give her the most pleasure. It's beautiful when she finally lets go. Her eyes roll back. Her lips part. She stutters and makes little half-word noises. I slow my pace and drag it out for her. Pressing deep and steady.

When she's calmer, her eyes flutter open. She places her hands on my cheeks, forcing me to look into her eyes. All I see is the deep well of love she has. For me.

My goal was to make her come, but now I'm the one coming apart.

"I'll be by your side no matter how dark our road may be," she whispers.

Burying my face against her neck, I kiss her shoulder. "You're all the light I need, Trinity."

MY HEAD ACHES from exhaustion, but no matter how hard I try, I can't sleep. My constant tossing and turning has to be waking Trin up, so after kissing her sleepy cheek, I slide out of bed, take one last look at my girl safely snuggled in her mess of blankets, then walk down to the living room.

I shouldn't be surprised to find the war room door open, but I *am* surprised to hear Rock and Z inside. I figured Rock would be at his house and Z would be...wherever Z is these days.

"What're you doin' up?" Z asks as I push open the door.

I give him my *you're-kidding* stare. "How the hell am I supposed to sleep?"

"Make up with Trin?" he asks. He'd given me shit as soon as he returned from dropping her off earlier. If I hadn't been so consumed by everything else, I definitely would've kicked his ass, although secretly, I kind of liked the way he stuck up for Trinity.

I'm complicated that way.

"We're fine," I answer. "Thanks for your concern."

Rock's eyes follow my movements as I pull out my chair and drop into it, but he's silent. I take him in—he looks more beaten down than I feel. "What's up, prez?"

"I'm tryin—"

I take note of the bottle of Scotch on the table. Doesn't look like either of them have touched a drop yet. "I know you are."

He lifts his chin at the phone in front of him. "I spoke to Tony earlier. He's got a contact in the Criminal Investigation Unit. Gonna get us some info on that Brand asshole."

"You think they're gonna charge *me*?"

"Hope didn't like the arson investigator's questions. I don't want you blindsided by any bullshit."

"Thanks, brother." I must have been more out of it than I realized. Although the guy's attitude was annoying, I didn't get the feeling he seriously suspected me. He seemed more focused on the body they'd found.

The body that probably belonged to Twitch.

Twitch. The kid I brought into the club.

"Did he say when they thought they'd get an ID on the body?" Rock asks.

"Couple days."

"They really seemed to think Twitch set the fire. It makes no sense. He was all about the club. Had no real family."

Z shakes his head. "You caught him breakin' in there once before."

"Yeah, because he had nowhere else to go. It was like a game to him. Breaking in to places he shouldn't be. Settin' fire to my business? Killin' himself in the process? I don't see it."

"I'm inclined to agree with you," Rock says.

Z shrugs and meets my eyes. "He could have been working with someone else. Money's a powerful motivator when you don't have any."

Murphy and Teller stop by a few minutes later. "What're you doing here?" Rock asks, directing his question to Murphy.

"Girls are asleep." He barely glances at me as he rounds the table and drops into his chair.

"You need anything, brother?" Teller asks as he takes his seat.

"I don't know." I focus on Murphy who's busy studying his hands. "What was Twitch like when you left last night?"

He lifts his shoulders and still won't meet my eyes. "Twitch was Twitch."

"You two get along?"

"Yeah."

Rock sits forward, obviously concerned about Murphy's mood. "He seem edgy? Or try to talk you into leaving early?"

Finally, Murphy looks at me. "No. I left early all on my own. I'm so sorry, brother."

"Shit, Murphy. I ain't blaming you."

"I should've stayed."

"From what I overheard," Rock says, "it wouldn't have mattered. The fire started early in the morning."

Z slaps Murphy's arm. "Or *you* coulda been hurt. We don't know if Twitch was working with someone."

"He wasn't," I insist.

Murphy nods. "I liked giving him shit, but he worked hard. All he talked about was patching in to the club." His mouth turns up into a smirk. "He thought *you* fuckin' walked on water," he says to me. "No way he torched your place."

We're all staring at Murphy by the time he finishes his speech. He sits back, lacing his fingers together. "He didn't do it."

"All right," Z says. He taps the table to get everyone's attention. "Who else?" He lifts his chin at me. "How's your relationship with Whisper?"

It takes a second for me to get my words in order. I don't want to throw shade on Whisper with nothing to back it up. "I'm not sure. He's always been laid back. Hands off. Collects his check. Signs off on whatever I want to do. It's always been a way for him to wash some cash and bang hot chicks."

Z chuckles. "That ugly motherfucker would never get laid otherwise."

I flash a quick smile. "True. Lately, he's been a pain in the ass though. Buggin' me about every last fuckin' nickel." I shake my head trying to come up with something more specific. "He wasn't okay with the expansion." My gaze strays to Murphy. "Wasn't thrilled about me bringing you in."

"He's an asshole, for sure," Rock says. "But burning down his own business is pretty extreme."

"Personality flaws aside," Teller says, leaning forward and placing his elbows on the table. "Whisper isn't stupid. Even if he's having cash flow issues, he knows as well as any of us an obvious arson won't net him any insurance money."

"*Fuuuck,*" I mutter.

Rock gives me a sympathetic look. "Even after we get you clear of the criminal investigation, you're in for a hell of a fight with your insurance company."

"I know you don't want to hear this, bro," Z says. "But if they determine Twitch did it, you're gonna have to distance yourself from him."

I nod to indicate I heard him, but that's it. I already considered that earlier.

"We'll figure out a way to pay for his funeral and keep you out of it," Rock assures me. He leans forward. "Now, what about the new guy?"

"Sully? Jake's brother? No way. He's a straight arrow. Does self-defense training with the Sheriff's department out in Johnson County."

"Got his own place," Teller reminds me.

"Yeah, but it's far enough away. We're not in competition with each other."

Rock picks up the bottle of Scotch and tips it into his glass, then passes the bottle to Z. He nudges the glass my way, but I shake my head. "I'm good."

Murphy stands and grabs a couple glasses from the cabinet, setting them down on the table with a thunk.

"You even old enough to drink yet, bro?" Z jokes.

"Please." Murphy snorts and snatches the bottle out of Z's hand. "I feel about a hundred."

Rock chuckles into his glass. "Cry me a river, kid."

After a few sips of Scotch, Murphy leans back. "Ransom."

Teller nods. "He's the only one who makes sense."

I'd been having that same thought all day. He's the only person alive who has a reason to come at us so hard.

We're all silent as we let that sink in.

"How was your trip?" Z asks.

"Fine until this morning."

"Sorry, bro," Murphy says.

"What'd you guys do?" Teller asks.

My lips curl into a smirk. "What do you think?" After a couple seconds, I drop the cocky attitude. "Looked at a couple of cabins for sale. Did some hiking—"

"Wait," Z throws up a hand to interrupt me. "Go back. Cabins?"

"Don't worry, we're not moving away from our happy little compound. Just a vacation-weekend-type place. Think I'll have to wait on that now."

"Hey." Rock reaches over and pops me on the arm. "We're all here. Whatever you need."

"Thanks. Oh, we did have one weird thing happen. Ran across a pot farm while we were on our hike."

Z's eyes widen. "No shit?"

"Like a big operation or some personal supply?" Teller asks.

"We didn't exactly stick around to take inventory. Looked like it operates as a Christmas tree farm."

Z nods slowly. "Good cover if they do surveillance."

"They had security cameras and fucking bear traps around the perimeter, so I think it's more than just someone's personal op."

"Tell Sparky," Rock says, drumming his fingers on the table. "Let him check his weed-buddy network."

When he finishes laughing, Z glances over at me. "Give me the address, I'll look into it. You ask Sparky to do it, he'll forget by the time he gets back downstairs."

There's a soft tapping at the door, and I lean back, wrapping my fingers around the knob and yanking it toward me. Hope's on the other side wearing a LOKI sweatshirt, flannel pants and an uncertain expression.

"Hey, baby doll," Rock greets, waving her inside. "What are you doing over here?"

"I woke up and you weren't there." She casts a glance at the five of us while rounding the table. "Figured you were over here." She reaches over and touches my shoulder. "How are you?"

"Fine."

Rock pulls her into his lap, and she gives him a quick kiss. "Am I interrupting?"

"No," we all answer almost at the same time.

She chuckles and leans back against Rock.

"Everything all right at the house?" Murphy asks.

"Alexa was up." She hesitates. "That's why I—"

"Shit. I'm sorry, Hope."

"It's fine. I wasn't sleeping well anyway."

Murphy stands, pushing his chair in. "I'm gonna go help Heidi." He meets my eyes. "Unless you need me?"

"No. Go take care of your girls. I'll see you in the morning."

Teller lifts his chin Murphy's way. "You need me?"

"Nah." Murphy taps his cheek. "She's just teething. It's been a rough week."

Teller sets his phone on the table. "You guys need something, let me know."

"I'm sorry," Hope says after he leaves. "He didn't have to go. That's not why I came over."

Rock squeezes her closer. "No? Why'd you come over?"

"To find you." They nuzzle each other and generally behave as if they've been apart for days instead of a few hours. Z, Teller, and I entertain ourselves by rolling our eyes and making barf faces at each other.

"Is Trinity up?" Hope asks after she and Rock finally calm the fuck down.

"She wasn't when I came down here." I cock my head and wait for her to spit out whatever's bothering her. "What's wrong, Hope?"

"Nothing. Are you meeting with the adjuster tomorrow?"

"I'm supposed to, yeah. Why? You need to be there with me?"

She sits forward, and all traces of lovey-dovey Hope vanish. "No. I think if you bring a lawyer it's going to send the wrong signal. You might want to check with Glassman, though."

"Okay. Anything else?"

"If it's an *attorney* who wants to take your statement, I want you to call me right away. I'll come down, or we'll have Glassman get his overpriced ass down there."

I chuckle at her contempt for the club's lawyer. "Will do."

"I've only worked on one arson case—and by work, I mean read through a bunch of dusty files—so it's not really my area, but please be careful what you say to them. Cooperate without making unnecessary comments. Be civil."

"Yeah," I answer slowly. "You do realize we've dealt with cops and shit before, right?"

Pink stains her cheeks, but then she shakes her head. "I understand that. It's just...I know it seems like the insurance company should be on your side. But they're not. The adjuster's job is to do whatever he can to give the insurance company a basis to deny your claim."

"If Empire's investigator clears me, that should help though, right?"

"Brand?" She crosses her arms over her chest. "What a dick," she mutters, making all of us laugh. "It's possible the insurance company will ask Brand to "assist" them," she says complete with air quotes. "That way they can make their findings look more legitimate. I don't know if Brand's the type of guy to fall for that or not."

My impression is that Brand won't take kindly to being manipulated, so I'm not overly worried.

"You might want to think about hiring your own fire investigator now, while the scene is still fresh," she advises.

"All right."

"I'll see if Tony can recommend someone," Rock says. "You have enough going on with that and the wedding."

"Is the wedding still on?" Z asks.

"Fuck, yeah it is." There's no room for argument in my tone, and Z puts his hands up.

"Just checking."

Hope lets out a big yawn, and Rock catches my eye. "We're gonna head back. I'll see you first thing in the morning."

"I'll be here. Doubt I'll get much sleep."

I STUMBLE INTO our room as the sunlight's peeking through the edges of the blackout shades Trin keeps pulled down tight. Her blonde hair spread out over the pillows and the shape of her body are all I can make out. I slip into bed, trying not to jostle her too much. She rolls over anyway, tucking herself against my side.

"Wyatt," she mumbles.

"I'm here, angel."

After a few minutes she turns over, and I pull her close, wrapping her up so tight, she wiggles in her sleep and adjusts the arm I slung over her ribs.

"Are you okay?"

"I'm fine," she answers. "Are *you* okay?"

"Better now." Can't seem to feel a damn thing, but having Trinity next to me brings me back to life.

I don't know if she does it on purpose, but she stretches, bumping her ass into my groin. My hand slides up her side, reaching under the arm she tucked close to her chest to cup her breast. My thumb absently slides over the fabric covering her nipple until it hardens under my touch. "Are you okay?" I ask again. This time I whisper the words against her ear. "We had a pretty…intense couple days together. We were talking about some serious stuff. I'm sorry all of it got ruined."

"Wyatt," she breathes out, her breath warm and soft against my arm. She struggles to turn her body, and I loosen my grip on her. When she's facing me, she places her hand on my chest, her arm tucked between our bodies. "I still can't believe it. Yesterday everything was so perfect. And now…" she trails off.

I brush the hair off her face. "I'll make it perfect for you again, Trinity. I promise." My hand cups her jaw, angling her face for a kiss.

She gasps as our lips meet, one of her hands grips my arm, pulling me closer as if the few centimeters of space between us are too much.

My cock hardens in an instant, and I groan loudly when she pushes her pelvis into me. I break the kiss, resting my forehead against hers.

"What do you need?" she whispers.

"Let me love you, Angel Face. That's all I need right now."

CHAPTER TWELVE

Five days before the wedding...

WRATH

THE CLUB'S PRETTY solemn when I enter the war room for church a few hours later.

Each of my brothers offers a nod or words of support. At one time or another, almost everyone in this room has helped out or worked at Furious. They're all feeling the loss.

"What do we know, prez?" Dex asks, getting down to business.

"Gotta be Ransom. Gotta be tied to the shooting," Murphy says, still committed to the same theory he floated last night.

"We really think Ransom's even alive?" Ravage asks. "Figured someone woulda put a bullet in his brain by now."

"They ID the body yet?" Teller asks.

"Don't know," I answer. "But it's gotta be Twitch. No one's been able to reach him."

"Sparky, give us some good news," Rock says.

Our stoner brother's usually animated and practically bouncing out of his chair when he's asked to talk about his plants. Today, he's wearing a kicked-puppy expression. He swings his bleary gaze my way. "Sorry about Furious, man."

"Thanks."

"You still having the wedding?"

"Yeah, why?"

"No reason."

I remember how Sparky'd been worried the place we'd originally planned to get married at burning down was some sort of bad omen.

Guess it doesn't matter now.

Finally, he perks up. "So, the plants we got from the Iron Bulls are still producing. I kept some totally pure, but as an experiment, I spliced them with a couple of our better strains, and the results are fucktastic." He launches into a lengthy lecture about THC percentages, and even though I tune most of it out, it's nice to be doing something normal.

"Okay. Wrap it up, Sparky," Rock orders. My cue to tune back into the conversation.

"That's it. If we swap with them again, they're supposed to come up here."

"Oh, great. Just what we need," Ravage bitches.

After they hash that out, Murphy raises his hand. "I got something I want to bring to the table."

"Christ, you didn't set a wedding date already, did you?" Ravage asks.

Murphy scowls in his direction. "No, fuckhead. That ain't club business."

"Go on," Rock urges. I get the feeling he's not aware of whatever Murphy plans to say.

"I'm entering into a fight." He glances around the table, assessing our reactions, somehow avoiding my eyes. "Should bring some cash to the club, since we seem to be hemorrhaging it lately."

When he finally meets my eyes, I raise a brow. Brother has some balls. Doesn't even flinch. "What the *fuck* are you talking about?" I ask, dropping each word so slow, all noise in the room comes to an abrupt stop.

"Jake's setting it up." As if that explains anything.

"You got any idea what those underground fights are like? No one worries about skill level or weight classes. They'll throw you in the ring with any psycho who signs up."

"Yeah, I watched *you* do it for years."

My hand slaps the table hard enough to make it rattle. "No."

Murphy's eyes widen. "I wasn't *askin'* your permission, brother."

"No fuckin' way." I turn to Rock, hoping he'll help me talk Murphy out of this. He shrugs and throws his hands up, so I turn to Teller. "He's got a fiancée and kid to take care of. He can't be gettin' in the ring."

Murphy thumps his fingers against the table, a sign he's getting seriously pissed. Too fuckin' bad. "It'll help Furious get back on track."

"How? There's no gym left for you to train at."

"I'm gonna train at Sully's place."

Next time I see Jake, I'll fucking gut him for roping Murphy into this. Sully, too. *Assholes.*

"All right," Rock says, holding up one hand to silence us. "Let's worry about the investigation and finding whoever's responsible. We can sort knucklehead out later." He doesn't glance in Murphy's direction, but I know that's the knucklehead he's referring to.

Teller flicks his hand up. "You remember my friend Bree from high school?" he asks me.

I nod because I vaguely remember him mentioning her before.

"Her boyfriend knows this investigator Brand. Says he's a hardass, but smart and fair."

My eyes narrow. Now I know why I remembered the chick's name. "She the one with the cop boyfriend? Please tell me you didn't talk to her about this."

"No. Fuck no." His face creases into a scowl. "Her boyfriend knows Sully and Jake. Heard it from one of them, quietly asked some questions and she gave me a call."

Interesting I haven't heard from Jake yet today.

Teller shrugs as if he realizes I'm less than impressed. "Just didn't want you to have the extra stress of this investigator breathing down your neck. Doesn't sound like someone who'll go along with whatever the insurance company wants."

Everyone's trying to do what they can for me. And I realize he only brought it up because he thought it might help. So I say the only thing I can, "Thanks, brother."

Rock glances around the table, silently asking if anyone else has something to add.

"You know I'm meeting with the insurance adjuster in a few hours." My way of saying *don't even think about giving me any assignments today.*

"Reach Whisper yet?"

"Yeah, he finally called early this morning. Said he was on a run down in Mississippi, but he should be back day after tomorrow."

"Convenient," Teller mutters. No surprise. He's not a big fan of Whisper's.

"We'll dig into that later, too," Rock says. "I spoke to Loco earlier. He's running down leads with some of his contacts. Seeing if anyone has information. In the meantime, he requested a sit-down." Rock grits his teeth. "Of a personal nature."

"Aw, prez, maybe he's ready to confess his love for you," Ravage jokes.

Ignoring him, Rock turns my way. "He specifically requested *your* presence."

"Me? Why? I don't have time for that shit."

"Go after your meeting." He waves a finger in Teller and Murphy's direction. "I want you two with him."

"Why me?" Teller asks. "Still can't fuckin' walk right. Ain't no good if Loco gets trigger-happy."

"Your hands work fine, dickhead," Murphy says under his breath.

Rock clenches his jaw and stares the two of them down. "Can someone at this table do what they're fucking asked to do without giving me lip, or do I need to start cracking your skulls?"

"Where you gonna be, prez?" I ask.

He glares at me, not happy about being questioned. I'm not trying to be a dick, I genuinely want to know why he's not meeting with Loco.

"I'm meetin' up with Tony. Then Sway. Need to have Z with me."

Rock rattles off a list of places he wants everyone else covering today. Ravage at the burned out carcass of my gym just in case. Dex, Bricks, Hoot, and Birch at Crystal Ball. "We have extra guys coming up from Sway's place, and Chaser's sending a few of his guys to help us with security there."

It doesn't surprise me guys from the Devil Demons MC are helping us out. Their VP's son has been working at my gym for a while. I'm sure the first call Dylan made yesterday was to his dad.

I raise my hand. "Trin has some wedding stuff to do, and I'd really like a brother with her when she goes out."

Rock huffs out a laugh. "According to Hope"—he stops to roll his eyes—"they have a *billion* errands to run—"

"Rock," Dex says, drawing our attention his way. "You know I won't let anything happen to them. If you think you can spare me from CB."

"Yeah. If you don't mind."

Thank fuck. I trust all my brothers, but if I can't have Z or Murphy watching them, Dex's who I'd pick. He'll take the job seriously and won't let the girls push him around. "Thanks, brother. Appreciate it."

Just when it looks like Rock's gonna release us, Bricks raises his hand. "Prez, I gotta mention, we're behind on our custom work."

"Fuck. Yeah, I know." He glances around the table. "We'll talk about it later." He throws a glance at the rest of us. When no one else pipes up, he ends the meeting.

I stand and stretch. Sitting for so long leaves me feeling every one of my thirty-eight years.

Outside the war room, I stop Murphy with a hand to his chest. "What are you doing, bro?"

"Christ, you act like I've never been in a ring before. What's with you?"

"Fightin' down at Sway's for fun is not the same as gettin' in the ring with the guys who sign up for these fights."

"Trust me, I wasn't fightin' for *fun* down there," he growls. "Why are you so up in my business? Don't you have enough to worry about?"

I can't explain why it bothers me so much. Yeah, I don't want him getting hurt. But it's more than that. I spent years in the ring as a way to punish myself and unleash my rage. I can't wrap my head around why Murphy would want to do this *now*.

Taking him by the arm, I drag him away from the war room door, so no one's sticking their nosy ass in our conversation.

"Why now?"

He shakes off my hand. "Stop with the big brother bullshit. I know how to handle myself."

Yeah, I'm getting dangerously close to calling him a pussy by making such a big deal out of this. If someone had tried to talk me out of fighting at his age, I probably would have knocked them out by now. "I'm not questioning your ability. I'm...worried about you." That's as close to an apology as he's getting from me.

"I'm fine."

"If you need money, I'll give you money."

He blows out a frustrated breath but drops some of his defensive attitude. "It's not that. I hear what you're saying. I'll think about it, okay?"

"Fine." He's not fooling me one bit. He's just sayin' it to get me off his back. He's right—I have a lot of shit to get done today. So for now, I back off.

I hate to break it to Murphy, but we're not done with this conversation.

Not at all.

Trinity

I WOKE UP terrified. Fiery nightmares suffocating me for the first time in a long time. Thankfully, Wyatt was already up and at church. I still can't shake off the ugliness in my head, but I can't seem to put any of what I'm feeling into words.

Hope, Heidi, and I are already sitting down for breakfast when the guys flow into the dining room after church. Conversation has been limited. Everything we talk about seems to lead right back to the fire.

I nod at the counter where Swan and I set up a buffet earlier. "Serve yourself, guys."

Shaking my head, I turn to Hope. "I should have thought of that years ago. Let them fetch their own food."

She chuckles and pulls out the chair next to her for Rock to take.

The guys are all seated and immersed in their breakfast and club stuff when Heidi leans over. "I'm almost done cataloging the photos, Trinity."

"Thank you." With everything going on, I've neglected all of my clients. Not good for business. At least now I'll be able to give a few of them links to fresh galleries.

"Your notes said not to use Uncle Wrath's real name or his road name, so I labeled his gallery "Big Blond Viking Guy." A teasing smile forms at the corners of her mouth. The first time she's lightened up all morning.

I choke on my orange juice and don't have a chance to answer her. Wyatt must have caught the tail end of her comment because he turns my way with a smirk and a raised eyebrow. "What was that, Heidi?"

Her cheeks turn red, but her eyes glitter with mischief. "I went through your portfolio the other day. At first I was like 'Wow, this guy's smokin' hot,' then I realized it was *you* and needed a hit of brain-bleach." She gives an exaggerated shake of her head. "Some things can*not* be unseen."

Murphy pokes her in the side. "Who's smokin' hot?"

"You, babe," she answers quickly, leaning over to give him a kiss.

"Wait a second," Z says, picking up on the conversation. "*He's* one of your beefcake models?" He jabs his fork in Wrath's direction. "Why didn't you ask me? I'm way better looking."

"You wish," Wyatt grumbles.

"I *did* ask you, Z. You're always too busy making fun of me."

"You'd rather have big, blond, and scary on your covers instead of tall, dark, and handsome?" he says, running a hand through his hair.

"Do people still say 'tall, dark, and handsome?'" Hope asks.

Ignoring her, he jerks his chin at Wrath. "So somewhere out there, he's on some book covers?"

I grit my teeth because I hate talking about my work with anyone besides Wyatt and Hope. "Yup. Nothing you'd ever read, though."

"What? I'm a romantic at heart."

"Yeah, about seventy-five percent of the females in New York under thirty-five can attest to that," Teller says, ducking out of the way of Z's fist.

"I don't discriminate based on age," Z says, throwing an impish smile at Hope. She shakes her head in disgust, but laughter tugs the corners of her mouth up.

"Ew. Really, Uncle Z? There are some things I don't need to know."

"Your brother started it."

Wyatt jabs a finger toward Heidi. "No, technically *she* started it by bringing up the photos in the first place."

Heidi straightens up. "I was discussing a *work* assignment with my boss," she says, in a haughty business tone that makes all the guys laugh. "I can't help it if you have bat ears," she mutters, turning my way and mouthing "Sorry."

I glance up at Rock then Wyatt. They're both quietly laughing.

Something neither of them have done lately.

Even Alexa lets out a few happy baby-squeals, making things almost feel *normal* this morning.

"It's okay, Heidi. We needed the comic relief."

WRATH

THE ADJUSTER CALLED after breakfast and needed to reschedule our meeting. With my newly freed-up time, I decide to get the meet with Loco out of the way.

The easy feeling that settled over me during breakfast with the girls vanishes as I ride to Loco's place in downtown Ironworks. Murphy's in Teller's truck with him. I, adversely, couldn't stand the thought of being caged up even for the short trip over the county line.

I almost don't recognize Loco without his gangster swagger and pimp clothes. He insists on doing this weird secret handshake thing and slapping me on the back like we're old pals. Then we follow him inside the old brownstone he runs his prostitution ring out of.

Oh, sorry. Escort service.

Whatever.

Murphy and Teller follow in behind me. Girls rush over to say hello, but Loco waves them away. "Later."

Yeah, *no*.

"What's with the businessman look?" I ask when we're seated in his ridiculously ornate office at the back of the house.

He glances down at his navy suit and laughs. "Had a meeting at town hall this morning."

I don't ask for details, because honestly, I don't care.

"So why'd you drag me down here?"

I'm forced to lean over Loco's desk because he lowers his voice and gets all dramatic. "I got a family issue."

I nod for him to continue and try not to choke him. I am *not* in the mood to be doing favors for this prick.

"My cousin, Kidd?"

"Yeah, I remember him." He's a lazy little punk.

"He's missing."

I resist the urge to ask why the fuck that's my problem. Just barely. Murphy does it for me.

"Yeah, and?"

Loco casts a dirty look Murphy's way but otherwise ignores him.

"Few of my guys been complainin' 'bout him lately. Sayin' he's been actin' shady. Going off to meet folks without telling anyone. Figured it was just internal power struggle bullshit." He waves a hand toward the door. "Feel like I'm their dad and they're all fighting for my attention sometimes, you know?"

I snort, because no, *I* don't know, but I suspect Rock could relate to that feeling.

"Anyway," Loco continues. "I didn't take certain concerns seriously. Now, I gotta wonder. Night before your gym got torched, someone tried to set my diner on fire."

"Shit." Now he has my attention. "You catch 'em?"

"No. One of my guys stays there round the clock and scared them off. Only managed to light the dumpster in the back on fire. Kept it away from the cops."

"You think it was some sort of test-run?" Teller asks.

"Don't know. But arson's pretty rare 'round here. Know what I'm sayin'?"

"You think your own cousin would do that?"

He flaps his hands in the air. "Ain't Rock always sayin' no one can fuck you over better than blood?"

I snort because yes, he does, and yes, that's the truth.

"But yeah. We been bumpin' heads because he wanted to start

cookin' meth in Ironworks, and I told him no. We finally got that shit *out* of Ironworks. We ain't bringing it back."

Well, at least there's one thing we agree on.

"Some of my girls complained about him, too, but I figured they was just bein' dramatic."

"God damn, Loco. Seems like you got an awful lot of problems with him that you've been ignoring. That ain't like you," I add to seem like I'm trying to be helpful.

He glares at me for a second, then lets out a sigh. "Yeah. His mom—my aunt—she was like a second mother to me. Been tryin' to look out for him, ya know?"

That's probably the most personal information Loco's shared with *me*. Who knows what kind of heart-to-hearts he has with Rock.

"So what are you asking, Loco?" This whole conversation's gone on way longer than it needed to.

"If you see him. Or if you get a hint he was involved in the fire. I'm respectfully requesting you hand him over to me."

It's a reasonable request. Since I doubt Kidd's lazy ass had anything to do with the fire, I agree to it.

After turning down offers of "comfort" from the girls, the three of us head outside.

On the sidewalk, Teller shakes his head and I tap his arm with my fist. "You're a free agent. That little redhead liked you. Why'd you turn her down?"

He shoots a glare at me. "What are you, the social activities director of my dick?" he bitches, making Murphy snort with laughter. He turns his pissed-off face Murphy's way and cracks a smile. "I'm trying to set a good example for this fuckwit."

Murphy stops laughing. "Fuck you." I can see he's dying to add another comment. Maybe a reminder that his dick's getting plenty of social activity these days.

Before they trade more insults, I smack both of them in the back of their thick skulls.

"Concentrate."

Teller straightens up and shuffles closer to the truck so he can lean on it. "Kidd's a little punk," he says in a low voice. "But no way he pulled that off by himself."

"Agreed. Let's not discuss it here, though."

We tap knuckles and get on the road.

CHAPTER THIRTEEN

A FTER BREAKFAST, WYATT explained that Dex had volunteered to
take us to run our errands today. He also asked us not to give Dex a
hard time, something I accepted without a thought. Hope, not so much.

"You promise to behave, right?" Dex asks, towering over us, hands
on his hips, stern expression in place.

Next to me on the couch, Hope lets out an audible, *irritated* sigh.

"Dex, man, livin' dangerous." Ravage snickers into his hand.

Dex blows out a frustrated breath. "You know I don't mean any
disrespect. I gave my word I wouldn't let either of you out of my sight."

Hope's mouth flattens into a line.

"Come on, First Lady, you don't want to get me in trouble with
Rock, do you?" he pleads.

"No," she grumbles.

"Then let's go." His gaze returns to me. "You said three places, right?
Post office, hair salon, dress shop. That's it."

"We need to stop at the drug store, too," Hope insists.

Dex plows his fingers through his hair. "You're killing me."

Ravage flops down next to us, chuckling.

"Aren't you supposed to be at Crystal Ball?" Dex asks.

"Not until noon."

Hope jumps up, grabbing her purse and bridesmaid binder. "Let's go, Dex. We're losing daylight, and I'm sure we're supposed to be back before dark."

"What the fuck did I sign up for?" he mutters as he follows us out the door. "You hassle Murphy this bad?" he asks her as he opens the door to his SUV.

She pats his cheek. "Of course."

"Where did I go wrong?" he whispers to me.

"I think it was the 'behave' part."

"She's going to make me pay for that, isn't she?"

"Probably."

"Post office first?" he asks once we're on the road.

"Please."

"So, Dex," Hope says, leaning forward and placing her arm on the back of his seat. "Are you bringing Swan to the wedding?"

He chuckles before answering. "Am I picking her up and driving her to the park? Yes."

"That's not what I'm asking and you know it."

Hope pries some more, and Dex evades all her questions. I poke her in the side. "We'll get the story from her."

"There's no story." Dex says. "I don't date employees. You're a lawyer, Hope. Isn't that a rule or something?"

She snorts. "No." I barely catch the hint of a sly smile that curves her lips before she asks her next question. "What if she wasn't an employee?"

Neither of us miss the way his entire body tenses up. "You know something I don't? She plannin' to quit?"

I barely hold in my laughter. "What's wrong, Dex? There must be hundreds of dancers in the Capital Region dying to work at Crystal Ball."

"Not good ones who show up on time and don't cause problems, besides...she's talented."

"That's sweet." Hope sighs.

"Did you think I was going to say something else, Hope?"

"You? No."

Dex seems to appreciate that.

"Don't worry. She hasn't said anything about leaving. I just figured she's starting to teach more yoga classes, so—"

His eyebrow quirks. "She is?"

"Yes. We've been taking classes from her for a while now." Hope stops and tries to twist herself into this completely ridiculous foot-behind-her-head pose that she hasn't been able to do in class yet, so why she's trying it in the backseat of the SUV I don't know. "I'm not as flexible as she is, but…"

Dex's booming laugh fills the car. "For fuck's sake, put your feet on the floor before you hurt yourself."

As miserable as I'm feeling today, even I can't help laughing.

"Anyway, I know she's going to start teaching at Wrath's new place when…" her voice falters and she glances over at me. Suddenly all her silly behavior makes sense. I reach over and squeeze her hand, appreciating her efforts to take my mind off things.

"Your man trying to poach my employees, Trin?"

"I might have mentioned how good she is." I scoot over closer to Hope. She wraps an arm around me, and I rest my head on her shoulder.

"Oooo," Hope says, like she just came up with the best idea ever. "We should ask Wrath to add pole-dancing classes."

"Dear God," Dex mutters.

I lift my head. "I feel like Rock's answer would be something like 'the only pole you're dancing on is mine.'"

Hope turns pink and bursts out laughing. "Yeah, probably."

We finally arrive at the post office. Dex holds his hand out. "Give me the slip," he says, pulling into a spot in front of the building.

I dig the pink postal slip out of my bag and hand it over. "There should only be one small box."

"I'll get it sorted. Stay here." He glances at Hope. "Please." He barely hides his smirk.

"Swan's going to kill you," I say after he shuts the door.

She waves off my concern. "How are *you*? You've been so quiet all morning."

"I don't know. The gym isn't mine, so I feel bad that I'm this upset, you know?"

"Trin," she says with exaggerated patience. "It's your husband's business. A place he poured a lot of love into. Of course you have a right to be upset."

I'm quiet while I think over her words.

"How was your trip?" she asks. "You never had a chance to tell me."

I lean back against the seat and briefly close my eyes. "Amazing. We had the best time. It was perfect...until—" A few tears slip down my cheeks, and Hope wraps her arms around me.

"Oh, Trin," she whispers. "It's going to be okay."

Then I finally admit what I didn't want to voice yesterday. "I'm scared, Hope."

"Of whoever did it?"

Shit, I hadn't let myself think about *that*. "Yes, but I'm also worried about the investigation. *I* know he had nothing to do with it, but I'm worried once the cops realize..." my voice trails off and she sighs.

"The club?"

"Yes."

"I'm worried about that, too," she confesses.

"Someone died in the fire, Hope. That makes it—"

"Felony murder." Her voice cracks on the last syllable.

My stomach lurches at the words. I didn't know the correct term. Now that I do, it sounds so awful more tears fall.

In a softer voice, Hope admits, "I'm worried I didn't do him any favors by sticking around when he was talking to the investigator yesterday or that I missed something important in his questions because I'm not a seasoned criminal attorney."

I hadn't considered that, either. "I'm glad you were there. I'm sure it helped."

"I think Rock's talking to Glassman today." She must see the panic racing across my face. "Just as a precaution," she assures me. "He won't get involved unless he has to, but it's good to give him a head's up."

Dex returns with two packages, ending our conversation.

There's one huge box and one small. Hope seems to shake off the gloom from our talk and makes a squee noise as he passes the boxes to her. She hands me the small box and sets the other one on the floor. "Open, open. I can't wait to see them."

"Oh, wow. These are gorgeous." I carefully pull the neatly packed, handmade leather ballet flats out of their teal-blue box.

Dex glances over. "They look like black shoes, Trin."

"*Pshh.*" Hope smacks his shoulder. "Quiet. You don't know anything about shoes."

"Thought for your wedding day, you'd want like glittery whatever heels," he says.

Hope chuckles. "I'm impressed you've given so much thought to women's footwear."

He rolls his eyes as he backs out of the parking spot. "Please, you know how much shoe talk I have to listen to down at CB?"

"No stripper heels for me," I mutter as I toe off my sneakers and slip on the iridescent ballet flats. "I don't want to face-plant at my wedding in front of everyone. Heels outdoors are a bad idea."

Hope breaks into giggles. "So, they're only for *indoor* use. I see."

"Shut up." I give her a playful push, and she laughs harder. "That's not how I meant it."

"Is someone going to tell me where this dress shop is?" Dex asks.

We make it there without too much trouble. It's actually not far from Crystal Ball, which makes Dex groan. "Why didn't you just say that?"

"I didn't think of it."

He eyes the tiny dress shop, then sweeps his gaze around the near-empty parking lot. "I'm going to wait right here." He holds up his phone. "Text me if you need something."

Thankfully this is a quick stop. I'd picked the dress out months ago, but when I tried it on last week it was too loose up top, so I'd brought it back to be taken in.

"Hi, Gloria. We're back," Hope announces after closing the front door.

The shop owner fusses over me for a few minutes before handing over the dress and pushing me into a private room to try it on.

"Hope, can you help me?" I call out when I can't get the last few inches of the zipper up.

She slips into the room and fixes the zipper. For a few minutes, she stares at our reflections in the mirror.

"What do you think?" I ask.

"I think I'm really jealous that your boobs defy gravity better than mine," she says, placing her hands under her breasts and staring down at them.

"Hope, I'm serious."

The corner of her mouth slides up, and she drops her hands. "You're *beautiful*. I mean, you're always pretty, but the dress is spectacular. Wrath will love it."

"Are you sure you don't know what he's wearing?"

"All I know is he's not wearing shorts."

"Thank God." I meet her eyes in the mirror. "You swear you didn't tell him about my dress."

She slaps her hand over her heart. "Swear."

I chuckle. "You think it's weird neither of us wanted white dresses?"

"Nah." She picks my hair up, twisting it into a makeshift bun. "We're trendsetters."

I turn and glance over my shoulder, then do a full spin. The layered skirt twirls with me, then settles into place right above my knees.

Bending over, I pull the shoes out and slip them on.

"Oh, they look perfect, Trin."

She's right. The shoes have a deep blue base, but the iridescent patent leather shines with various jewel tones as I move. They complement the embroidery of the dress perfectly.

"You think the gold ones would look more bridal? These were so freakin' expensive I'm afraid to wear them."

She rolls her eyes. "It's your wedding day. You *have* to have special shoes. And no, they're perfect."

"You think heels would be better? Do these make my legs look stumpy?"

"What? No. You have gorgeous legs. Stop being ridiculous." She fusses with my hair a bit more. "Is Krystal adding more blues and teals to the ends of your hair?"

"Yes, and we're supposed to go over my makeup. She wanted me to bring the dress."

"Awesome." She claps her hands and bounces up and down a few times. "Let's get going before Dex drags us out."

Dex is waiting patiently in the SUV but jumps out to open the door when he sees us.

"Got your dress?" he asks, taking the garment bag out of my hands.

"Yes. Don't peek."

He chuckles, then stops me from getting into the truck with a hand on my arm. "Hey, you make him really happy, you know?"

"I hope so."

Once we're back on the road, he glances in the mirror at us. "Do you ladies mind if we stop by Crystal Ball before we go downtown?"

Not exactly where I want to spend time, but I can't say no to Dex when he's been so good to me all day.

Hope doesn't seem to mind the stop. Even though Dex wants us to wait outside, she follows him into the club. "I want to say hi to Willow," she explains.

It doesn't escape my notice that the club has a lot of extra muscle stationed at the doors and around the interior. Many of them are Lost Kings. Some I recognize from downstate. Other guys look familiar, but I'm not sure where they're from.

Obviously what happened to Wrath's gym has the club on alert. A shiver of fear sneaks down my spine. I'd been so torn up about *Wrath's* loss, and possible legal trouble, it hadn't occurred to me that the whole club might be a target. Suddenly, I feel absurdly self-centered for going ahead with the wedding in the midst of all this chaos.

Hope tugs on my sleeve, pulling me out of my thoughts. I follow her over to the bar, and I'm amused by the way she doesn't seem flustered here. She hops up onto one of the bar stools and smiles when Willow approaches.

"What are you two doing here?"

"Wedding errands," Hope explains.

Willow reaches over and gives me a big hug. "I'm so excited for you two."

"You're still coming, right?" I ask.

"Wouldn't miss it."

"All right, ladies," Dex says from behind us. "Let's go."

Hope takes a minute to finish her conversation with Willow, and I pull Dex aside. "It's bad, isn't it?" I gesture to the extra muscle stationed at the front door. "I feel awful doing frivolous wedding stuff. I should be helping the club—"

"Don't," he says, cutting me off. "He needs you now more than ever. Getting ready for the wedding is how you help him. Whole club knows it. You're doing exactly what you're supposed to be doing."

His words help lift my guilt. "Thank you, Dex."

"Any time."

On our way to the hair salon, Dex glances at Hope. "If you really want to play matchmaker, Sparky's into Willow." His mouth twists into a cocky grin as if he thinks that will be enough to get Hope out of his business.

"Aww." Hope sighs. "She's such a sweetheart."

My foot accidentally kicks the big box Dex picked up at the post office. "What the heck is in there?" Hope asks.

"I don't know. Maybe Wrath ordered something." I pick it up and don't recognize the return address on the attached card.

"Open it."

Sighing, I pull the card off and pry it open. "What if he wants it to be a surprise?"

"Then we'll tape it back on."

"Oh, shit. It's from Lilly."

Hope leans over to read the card. "That's so sweet."

"Her invite got returned. How'd she even know about the wedding?"

"I emailed her for her new address."

"Oh." Lilly and I had gotten to be pretty good friends when we were in Hope's wedding. But I haven't heard much from her since then, so the gift is a surprise.

"What is it?" Hope asks, poking at the box.

Dex hands me his pocket knife, and I carefully slice open the box to find something soft and squishy inside. "What the hell?"

Hope grabs the papers stuffed on top and after giving them a quick glance howls with laughter. "It's a sex pillow."

"What?" I reach over and snatch the papers and Lilly's card out of her hands. "May your married sex never be boring," the card reads. "Very funny, Lilly." Even though I said the last part under my breath, Hope hears me and laughs. I flip through the other papers and snort at the part where the pillow claims your partner will be able to "achieve deeper penetration than ever before."

"Jesus, I don't think I can take it any deeper." I shake the box. "He'll probably split me in two if we use this thing."

From up front, Dex chuckles uncomfortably. "Girls, really. There're some things I don't need to know."

Hope's still laughing so hard she has trouble catching her breath. I move to take the squishy mass of foam and fabric out, and Hope stops me. "It will expand to its full size, and you won't be able to get it back in the box," she warns.

I give her the side-eye. "*Why* do you know this?"

"Please don't answer that, Hope," Dex begs.

WRATH

MURPHY AND TELLER follow me to the meeting with the adjuster. They promise to stay out of the way. Not that I'm nervous about the appointment, but I appreciate the support.

We meet at the gym, and I'm not surprised to find the adjuster already there poking around the scene. He's a tiny, bald dude. I could easily pick him up and snap him in two if he gives me a reason.

"Eric Sanders," he introduces himself and shakes my hand. "I spoke to your agent yesterday and he filled me in." He glances at his notebook. "I spoke to Mr. Wallace this morning and haven't been able to reach your third partner—"

"He's on the road but should be back tonight or tomorrow."

He flips through his notes. "I see you recently withdrew a large sum of money from your personal checking…"

My jaw clenches tight. These assholes somehow already started digging through my finances.

"It was the final payment on the house my fiancée and I just built." Boy, does it burn my ass to have to explain myself to this fuckwad. "If you go back a few more months, you'll see other similar withdrawals."

"Oh." Some of his smug smile disappears. "Who'd the money go to?"

"Our contractor." I rattle off the name and phone number. "Feel free to call and ask."

"You also had a large withdrawal from the business account recently."

I nod at the buildings next door. "It was a deposit. We're expanding the gym." My gaze strays to the scene in front of us. "Or, we were. Ask Jim, he can confirm it," I say dropping our insurance agent's name.

"Oh, I will be combing through Jim's files carefully," he assures me.

As Hope predicted last night, the conversation gets ugly fast.

"It seems awfully convenient you were out of town when the fire occurred."

I hang on to my temper by a thread. "I reserved the cabin months ago."

"So what?"

That seems less than professional, and I ignore it.

Investigator Brand joins our happy party an hour later. He has more questions about Twitch.

Now I have two assholes to deal with.

CHAPTER FOURTEEN

Four days before the wedding...

AFTER MY SHITTY afternoon getting grilled by both the insurance company and the arson investigator, I was in a hell of a mood. It's a miracle I didn't end up handcuffed and tossed in a cell.

Rock calls me down to the war room early the next morning. I find him in his regular spot on the phone and he holds up a finger, then points to my chair. So far, I'm the only other one here.

Murphy comes in as Rock's hanging up the phone. "What's up, prez?"

"You might as well hear this, too." He tips his head toward the door. "Close that."

As soon as I take my seat again, he hits me with the news. "Got a call from Tony. Coroner's office identified the body. It's Twitch," he says.

"Fuck. I knew...*fuck*." My fist slams into the table, and I barely feel the impact.

"I'm sorry. They're waiting until they notify his family before—"

"Yeah, good luck with that," I snarl. Even if the cops manage to find Twitch's useless family, they won't give a shit.

"I think we were the closest thing he had to family," Murphy adds.

"I know." Rock sighs and sits back. "You're not gonna like this next part."

I shoot a glare at him. "I don't like any of this."

"From what I understand, they're having a hard time determining whether the fire was intentional or a prank that got out of hand."

155

"So, they want to lay all the blame on Twitch."

"Brother, that will be the easiest way for it to go down and you know it. Now let me finish."

I nod for him to continue.

"The gym was successful. There's no motive. From what Tony says, unless the DA's office thinks they can get a conviction, they *might* not keep investigating."

"Let me guess, for some cash, Tony can convince them to definitely drop it."

"Right."

"How much we talking?"

He shakes his head. "I'll handle that part of it."

"Rock—"

He holds up a hand, cutting me off. "Don't argue with me. I'm not in the mood."

"You think Brand can be called off that easy?" Murphy asks.

"Fuck him," Rock growls. "He gets told to back off, he better back the fuck off."

Teller, Dex, Stash, and Sparky join us.

"Where's everyone else?" I ask.

"CB," Dex answers. "I'm headed down there next."

Dex drops into the chair next to me, and I turn toward him. "Thanks for helping Trin out yesterday."

"No problem." He sneaks a look at Rock. "Trin was fine."

Rock chuckles. "You tryin' to say something about my woman?"

"Noooo, prez. She was a delight."

Murphy chuckles and tips his chair back. "Unless you had to go to the spa and dress shop with them, I don't wanna hear your bitching."

"You planning to bring that up forever?" Teller asks.

"Yes."

I sit back, covering my face with my hands and stare up at the ceiling for a few minutes. Figure the odds of me not kicking someone's ass are better this way.

"You need one of us at CB, too, boss?" Sparky asks. The question makes me open my eyes. Sparky almost never volunteers to leave the basement.

Rock's staring at him. Actually, everyone's staring at Sparky. "What?" he asks, glancing down at the table. "I just want to help out."

"You *are* helping out. We need a healthy crop now more than ever," Rock says.

That seems to satisfy Sparky. He turns my way. "Your counters are in if you want to take Trinity over to your house today."

"Yeah? When'd that happen?"

"Finished up last night."

"Thanks." Finally something good I can tell Trinity. "You done with me, prez?"

The corner of Rock's mouth twitches. "Yeah. Go."

Last I knew, Trinity was in our room and that's where I find her. "Hey, babe. Come take a walk with me."

"Where?" she asks as she throws on a sweatshirt and follows me out the door.

"You'll see."

I don't have a key to the house, because honestly, who the fuck would have the balls to break into anything up here?

The floorplan is open like Rock's house, but we had a lot more windows and skylights added. Sliding glass doors open to a large deck and wrap around porch. Whatever Trin wanted I made sure she had.

"Oh my God." Trinity hurries over to the kitchen. "These aren't the counters we picked out."

"I wanted you to have something nicer."

"Nicer? These are beautiful."

She has her elbows on the counter, cute little ass tipped up, and she's running her hand over the colorful granite swirls when I step up behind her. "It's called Peacock Blue, even though it's more black with blue and green flecks," I explain as I trace my fingers over the peacock feather tattooed on her shoulder and down her spine. She shivers under my touch and turns to face me.

"I love it."

I fit my hands into the curve of her waist and lift her onto the counter.

"Hmm, interesting height," she teases, wrapping her arms around my neck.

"Huh. Look at that." The corner of my mouth turns up in a lopsided grin as I grind my hips into her.

I lean over and press a kiss to her lips. "We'll move the last of our stuff over after we get back from our honeymoon."

She pulls away, worry creasing her brow. "Can you even go? They told you to stay local—"

"Fuck that. We've had that trip booked for months."

She hesitates. "Do you have any news about—"

I cut her off with another kiss. "No. No bad stuff in our house. We'll talk about it later."

Her eyes search mine for a few seconds before she nods in agreement.

There's nothing except Trinity and me right now. In the house where we'll spend our life together. Our eyes meet and I'm done. Every time. Those eyes hold me captive and fucking *own* me.

She hooks her legs around my hips, drawing me closer. "What're you doing, angel?"

Her hands drop to my belt, expertly sliding it open while her eyes never leave my face. Once again, the riot in my head quiets because of her. Her fingertips feather over my cock as she takes me out, teasing at first, then gripping me harder.

My fingers hook into her pants and drag them down her legs. She helps by kicking off her shoes, and I drop her pants to the floor. "No panties, Trin? Bad girl," I tease.

"Well, I was hopeful."

"Hopeful for what? Did you want to get dirty in the woods?"

"Maybe."

I stop and admire her little naked ass on the counter. Fuck, she looks good like that. "Next time."

"How did this happen?" she asks, knocking me out of my lust-fog.

"What's that?"

"Somehow I'm naked on our new kitchen counter and you're standing there—"

"With my dick out?"

Her soft laughter rocks through me, while she wraps her hand around my cock again. "Fuuuck, that feels good, angel."

She strokes me slow and even, as if we have all the time in the world. I'm dying to bury myself in her but enjoying myself way too much to stop.

"Take your shirt off, Wyatt," she whispers.

I pull it up over my head, drop it on the floor and take her in again. Flushed cheeks, teasing eyes, tempting lips.

I crouch down, cursing the loss of her hands on my cock. "Lean back."

"Wyatt?" Nervous laughter follows.

Gently, I wrap my hand around one foot, then the other and place her heels on the counter, spreading her wide. "Perfect, Trin."

I slowly brush my mouth against the inside of her knee and up her inner thigh. She's moaning before I even get my tongue on her. Her body jumps when I flick her clit with my tongue. The muscles in her legs flex and quiver. I can't keep my fingers out of her. She's drenched. So ready for me. I lick, suck and swirl my tongue around her clit, while my fingers drive into her.

Her breathing's ragged, and she lets out a bunch of high-pitched noises, so close to the edge. I can't wait another second. She whimpers when I stand, but a second later, I fit my hands over her hips and drag her ass to the edge of the counter.

"Keep those legs spread." My voice is so damn rough, but she responds to it perfectly, staying open the way I want her. "I need to bury my dick in you."

"Do it." She stares into my eyes, daring me.

Slipping my hands under her legs, I tilt her to the angle I need and slide in. A low groan works out of my throat.

"Fuck, fuck, fuck, Wyatt." Her head drops, and she watches me slide in and out.

I take one of her hands, placing it over her clit. "Touch yourself."

At first she's tentative. I pick her hand up and suck her fingers into my mouth, then put them against her pussy. Her fingers dance around for a few seconds. Finally, she circles her clit. She bites her lip, and her eyes flicker up to meet mine. That's all it takes, her body trembles, ready to go over.

"You gonna come for me already?"

"Please?"

Cupping the back of her head, I lean down and kiss her. She responds eagerly, gripping my arms, holding on to me while she comes apart. A few second later, lights gather in my vision and I explode. After coming for what seems like forever, I stagger backwards. She reaches for me, and I take her hand.

"Give me a second."

Glancing around, I let out a curse. "There's nothing in the house to clean up with."

Her body shakes with laughter, and she falls against me. "You're going to regret doing the no underwear thing," I murmur against her ear, which only makes her laugh harder.

I hold her until her laughter fades, stroking her hair and back. Once we step outside, there's all sorts of shit I don't want to deal with waiting for me.

After we're dressed, she glances around the kitchen. "Every time I'm cooking in here, I'm going to remember this day."

"Should we build a shrine on this part of the counter?"

Soft laughter eases out of her. "No, but we should keep that one strictly for sex."

"Fine by me."

"Wyatt, I'm scared," she blurts out. Her soft, honey eyes stare up at me. I don't have to ask what she's afraid of.

"I know, baby." Inside I'm wrestling with whether I should tell her Rock can probably get me clear of the arson charges. But I hold back in case things don't work out.

"I'm scared to get too excited about this." She waves her hands around, indicating the house, our lives, the freedom to do whatever we want whenever we want. "In case it all gets ripped away."

It's almost exactly the way I feel. *Cautious.* I pull her into my arms and hold her, trying to reassure her with my body instead of words.

I need to be strong for her, so I keep my own fear locked down.

CHAPTER FIFTEEN

Three days before the wedding.

WRATH

ANOTHER PHONE CALL wakes me. I'm starting to dread the damn thing. If I wasn't waiting for information from the insurance company, I swear I'd chuck it in the woods.

It's not my regular cell, though. It's a burner I use for club business. I hope like fuck that means someone has a lead on who started the fire. My hands are aching with the need to snap someone's motherfuckin' neck.

I don't recognize the voice on the other end right away. "How's it going, Wrath?" He hacks and coughs into the phone.

"Who is this?"

Next to me, Trinity stirs and sits up, watching me intently.

"Who you think?"

Ransom. "What do you want?" I place one hand over the phone and mouth to Trinity. "Get Rock and Z to the war room."

She scrambles out of bed and darts out the door. My attention returns to the phone call.

"How's the fitness business? Hear it's been hot lately."

No fucking way. I can't believe this asshole pulled that off by himself.

"Sorry, we're closed to new members." I slip out of bed and pull on a shirt, while walking into the hallway.

"What's wrong? Gotta find your prez? Know you can't find your own dick without him. Go ahead, I'll wait."

Ignoring that, I ask, "Why're you bothering me this early in the morning?"

"I want my club back."

"From what I hear, you don't have a club no more."

"Your fault."

"I don't think so." I flick on the speaker and set the phone on the table as Rock and Z walk in. Quietly, they take their places. *What the fuck*'s written on both their faces. "Ransom," I mouth.

"Ah, your prez on the scene? Must like you, the way he got there all quick," Ransom says.

"What's up, Ransom?" Rock asks.

Crackling comes over the line. Ransom moving to another location maybe. "Your club's taken a lot from me in the last few years." No matter how hard Ransom tries to sound civilized, there's no way to disguise the evil in his soul. It bleeds into his voice every time he opens his mouth.

"It's your own fault, man."

"Took my girls," he continues, ignoring Rock's comment. "Pushed me outta my own territory. Killed my best friend."

"I don't know what you're talking about."

Teller and Murphy storm in, and I'm ready to jump out of my fucking chair. Sitting around talking, playing games with this asshole has me ready to kill someone.

Ransom's voice takes on a sharper quality. "At least own up to all the shit you done, Rock."

"Interesting advice coming from someone who ordered a hit on an innocent girl."

"Who? Mariella?" He spits her name out like a curse. "Whores ain't innocent." *There it is.* I knew this fucker couldn't pretend to be normal for long.

Rock's jaw clenches. "What do you want?"

"The pretty blonde girl."

My eyes go to Rock. *No.*

"You're going to have to be more specific."

"Wrath's girl," he says slowly, drawing the words out. "He used to bring her to his fights."

Once. One fucking time. I've been paying for it ever since.

"Fuck, no," I snap.

He chuckles. "Yeah, thought so. Figure fair is fair. You took out Killa. Now I take your girl."

Technically, Murphy took Killa out, but that's not relevant or helpful at the moment.

"Seems like you got some bad information, Ransom," Rock says.

"My info's solid and you fucking know it." Ransom's done toying with us. "Hand her over or I'll incinerate your other business. Maybe this time, it'll be full of dancers instead of just a pathetic prospect."

"Could you be any more predictable, you crazy fuck?" Rock answers in a bored tone, completely at odds with the fury burning on his face.

Rage turns my voice almost robotic. "Go ahead, motherfucker. Burn everything I own to the goddamn ground."

"Crystal Ball's a *club* business. You sure the rest of your brothers feel the same? Prez, you gonna let that arrogant, cocksucker enforcer of yours be the reason you're picking through rubble and charred remains of dead whore dancers? Can your club afford to have arson investigators sniffing around *another* burned-down business?"

"We'll get back to you," Rock says.

"No, we—" Rock holds up his hand, cutting me off, and my fist slams into the table. Z snatches up the phone, shutting it off.

"You out of your fucking mind?" I explode.

"Brother, we need to nail this fuck once and for all," Z says.

"You ain't doin' it using Trinity." I drill Rock with a stare. "Would you offer up Hope if he asked?"

He winces but holds my gaze. "No," he answers steadily.

"Then don't you dare fuckin' ask me to. I don't care how well we plan. All sorts of shit can go wrong. I won't risk her."

"I'm not asking you to."

"Not yet," I snap, because I know where we're headed as soon as everyone gets here. They'll take a vote.

Not happening.

"What the fuck is going on?" Murphy asks.

"Ransom slithered out from under his rock," Z explains. "Where's everyone else?"

"On their way."

"Please tell me I heard wrong?" Teller asks.

I can't even say it. I don't want anyone else knowing about Ransom's threat or his demand for Trinity.

Z fills them in on the parts they missed.

Teller sits back in his chair. "No fucking way. Absolutely not."

A fraction of my anxiety fades with his words. Maybe in the back of my head I'd been worried he'd be eager to offer Trinity up since he can't have her. It was a shit thing to even think. "Sounds like a bullshit distraction. We need to focus on what he's planning while he thinks we're distracted with this," Teller says.

"He'll burn down Crystal Ball anyway," Murphy adds. "He'll keep coming at us."

Z whips out his phone. "I'm telling them to shut it down early."

"Jesus Christ." Rock sits back, pinching the bridge of his nose.

"I'll do it." Trinity's soft voice comes from behind me, and my anger spikes.

Why the fuck is she in here?!

My racing heart won't calm down. Rage, unlike any I've felt in a long damn time blows through me. My body jerks around in my seat. Seeing Trinity standing in the doorway doesn't calm me down like it normally would. No, if anything I'm even *more* enraged. By sheer force,

I keep my ass in my chair so I don't toss her the fuck out of the room. She's pale, shaking, scared as fuck, yet she just made this insane offer. Through clenched teeth, I spit out the only response I can.

"Get. Out. Now."

WHATEVER THIS IS, by the look on Wyatt's face and the way he told me to find Rock, it has to be bad. I'm standing outside the war room door, the only sounds coming through the thick wood are angry voices.

A few seconds later, Teller and Murphy slam into the clubhouse. They zero in on me right away. "They at the table?" Teller asks.

I can only nod.

They go inside without another word, but Teller leaves the door open a fraction.

Not once in the ten years I've been with the club have I ever been tempted to listen in while the guys were at the table. Whatever they discuss in there isn't my business. If they want me to know something, I trust Wrath or Rock will tell me.

Now, I creep closer to the open door.

"Wrath's girl. He used to bring her to his fights."

What the hell?

The guys go back and forth with whoever's on the phone while I stand there puzzling it all out.

And then it hits me.

Ransom. The former Viper MC president. Wants me? Why?

"Go ahead, motherfucker. Burn everything I own to the goddamn ground."

My heart squeezes at Wyatt's words. I've never been consumed with so much love. There's nothing I wouldn't do for him.

"He'll burn down Crystal Ball anyway." Murphy's voice shakes me out of my fear. *"He'll keep coming at us."*

There's nothing I wouldn't do for the club that's given me shelter for years. The club Wyatt's put his entire life into.

I have every confidence the club won't let anything happen to me. Ransom's crazy and stupid if he thinks the Lost Kings will hand me over like something disposable. I've trained with Wrath on how to use a variety of weapons for years now. Taken personal defense classes with Wrath and Jake. He won't expect that.

At the gym. Wrath's business that Ransom destroyed.

My mind strays to how helpless I felt seeing everything Wyatt's worked for reduced to ashes.

The thought of offering myself up to a Viper, even for a few seconds, is terrifying.

The thought of Ransom hurting any more people I care about is worse.

My heart hammers as I approach the war room door. I place my hand on the smooth wood and give it a soft push.

Z glances up, catching my eye, but his face is unreadable.

"I'll do it," I announce with a hell of a lot more confidence than I'm feeling.

"Get. Out. Now." The ice in Wrath's voice chills me, but I already knew that'd be his answer.

I can't back down. Mariella deserves justice for what was done to her. The club needs to eliminate this threat. And I can help them do it.

I won't back down.

I *need* to do this.

"Wyatt—"

"No!" he shouts, turning and glaring at me again.

Rock's gaze darts between Wyatt and me, but he remains silent.

"I know you guys won't let anything happen to me."

Z shakes his head. "I appreciate you'll do anything for the club—"

"I'll do anything for Wyatt," I correct.

Z's mouth twitches. "I know, but—"

Murphy and Teller both shake their heads.

"No fucking way," Teller snaps. "I know what they put Mariella through. As much as I need payback for her, risking Trinity isn't the way to do it."

Damn. I'd been counting on Teller to understand why I need to do this and take my side.

Rock's gaze lands on me again. I'm shaking so hard, it's a miracle my voice comes out steady. "At least see what he wants."

Wyatt explodes out of his chair. "We know what he wants! He wants to rape you and whore you out. I'm not lettin' you anywhere near him. No."

"Trin, can you wait outside, please?" Rock asks.

Wyatt whips around to glare at Rock. "She doesn't need to wait anywhere. She's not doing it."

"I can do it." Oh, it kills me to argue with him in front of his brothers. Especially Rock. But this is too important. "I'll carry my Ruger. Maybe another smaller gun. Z can put a tracker on me—"

"No fucking way. Too easy to toss." Teller cocks his head. "What if he strips you down the second he gets his hands on you? Bye-bye guns. Bye-bye tracker. We can't take that risk with you. Listen to your man, Trin. He's right."

"If anyone can do it, Trinity can—" Murphy starts.

"Fuck you. You wanna send in Heidi?" Wyatt shouts.

"No, brother. I don't want to send anyone."

Z stares at me for a few seconds before addressing Rock. "She might be our best shot."

Wrath shakes his head while Rock looks to me. "I trust you, Trinity. I know how capable you are." His gaze lands on Wrath. "Final call is yours."

"No."

"Wyatt—"

He takes my arm and hustles me out of the room, slamming the door behind us. "What the fuck is wrong with you?"

Shaking out of his grasp, I stand my ground. "Wyatt, please. He'll keep coming after the club. This way, we can control it. We can end this. Stop looking over our shoulders all the time, waiting to see what fucked-up thing they do next."

"Ransom's the last one who's a threat to the club, Trinity." This is probably the most specific information about a club beef he's given me in a long time. "We'll handle him without putting you in danger."

"You've done so much for me. Please let me do this."

"I can't, Trinity. Don't keep asking me." I swear he sounds closer to begging than I've ever heard him.

A whirlpool of emotions spin inside me. Fear. Frustration. Determination. Faith. "You *know* they won't let anything happen to me." I point at the closed war room door. "I trust you to keep me safe."

"*Not* letting you do this is how I keep you safe."

The next thing I say is cruel, but I say it out of love and I hope Wyatt understands. "Keeping the club safe is also your job, and this is a way to do it."

The anger shining in his blue eyes levels me. "That's low, Trin."

WRATH

I'M A POWDER keg about to blow if Trinity doesn't drop this craziness. Does she seriously think I'm going to allow her anywhere near a psycho like Ransom?

She struggles out of my hold, and I release her arm. "I'm so sorry I'm putting you in this position. You know I'd never challenge you in front of—"

I wave her concern aside with a flick of my wrist. "I don't give a fuck about that."

"You have to let me do this, Wyatt."

Visions of all the horrible things that could happen to Trinity flash through my head. "No, I fucking don't."

"I can handle it. I swear. You—"

"No! Don't you get it? You're asking me to do something that goes against everything I am."

"Wyatt—"

I take her outstretched hands and back her up against the wall. "Are you mine?"

"Yes," she whispers.

"Do you love me?"

Her face softens, and she reaches up to run the back of her hand over my cheek. "More than anything in the world. That's *why* I have to do this."

"No, you don't. You don't *owe* me anything."

"That's not it. I love you. I'd do anything for you."

We stare at each other for a few long moments. "If you love me, you understand—this is who I am, Trinity. You can't pick and choose which parts of me work for you. You're *mine*. I keep you safe. I protect you. I can't turn that off."

"Please listen to me."

"No, *you* need to listen to me. You know how tight I hold you at night? It's because even in sleep I want to keep you safe."

"Wyatt, I've never felt safer than I do with you."

"Good, that's what I want. Me to take care of you and protect you. Not put you in the middle of club business."

"But this is the life we choose to live. I know this. You're worth the risk."

For the first time, Trinity's voice falters. Thank fuck. Does she finally get it?

"You have to let me do this, Wyatt." She places her finger against my lips to silence the *fuck no* already forming.

This determined glint shines in her eyes, and I steel myself against whatever argument she's about to make. "You have to trust that I can handle it. Otherwise, this will never end." Her voice comes out low and steady. Almost hypnotic. "Maybe he doesn't burn CB down, but because everyone's focused on that, he slips under the radar and does something else to hurt the club."

Jesus Christ. She really has learned too much from me, because that was one of my first concerns.

"What if while all the guys are busy securing CB, Ransom grabs Heidi when she's out with the baby? Or Hope when she's on her way to court? He could ambush me some other time. When we don't know it's going to happen and we aren't ready for it. God only knows where I'd end up." Her bottom lip trembles as she asks her next question. "What happens then?"

"I won't let it happen."

She shakes her head. "What if he really does burn CB down and hurt those girls? I couldn't live with myself."

I drop my gaze to the floor. "Fuck," I mutter. Why does she have to make so much fucking sense?

Knowing what damage Ransom's capable of inflicting, the thought of him grabbing Trinity when we can't see it coming…makes me want to lock her up tight for the rest of her life.

The night we rescued Mariella comes back to me in vivid, horrifying detail. Trin's suffered enough in her life. I don't ever want anyone hurting her again.

I'm coming apart, bursting out of my skin while I think this through. The only person in the world who can make sense of all the noise in my head is standing in front of me, quietly asking me to do the unthinkable.

Now that I know Ransom, for whatever twisted, fucked-up reason, has her in his sights, he won't back off. Not until he has her.

Or he's dead.

Burning down my gym? Whatever. In the end, it's nothing more than a big box of stuff.

Threatening Trinity? When she's everything in the world to me?

He. Is. Dead.

My traitorous brain remembers how fucking fierce Trinity is. How accurate she is with a gun and a knife. My hands travel over her arms, gently squeezing muscles toned from hours spent at my gym. She's strong. Quick on her feet. Smart.

She *can* do this.

I hate it. Everything in me says it's wrong to use my woman to take Ransom out. To put her in danger.

But she's already *in* danger. Just by Ransom knowing who she is and what she means to me, she's in danger.

"Why can't I have a nice, complacent old lady who does what she's told?" I finally ask.

She sucks in a deep breath.

"Why does mine have to be so fucking smart and brave?"

"Because I have you," she answers. Her hand squeezes my shoulder. "Nothing and no one will take me away from you."

Finally, I pick my head up and stare into her brave, honey eyes. My mouth stretches into a pained smile. "You have to do everything I tell you to do."

"Thank you." She closes the distance between us and hugs me tight.

"I hate this," I murmur against her hair. Pulling back, I cup her face between my hands. "He could hurt you."

"I'm a fighter, remember?"

"Yes, you are."

"I won't lie to you, Wyatt. I'm terrified, but my faith in you…my faith in the club, they're both stronger than my fear."

Fuck, if that's not the one thing she could say to convince me I'm making the right decision.

CHAPTER SIXTEEN
WRATH

I CAN'T WAIT to rip Ransom apart with my bare hands.

Because once I catch him, that's exactly what's gonna happen. If he does anything to hurt Trinity, it'll be a long, slow slide into oblivion for that cockroach.

There are so many emotions stirred up inside me, I can barely think as I lead Trinity back into the war room. Rock raises an eyebrow but doesn't speak.

No one says a word.

Finally, Z meets my gaze. "We're working on another plan."

I almost say "good" and push Trinity out of the room. But she squeezes my hand. Z's trying to give me an easy way out, and we both know it.

"She's in. But if anything happens to her, I'm taking it out of your ass. After I dismember Ransom."

Z rests his folded hands on the table and stares at them for a few seconds. "It all depends on how soon he wants to do this, brother. My preference is multiple tracking devices. Even if he wands her, which I doubt he'll bother to do, he won't catch all of them. If he does later, she can pretend she didn't know."

"All right," Rock says, drawing our attention to the head of the table. "Planning anything is useless until we know how Ransom wants this to go down."

"I say, follow his lead," Teller suggests. "That asshole has a giant fuckin' ego. Let him think he's got us by the throat."

Sparky and Stash show up next.

Z greets them. "Called you like half an hour ago, ya fucks. All you gotta do is come up a flight of stairs."

They apologize to Rock. And while he accepts their apology, he doesn't tell them why they're upstairs.

"Let's wait until everyone gets here first."

Slowly, brothers trickle into the room and take their seats. The tension in the air stops anyone from asking questions.

Last to show up is Ravage. "Sorry, two of the girls got into a fight out in the parking lot. Had to make sure they both left..." Ravage trails off as he looks around the table and takes in our expressions. His gaze lands on Trinity in the chair next to me, and he drops into his seat without uttering another word. By the graveyard silence in the room, he knows Trin ain't sitting here for some last-minute wedding details.

Trinity squirms and attempts to leave, but I reach out and grab her arm. I turn to Rock and he nods.

"Trin, I need you to stick around. What you're doing for us is huge. I want you informed of everything that's going down," he says.

Once he's sure Trinity's staying put, Rock finally explains why we're all gathered here. Every word he drops intensifies my urge to grab Trinity and run.

And I've never run from a threat in my life. Removed myself from a bad situation until I could regroup, sure. I consider that smart. Outright run and hide? It's an unfamiliar feeling. But I'm willing to do anything to protect Trinity.

I'll give Sparky credit because as soon as Rock finishes he shakes his head. "There has to be another way, prez." He swings his bloodshot gaze my way. "You cool with this, bro?"

"No. I'm not fucking cool with this."

All eyes are on me after Rock wraps up the discussion.

"You're sure?" he asks.

My hand settles over Trinity's. "We're ready."

"Let's get this over with." Rock keeps his eyes on us while he dials Ransom. No one in the room needs to be told to be quiet. A hush falls over the table as everyone watches Rock.

"Surprised you made a decision so fast, prez," Ransom answers.

"Let's make this quick. I only have a few minutes. I can't have this blowing back on me. I think you understand why."

"Going behind your SAA's back?" he taunts with fake surprise.

"Gotta think of the entire club," Rock snaps back. "How do you wanna do this?"

"Day after tomorrow." Ransom rattles off the address of a grocery store in South Ironworks. Not far from the Vipers' old clubhouse/meth lab. "Send her there. I'll take care of the rest. Don't even have to get your hands dirty."

"How the fuck am I supposed to get her there?"

"Don't your bitches listen? You gotta give her a fuckin' reason to do what she's told?"

Rock snorts.

"You sure about this, Rock? Why you so eager to hand one of your girls over to me when you think I'm such a bad guy?" Ransom's brazenly disrespectful tone would get him shot if he were standing in front of us.

"Come on. You know how uppity these whores get when they start fuckin' one guy on the regular." Rock keeps his steady gaze on both of us as the words flow out of his mouth. His expression doesn't change, and only because I've known him so long do I know how much it bugs him to talk about Trinity that way. Even though I know why the words are being said, it doesn't stop my hands from curling into fists.

Trinity doesn't even flinch.

Ransom, scum that he is, laughs—loud and harsh. "Yeah, prez. I know exactly what you mean."

"Who's gonna pick her up?" Rock asks.

"Now, prez, you're not plannin' to double-cross me, are you?"

"No, you fuck. You're asking me to hand over a brother's girl. I wanna make sure the right person gets her."

"Oh. Yeah. I'll be the one to get her. Me and my associate." He pauses and hastily adds. "Don't get cute, I got other people in the area watching my back while I'm down there."

Hard to tell if that's true or bullshit.

Rock doesn't press for details. Even though we're all curious, he won't risk raising any more suspicions.

"Is this number good?" Rock asks.

"For now. Why?"

Frustrated with Ransom's denseness, Rock shakes his two fists at the phone while silently mouthing "stupid motherfucker. "I was gonna text you with what she's wearing, so you know what to look for," he answers calmly.

"Oh. Yeah. This number's fine. Don't stress, prez. I remember that bitch real good. No way I'd forget a face or an ass like hers."

Fuck me. This motherfuckin' prick needs to die. *Hard.*

Silence clings to the room even after Rock hangs up.

"Anyone else find it curious he's comfortable meeting in Ironworks?" Teller finally asks.

Rock nods slowly, his gaze straying to Trinity. "Yeah. We'll need to speak to our friend over there about that at some point," he says, meaning Loco. Ransom shouldn't be able to show his face anywhere in upstate, New York, and definitely not in Ironworks without it getting back to us.

Murphy shrugs. "South Ironworks has always been sketchy and that's where their—"

"Yeah, yeah," Rock says, cutting him off.

I sit up and pin Rock with a stare. "Lot of buildings down there. Could set up camp with a sniper rifle and take him out before he even touches Trinity." It's a weak plan and I know it, but I have to explore every other option.

"You're solid with a rifle, no doubt. But Ironworks?" Rock slowly shakes his head as he thinks it over. "Too many narrow, one-way streets. Way too hard to get out clean."

"You snipe someone in Ironworks in broad daylight, that's gonna bring a lot of heat," Dex says. "Police will know it's more than a random gang shooting."

"I know you're a good shot. But with Trinity so close to him. No way," Z mutters.

"I won't take the shot if she's too close."

Z pulls up a map of the store where Ransom wants to meet and studies it for a few seconds before turning his tablet around for the rest of us. "Place isn't far from the onramp to Route Seven. Cop presence is weak there...I can go scope it out today..."

Dex leans in, staring at Z's screen. "Buildings around there aren't tall enough. Besides, we don't know that he won't have his own people spread out in case we try to do something exactly like this," Dex says. He lifts his gaze to me. "Believe me, brother, I'd risk you over her any day, but I think it's best to take him down away from the city if at all possible."

"We don't know he's taking her out of the city," Sparky shouts. He shakes his head vigorously. "I really hate this."

Me too, brother.

Dex growls with frustration. "It's hard to tell, but he sounded like he's planning to leave Ironworks as soon as he has her."

"I can do it, Sparky," Trinity says softly. She places her hand over mine. "Wrath's trained me well. Not just with guns." Her gaze flicks to Teller. "He's not used to girls fighting back."

Teller acknowledges that comment with a slight nod. Trin and Mariella were close. My girl probably knows better than any of us what she's volunteering to walk into.

We toss a few other ideas around, and then it's time to get serious and talk about what weapons she'll be taking. "She can carry at her back and her leg—"

Teller shakes his head. "Carrying at my six is how my legs got fucked, have her—"

"She's not gonna be wearing it long enough to have anything happen," Z says. "He'll pull that first. I doubt he'll expect her to have another weapon or two hidden."

My vision blurs red thinking about Ransom touching Trinity.

"Someone needs to keep a visual on her," Rock says.

"Gotta be someone he won't recognize immediately." Murphy points at Z, Rock, and Teller. "Can't be any of you." He glances down the table at Dex and Bricks. "He might recognize you two from CB."

Z's mouth quirks up. "Looks like Stash and Sparky gotta come outta the basement."

I love those guys, but I'm not real comfortable with the vampire twins being all that stands between my girl disappearing with Ransom and not.

Stash has sobered up considerably since he walked in here and seems to sense my hesitation. "We won't let her out of our sight, brother."

As Rock continues discussing the plan, my gaze drops to Trinity's lap. She twists the hem of her shirt between her fingers, hands trembling with the strain of the situation, even though her face remains calm. Pride and fear go to war inside me. She's so fucking brave, it scares the fuck out of me.

I swear, after tomorrow, once Trinity's safe in my arms, she's never leaving the property again.

WHAT DID I agree to do?

No, not agree. *Beg* to do.

I can't back down now.

I won't.

Not when all the guys are ready to die to protect me.

I need to follow through.

I swallow my fear and paste on a false smile. "Who's going out to the gun range with me?"

CHAPTER SEVENTEEN

Two days before the wedding...

WRATH

EVERY SECOND I spend with Trinity at the gun range reminds me what I agreed to let her do.

But I don't trust anyone else to be out here with her.

Z seemed to understand my struggle and followed us out to the range this morning.

He keeps up a steady stream of upbeat commentary while he runs through each weapon with her. I sit back and watch, hating every second.

My woman already has excellent basic skills—I've made sure of that over the years. She's a pro at quick and safe reloading, one-handed shooting techniques, and she's deadly accurate with almost any gun you put in her hands.

What we work on today are her skills shooting at moving targets, moving while firing, shooting at multiple targets, and most importantly quick draw from a holster. As soon as the sun starts going down, we'll work on shooting in low-light.

The plan is not to let her out of our sight. The plan is to wait until Ransom gets her wherever he's taking her, ambush him, and get her out safely.

Plans can go wrong.

So here we are. Practicing with three different handguns I know she's comfortable with.

She's so tentative as she walks over to me for a break, I coil up tight inside. I hand her a bottle of water, and she takes a few sips before handing it back.

Z walks up with her paper targets. The reactive targets we've been using are still out in the field.

"Christ, she's good, Wrath. Look at these."

"I know." I take the targets out of his hands and set them on the bench without looking at them. They don't matter.

Nothing matters if she takes a shot at Ransom and misses.

Ransom might be a cockroach, but he's also a cunning thug. He didn't rise to president of a club like the Vipers by accident.

"Trin, grab a couple of those holsters and bring them over. We'll work on quick draw next," Z says.

As soon as she moves away, Z punches my shoulder.

"What?" I snap, punching his leg.

"I get why you're unhappy," he says in a low voice. "But stop being a moody fuck. She doesn't deserve it on a good day. And she sure as fuck doesn't deserve it today with what she's doing for us."

"I know," I answer, not even bothering to defend myself.

"Here," Trinity says breathlessly, dropping a pile of five different holsters on the table in front of us.

"You should help her with this, brother," Z says, shooting me a don't-fuck-it-up glare when Trin's not looking.

"Come here, angel," I say once we're alone. I hook my fingers in the waistband of her jeans and slowly draw her closer. She wraps her arms around me, and I rest my head against her stomach. We stay that way for a few quiet minutes.

If I still knew how to cry, now would be the time. But that's something that had been beaten out of me a long time ago. Instead, I lift the hem of her shirt and brush my lips against her skin.

She quivers with laughter and strokes the side of my face. "That tickles."

It's as if her voice reaches inside, wraps itself around my heart and squeezes. Handing her over to Ransom is absurd. Insane. So very wrong.

Three quick blasts from Z's gun shatter our moment. Reminding me why we're here.

She runs her hands through my hair a few times then pulls back, picking up her Glock and pointing it at the floor.

No words need to be said about what either of us are feeling.

"Hold your shirt up." I turn my head to give myself a second and pick up one of the waistband holsters.

She does as I ask so I can secure it around her hips. I slip the Glock out of her hand and tuck it in the back pocket of the holster, then fix her sweatshirt. "Draw."

She expertly pulls the gun, aiming toward the grassy field. "Good. You're comfortable giving that one up?"

"Yes. I like it, but I'm more comfortable in a rushed situation with the revolver."

"Okay."

Her hand sweeps over one of the other holsters. "I'd rather not even try the bra one. Don't really want to give them an excuse to feel me up."

I think she meant to say it as a joke, but there's nothing funny about this and we both know it.

I take the holster off and replace it with a different one and have her repeat the process.

When she's finished, I take that one off and set it to the side.

"Okay, which one are you more comfortable with if you get to keep your weapon?"

She considers the question before answering. "The hip-hugger one feels more secure. But the lace waistband holster tucks in where it's easier for me to draw from."

"Let's go with that one then." I motion with my hand for her to lift her pant leg, and we do the whole thing over again with the ankle holsters and her favorite revolver. We're putting an awful lot of faith in Ransom's lack of respect for females. Maybe he'll be too lazy to do a full pat-down. Given my position in the club, even if he does find the weapons on her, it shouldn't come as a surprise. But I know how volatile he can be.

"Trin, if he hurts you—hurt him back."

She drops into a fighting stance I taught her and throws a light punch at me. "Promise, coach."

I fucking hate this.

Z finishes his target practice and joins us.

Trin finishes her practice draws and shakes her pant leg back into place. "Both ankle ones are fine."

Z stares at her for a few minutes. "Have her carry one on each."

"Guys, I'm not fucking Laura Croft."

Both of us stare her down.

"Fine. Christ, I'm barely gonna be able to walk with all this hardware strapped to me."

CHAPTER EIGHTEEN

One day before the wedding...

TIME TICKS DOWN fast.

Ransom sent a text to Rock this morning. *Four p.m.*

That's when Ransom wants to grab me.

My stomach heaves every time I think about it.

All the guys were called into the war room. After about an hour locked inside, they called me in and reviewed the plan with me again.

Wrath's not a particularly wordy guy with the rest of the world. In private with me, though, we rarely run out of things to talk about.

Not today.

He's silent. Brooding. He's been considering any other possible way to get Ransom without involving me. But we both know this is the best way to draw Ransom out and end this.

At two, Rock taps on our door, pushing it open. "Ready?"

"As I'll ever be." I slip a plain black sweatshirt over my T-shirt. Under that, I'm wearing a tank top. I want as many layers between Ransom and me as possible. The lace waistband holster is tight around my middle, and I tuck the pistol in its place. At my ankles, the other two guns are already secure.

Rock pulls me in for a quick hug. "You're the bravest woman I know, Trinny."

"I don't feel brave. I'm scared," I admit.

Behind me, there's a muffled crash. I'm pretty sure it was Wrath's fist hitting the wall.

"Wyatt," Rock snaps. I've only heard Rock call him by his given name a handful of times over the years. "Let's go."

I try to take Wyatt's hand as we walk down to the living room, but he shakes me off.

I get it.

I do.

But it stings.

"Trinity, it's bachelorette party night. Where are you going?" Hope calls out, as she hurries down the stairs.

I'm standing close enough to Rock to hear the "fuck" he mutters. Hope stops in her tracks as soon as she takes in everyone. It's pretty obvious from the guys' tense postures and expressions that we're not headed out for a celebration. Her gaze strays to Rock.

"Rock? What's—"

He pulls her aside, speaking to her in low tones. Wrath still won't touch me or even look at me. I know it's his way of coping, but it still burns.

A couple of the guys open the front door and step outside.

"Trinity?" Hope's eyes are full of unshed tears and hell, if she cries, it's going to mess me up.

How much did Rock tell her?

While I don't poke into club business with Wrath, I imagine Hope doesn't take kindly to being excluded from things on the sole basis of having a vagina.

"Don't," I warn.

She pulls me into a hug anyway, and I squeeze her back just as tight. "I love you, Trinity," she whispers.

"Love you, too." I choke out the words. Damn her for making me cry. I pull back. "You can't be late to help me get ready tomorrow morning. Make sure you set your alarm half an hour early."

A sad smile touches her lips, but she nods at my attempted joke. "I will."

"We need to go," Rock says gently. God bless her, Hope glares at him. "Dex and Ravage are staying here. You are *not* to leave the property until we come back." Her glare intensifies, but she nods and doesn't question him.

Murphy steps forward. "Heidi knows she needs to stay put, too, Hope." He's also rewarded with Hope's pissed-off glare.

She squeezes my hand one last time before letting me go, but she's looking at everyone when she says, "Please be careful."

Hope's fond of calling me the "little blonde badass." I feel anything but badass as I follow the guys out of the clubhouse.

"Trin, you're riding with Z and Teller," Rock says, pointing at Z's truck.

"I figured." I give him a small smile.

He knocks his fist into Wrath's arm. "We won't be far behind you."

The rest of the guys discuss their assignments while I work on controlling my racing heart.

Finally we're ready to leave. Z opens the back door for me. As I'm about to step up into the truck, Wrath jogs over, placing his hand on my shoulder and spinning me around. I'm swept up into his arms and crushed against his chest. "I love you so much, Trinity," he murmurs against my hair. "I'm so proud of you. Thank you for being so brave."

I choke on a sob as I hang on to him tight. "Love you, too."

"You're everything that matters to me, Angel Face."

My throat's so tight I barely force out a response. "If I'm an angel, it's only because you're my heaven."

Before I say another word, his mouth crashes against mine. My pulse races as he yanks me tighter against his body. I wrap my arms around him and hold onto him just as hard. Our tongues collide wildly. Both of us needing to taste each other, reassure each other with this last kiss before going off to deal with the devil.

I back away first, breaking our contact. He sets me down but keeps his hands on my waist and leans down to press his forehead against mine. "You got this, Trinity. Not a doubt in my mind. You got this."

His words are exactly what I needed.

For the first time, I truly believe I can do this and come home in one piece.

WRATH

"HOW MUCH DO you hate me right now?" Rock asks as we watch Trin drive off with Z and Teller. His low voice can barely be heard above the rumble of my truck's engine.

I glance over, taking in his pained expression. This is killing him almost as much as me.

"It's not you I want to murder."

"Should be. I've done a shit job protecting this club lately."

I let out a sigh, not really in the mood for Rock's martyr bullshit at the moment. "This prick's had it coming. Vipers have been a problem in this area for a long time now. Since before you took over. Every time they change leadership, they say it'll solve the problem, but it never does. After tonight, we're finally done with these fucks."

He glances over. "I'm the one who should be giving you the pep talk."

"I don't need pep. I need Trin to be okay and I need Ransom dead."

"Amen." He goes back to staring out the window.

I hated being so cold to Trinity while we were gettin' her ready. Handling a situation like *this* isn't in my nature. There's no other way to separate who I am from the things I do. Trinity's my peace. She's not supposed to be mixed up in this. I'm supposed to keep my woman safe, not use her to bait our enemies.

Thank fuck I pulled my head out of my ass and told her how much I love her, how much faith I have in her, before she left. I couldn't stand it if my actions made her hesitate or rattled her when she needed to be focused. Couldn't stand it if she doubted for one second how much she means to me and how grateful I am that she's willing to sacrifice for the club.

Guilt and pain from all the times I've fucked up in the past pummel into me. I can't afford to lose my focus. If I do that, Trinity gets hurt and that's not acceptable.

Acid boils through my veins. I can't stop picturing Ransom laying his greasy fingers on my woman, and it's driving me insane that we haven't had any updates.

Thoughts of how I plan to torture him to death soothe me.

For now.

CHAPTER NINETEEN

W E'RE ALMOST TO the bridge that leads into the city of Ironworks when Z breaks the tense silence in the car.

"What you're doing for the club is huge, Trinity," he says quietly. "We all appreciate it."

I'm not sure how to respond, so I nod and because he's watching me in the rearview mirror he sees it. "We love you, girl. We're not letting anything happen to you." In the mirror, our eyes meet and a lump forms in my throat. Z's my friend. My playful, prankster friend. He doesn't do mushy stuff.

Z drives around the block once. There's a small parking lot behind the little grocery store. He parks on the street across from the place and stares at it for a few seconds before checking the dashboard clock.

"Almost time," he says.

Game on.

I'm shaking so hard, I stumble on my way out of the truck. Teller catches my arm, holding me steady. "You're gonna do great, Trin."

"Thank you," I whisper, feeling less than confident.

The club's counting on me. Time to get my shit together.

I straighten my shoulders and toss my hair back, holding my hand out for some cash the way a seasoned club girl would do. The kind of girl Ransom expects me to be, in case he's somewhere watching. Teller slaps a few twenties in my hand before I turn and strut into the grocery store. It's not one I've ever been to, or would ever go to on my own. Even though the Lost Kings have moved into Ironworks since they pushed the Vipers out, Wrath still doesn't like me venturing over here, so I don't.

It's a small store. Finding my way to the spices only takes a few seconds of navigating through the narrow, dirty aisles.

My hand barely brushes over the chili powder when warm, soft lips graze my ear. "Do you need help?" Even though I'd been expecting it, the voice rattles me down to my toes. I've never been up close with a Viper before, but without a doubt, this is Ransom. His low, sinister voice crawls over my skin like spiders.

Act natural. I have to remind myself I'd be startled, but cool if I didn't know this was a set-up.

"Can you reach that for me?" I ask in a flirty tone, pointing at the bottle that's about two centimeters away from my fingertips.

Ransom's not as horrible as I expected. In my head, I've always pictured him short, with greasy, stringy black hair. Scrawny and pockmarked. Maybe even with a bad-guy mustache. I couldn't have been more wrong. He's a snake in a decadent bad-boy's body. Dark curly brown hair I'm sure lots of women love running their fingers through. Or yank when they're trying to pull him off them.

I shiver with revulsion at the thought.

Maybe it's because Mariella shared more than a few stories about the way he tortured her, but he gives me the creeps. Especially the way he studies me with his dark amber eyes for a few seconds.

"You don't really need that, sweetheart."

The crawling sensation returns to my skin.

"I was told to get it," I say, keeping my tone light.

"Reymond," he says, extending a hand. I have no idea if that's his real name or not. It doesn't really matter.

"Trinity."

"What an unusual name for such a beautiful woman."

None of this is what I expected. I was prepared for him to shove a gun in my back and march me out of the store. Apparently, he plans to go the seductive route instead.

I think I'd prefer the gun to my back, honestly.

Instead, he takes my hand. Like we're lovers or friends who happened to meet up in the spice section. Haha, what a romantic story.

"What're you doing?" I ask, remembering to pretend I don't know what's happening.

His hold on me tightens.

"Let go of me. I have people waiting for me outside." I lower my voice. "You don't know who you're messing with. My man will fuck you up just for looking at me."

He doesn't answer, just keeps pulling me toward the back door. I have to pretend to put up a fight.

"Hey! Let me go."

"Shut up," he hisses. "No one's gonna help you here. I still have connections in this fuckin' town."

"Who are you?" I ask, as he shoves me into a dark, filthy hallway. He pushes me along without answering my question. At the end of the hallway, he opens a heavy steel door, which leads to the alley.

I dig my heels in. "No. I'm not going with you."

Now he takes the gun out, pressing it into my side. "Easy or hard, whore. Your choice."

"I'm not a fucking whore, jackass. My ol' man's the enforcer for the Lost Kings MC. He's going to kill you for this."

"That would be a lot more convincing if his president wasn't the one who handed you over."

I gasp and pretend to think that over. "Rock would never do that to me."

He takes his hand off the door, allowing it to slam shut with a heavy clank.

"Why?" He uses his body to push me up against the wall and lowers his head so he can whisper in my ear. "'Cause you're such a good *fuck*?" He punctuates *that word* by thrusting his hips into me. I turn my head and try not to vomit.

He chuckles deep and sinister as he backs away. "You can't be that good. Kings gave you up to save their business."

I don't respond. The next time he shoves me into the alley, I don't offer any resistance. We stumble outside together. A young black kid leaning against a low brick wall across from the door waits for us.

"What took so fuckin' long, man? Her guys drove off, but we still need to get out of here."

"They ain't comin' back for this bitch." His smooth olive skin creases into a scowl. "Which ones?"

"The VP and the blond dude we ran off the road."

"Wait, what do you mean they drove away?" I ask, reminding myself to act shocked that Z and Teller would leave me behind.

Even though in my head, I know the guys aren't far away, true fear beats in my chest. I'm now truly alone with these two psychos.

It's up to me to keep the plan moving.

"Told ya, they gave you up." Ransom sneers and rubs his hand over my ass.

I keep my head down as they hustle me into the parking lot. While I pretend I'm not paying attention, I'm actually trying to remember every single word they say. Whoever this other punk is, he played a part in Teller's accident. Rage at the unfairness of Mariella's death pulses through me. My fingers twitch, eager to grab one of the guns Wrath strapped to my body and blow this kid's fucking head off.

We stop at a shiny black Impala, and I almost laugh at what a cliché these two are.

"Get in." Ransom digs the gun into my side a little harder.

"No. I'm not going anywhere with you. Who the fuck are you?"

"You give your man this much backtalk?"

"Never. I actually respect *him*."

His eyes narrow. "You'll learn."

The other guy grabs my shoulder and spins me, pushing me flat against the car. "You search her for weapons?" he asks.

Ransom snorts. "Why's Rock gonna have her strapped when he gave her up?"

"'Cause her man's one twitchy motherfucker," he says, patting my sides. I tense up, afraid this is an excuse to grope me, but from the knees up he's ruthlessly thorough. Almost professional. He finds my cell phone and hands it to Ransom. "He probably has her carry everywhere she goes." It worries me that whoever this kid is, he seems to know so much about Wrath.

"My back," I say, hoping if I give up one weapon, they won't search for more. At least that was the plan back at the house. It all seemed so simple when we were simply *talking* about this.

Now it's real and anything but simple.

The kid stops. "What?"

"I'm carrying at my six."

He lifts my sweatshirt and lets out a low whistle. "Got yourself quite a holster there."

"Yeah, well, we can't all just shove a gun down the back of our baggy jeans." I cast a dismissive look at his gangster uniform of low-slung pants and Timberland boots.

He cups my jaw with one hand, turning my head and applying enough pressure to make it hurt. "You're a sexy bitch."

"Hands off, Kidd. Wrath's bitch is all mine."

Kidd lets go of my face and runs a finger around the edge of the holster then pulls the gun loose.

Out of the corner of my eye, I catch him waving the weapon in Ransom's face. "See?"

"You're more fun than I expected," Ransom says to me, pinching my ass.

"Get your hands off me."

Kidd grabs my hair, yanking my head back. "What else you carrying?"

"Knife. Right pocket." This time the fear in my voice is authentic.

"God damn." Ransom's laughter echoes across the parking lot. I'm glad he finds me so fucking amusing. The chuckles stop abruptly, and he taps my arm with his gun. "Get in the fucking car."

Obviously, they don't expect me to be carrying any other weapons. I hang my head in what I hope looks like defeat and slide into the front seat when Ransom opens the door. As he shuts it, I look up through my lashes, giving him the saddest pound-dog eyes I can come up with.

He laughs.

I can't wait to put a bullet between his eyes.

CHAPTER TWENTY
WRATH

Black Impala.

I RECEIVE SPARKY'S text at the same time Z calls Rock.

"She's in the car," Z says. As fucked up as I am over the situation, even I can sense the edginess in Z's voice. He's hating this, too. "I'm following Sparky."

"Where's Stash?" Rock asks.

"Ahead of both of us."

Rock puts the truck in gear and eases out of our parking spot.

"They're turning onto Park Street."

"Seven. They're headed for route seven," I say to Rock.

He nods and eases his foot off the gas. If we keep going, we'll pretty much run right into Ransom as he's turning onto the highway leading out of Ironworks.

A few minutes later, my theory's confirmed by Z.

"They just got on Seven East."

My fist slams into the dashboard. "That's slow-going traffic until you're out past Tibbit's. Lot of chances for Sparky to lose sight of them."

"Trackers are working," Z says.

In the background, I hear Teller. "Still moving slow up Seven."

Rock presses down on the accelerator, and a few minutes later, we're also on Seven, somewhere behind Z.

"Motherfucker," Rock grumbles, slapping the steering wheel as we get stopped at a red light. "Rush hour traffic. He's hoping we won't be able to tail 'em."

"No shit."

"Ah, fuck," Z's voice comes through the line.

"What?"

"Stash got pulled over. He ran a red light trying to keep up with them."

The dashboard takes more abuse from me. Rock glances over. "Sparky and Z are still behind her. We're good."

"Tell Sparky to go easy," I snap.

The next twenty miles seem to take hours, but probably only forty minutes have passed.

Forty minutes Trinity's been alone with Ransom.

EVERY NOW AND then, my gaze strays to the side mirror, hoping to catch a glimpse of one of the brothers following behind us.

All I see is a stream of unfamiliar vehicles.

Ransom decided to drive, while Kidd sat directly behind me.

"Did your man cry like a little bitch when he saw what I did to his business?" Ransom glances over to see if I heard his question.

I'd love to punch the glee off his smug face for joking about what has to be one of the worst days of Wrath's life.

"Come on. That arrogant cocksucker's had it coming for years," Ransom taunts.

Behind me, Kidd sighs as if this game of *torment the kidnap victim* is beneath him.

"No," I finally answer, stretching out my hand and studying my nails. "He was getting tired of runnin' that place. I think you did him a favor." I glance over and flaunt a fake-as-fuck sweet smile.

His hands tighten on the steering wheel.

I should be more scared. The lack of fear swirling through my belly actually scares me more. Over-confidence will get me killed.

It's not myself I have so much faith in, though. It's the club.

Well, that's not exactly true. I survived some pretty fucked-up shit in my life. I spent years living with a numbness inside that no amount of hurting myself ever cured. With Wyatt, I've finally found peace. Found happiness. Safety. Security. And so much love.

I won't allow anyone to steal that from me. From *us*.

This time tomorrow, I plan to be Mrs. Ramsey.

The weight of the weapon strapped to each ankle comforts me. They won't be *easy* to draw if things get bad fast, but I can do it. I'm glad we spent the extra time at the range yesterday. In my head, I go over each step. Picture aiming at Ransom's crotch and pulling the trigger.

Mariella cried in my arms more than once about the horrible things she endured under Ransom's control, so yeah, I'm shooting him in the crotch before Teller takes him out. No one told me that was the plan, but I didn't have to be at the war room table to know that's the way it will go down. Unless Ransom hurts me. Then Wrath will kill him for sure.

Eventually, we leave the Ironworks city limits and the traffic thins out. Two or three cars still trail behind us. Whether they're Lost Kings, I'm not sure.

I sneak a glance at Ransom and find him checking out the rearview mirror.

Not good.

"Why did we leave Ironworks?" I ask to distract him, in case it *is* Z or one of the others behind us.

"Don't worry, chica. I got a nice place all set up. No neighbors to bother us. No one to hear you screaming. It's perfect."

"Sounds lovely."

He smirks at my sarcasm.

For the first time, my confidence slips. Mariella spent a week being raped and tortured by Ransom, before he tossed her to his Viper brothers. After they broke her, they pimped her out. I assume that's what Ransom thinks my future holds.

I'm so lost in the gory details I remember Mariella describing, I don't notice we've turned onto a smaller dirt road. Our speed slows to a crawl.

A glance in the mirror shows *no one* behind us now.

Don't panic.

They're close by. I know they are.

Z can track me through the two little bugs embedded in my sweatshirt and through my cell phone, which I'm pretty sure Ransom still has in his pocket.

Wrath would die before he let anything bad happen to me.

He's near. I can *feel* him.

Ransom stops the car.

There's an aging farmhouse to our left and a large dirt parking circle. Further back on the property, I notice a rusty, broken-down trailer. If I had to guess, it's where they've been cooking meth. Trees and overgrown grass and shrubs surround the parking area. Plenty of cover for the guys to use when they get here. Z's probably pulling up a map of the area right now.

"You need a landscaper," I comment, and Ransom laughs.

"Your club don't seem to control its women. You got a smart mouth for a whore."

"I'm *not* a whore."

"That's not what I heard." His voice comes out low and deadly this time.

No traffic sounds reach us here. Only the rustle of the trees and an owl in the distance. At the clubhouse, those sounds always soothe me. They mean I'm safe from all the dangers of my past.

Faith is stronger than fear. Faith is stronger than fear. Wrath has that saying tattooed on his chest, and it's always brought me comfort. It never meant as much to me as it does right now.

I have faith. Lots of faith.

Wrath will be here soon.

The club will be here soon.

"Come on, man. We doing this out here?" Kidd asks.

I don't bother to ask *what*. I think it's pretty obvious.

Ransom's gaze crawls over me, stopping at my breasts. Irritation flickers at the corner of his mouth when I remain still. His eyes meet mine, and I'm struck by how flat but familiar they are. Familiar like one of my mother's boyfriends who used to "accidentally" wander into my room at night.

I'm not the same scared little girl who hid behind the couch when her mother "entertained" her boyfriends.

Back then, I couldn't fight back. Now, I can.

Then, I had no one to fight for me or protect me. Now, I have Wrath. I have the club.

A smidge of confidence returns.

Kidd grips my arms and steers me toward the house. I relax and let him lead me. I'm terrified that if I fight back too much, they'll tie me up or worse. So for now, I remain compliant.

The door closes behind us with an ominous thud.

Faith is stronger than fear.

Kidd circles the room, looking behind furniture and flicking on lights as he goes. Ransom stays by the door, watching me.

He moves in closer and runs his hand over my cheek, traces my bottom lip with his finger. "Pretty girl. Gonna get me back in business and earn me a lot of money, aren't you?" he says in a low, hypnotic voice—hypnotic the way facing off with a crocodile might feel while you pray he doesn't bite you in half.

I'm too scared to move or even blink.

"Ransom? You questioning her or what?"

"Yeah, but get her undressed first. I want to finally see those tits," he says to Kidd without taking his eyes off me.

My stomach twists, but I don't react. He expects me to say something. He's waiting for a response to his crude demand. He plans to question me? Once it becomes obvious I don't know anything about MC business, I'm in trouble.

Wrath will be here soon.

I stay silent. On the outside.

Inside, I'm screaming. *Hell fucking no.*

Something Mariella told me rattles at the back of my head. *Fear.* Ransom gets off on it. Big time.

By sheer force of will, I stop my body from trembling.

I place my hand on my hip. "You want me to just strip? Or I can do it nice and pretty for you, Reymond." I lower my lashes and put a little purr in my voice when using his name.

"That's more like it, sweetheart," Kidd says from behind me.

I glance at Ransom, letting him know I think he's the one in charge. He nods.

Shit.

Kidd's behind me and to my left.

Ransom's blocking the door.

By some unspoken agreement they both circle me, switching positions.

Ransom settles on the couch and crosses one leg over the other, placing his ankle on his knee.

"Let's go, chica. We ain't got all night."

I'm frozen with fear.

Two guns or not, I'm not some movie, super-girl hero who can double-draw and shoot two people on opposite sides of the room.

Kidd.

He's the one on alert, while Ransom has been treating me like a joke all night. I should definitely shoot Kidd first.

"Come on, cunt." Kidd sneers.

Ransom claps his hands. "Hurry it up."

Where's Wrath?

CHAPTER TWENTY-ONE
WRATH

"Z, COME ON, man. We're wasting precious minutes here," Rock says.

He's tight with tension, but it's nothing like the fire-breathing beast uncurling inside me.

"Left up ahead," Z says. "It looks like a turn around, but you'll see a dirt driveway when you pull in. They went down there."

Rock curses then gives Z the order. "Wait for us."

I glare at Rock.

"I sent Murphy down to check it out," Z says. "We're waiting for you by the road."

Murphy's jogging back to Z's truck by the time we pull in.

"There's a house. One car in front. Same one that took her from the supermarket. Didn't hear or see anyone."

"Let's go," I snarl.

Rock stops me with a hand on my arm. "Easy."

Somewhere in my human brain I know he's being logical. We don't want to bust in there before we know what's going on. While the element of surprise is nice, it could also get Trinity killed.

But it's my Neanderthal brain in charge of my body as I break into a fast jog down the driveway. Everyone likes to joke about how, for a guy my size, I can sneak up on 'em. Well, tonight I use that skill.

I'm tall enough to be able to peer in one of the front windows. They're covered in yellowed newspapers, but there's a sliver that gives me an unobstructed view.

Ransom.

Trinity.

And someone over by the door, judging from the way Trinity keeps looking that way. I can't see who from this angle.

"She okay?" Rock whispers as he slides up next to me.

"For now."

"How many?"

"Two. Ransom and someone by the door I can't make out."

He throws up two fingers, signaling to Z and Murphy to get in position by the front door.

"Where's Teller?" I ask.

"At the cars so he can warn us if someone else shows up. Sparky's with him."

My gaze returns to Trinity. She's tight with fear. Ransom waves a hand at her in a *hurry up* sort of gesture.

Her fingers go to the edge of her sweatshirt, and she slowly lifts it.

An inhuman growl rumbles from the back of my throat.

I'VE STALLED AS long as I dare.

My fingers twist in the hem of my sweatshirt. My body curves in what I hope is a seductive way but probably looks more like I'm having a spasm.

I'm lifting the sweatshirt over my head when there's a crash at the front door.

Perfect timing, guys.

I drop to the ground, struggling to pull my shirt down so I can see what the fuck is going on. There's a deafening crack as the door slams open, hitting the wall. The thunder of boots storming over the hardwood floor fills the house.

When I finally peek up, Murphy has Kidd pinned against the wall with an arm across the jerk's throat. "Your cousin's lookin' for ya, fucker," he growls.

Wrath rushes over to me. Behind him, Ransom's on his feet, shock all over his face. He doesn't make a move toward Wrath, but I won't take a chance.

Jamming my hand inside my boot, I draw my revolver.

"Shit, Trin," Wyatt says, but his voice comes from a million miles away.

I drag a long, slow breath in.

Focus on Ransom's leg.

Air flows out of my lungs as I squeeze the trigger.

Ransom falls back on the couch, screaming and cursing. Warm satisfaction fills my chest, seeing him writhe in pain. It's still not enough, though. He needs to suffer a lot more to pay for what he's done.

"Keep your gun on him," Wrath says.

"No problem." Slowly, I rise from the floor. My eyes never leave Ransom, while Wrath helps the other guys secure Kidd.

"You all right, Trin?" Rock shouts from across the room.

I can't form any words. Doesn't matter. No one would hear me over Kidd's yelling and Ransom's cursing. My head bobs up and down once.

"Shut him up," Z says.

"Get him outside," Rock orders.

Someone silences Kidd, and he's dragged out the front door.

Wrath strides over and lowers my gun, gently taking it from my hands.

He gives me a warm smile. Pride etched into every curve and line on his face. "Nice shot."

WRATH

RANSOM'S STILL YOWLING while a good amount of his blood soaks into the dirty couch cushions.

Not enough blood.

I'm absurdly proud of my woman. Not that I ever doubted her, but damn, my girl is fierce as fuck.

I take a second to grab her by the shoulders and haul her against me for a rough kiss. "You did good, baby. So fuckin' proud of you."

Her dazed eyes meet mine, and she wraps her fingers in my shirt, pulling and twisting until our lips meet again. Hungry, desperate kisses that almost make me forget that this isn't the time or place.

She's panting when we part. "I love you so much, Wyatt."

"Love you, too."

Ransom groans and rolls to the floor with a thump. "Love you, baby. You too, snookums," he mimics in a high-pitched voice. "Put a fuckin' bullet in me now so I don't have to listen to this shit."

Trin moves in and kicks his leg, right above the place she shot him, and he lets loose with an ear-splitting scream.

"I was planning to shoot your tiny dick off." She draws her remaining pistol. "We can still make that happen."

I snuff out my laughter and seize Trinity's arm, turning her away from Ransom. "He touch you?"

Before she answers, Ransom laughs. "Yeah. Grabbed that sweet fucking ass of hers." He throws a hand up in the air, opening and closing it to demonstrate exactly how he violated my woman. "Real firm. Too bad she has to find a new gym."

Rage obliterates every other sound in the room as I unsheathe the knife at my side. Ransom's still busy running his mouth. He only shuts it when my boot slams his wrist to the floor, pinning him in place.

205

"This the hand you touched my woman with?" I ask in a low voice.

Uncertainty, maybe a hint of fear, enters his cold eyes.

"Not so chatty now, huh?" I thrust the knife through his palm. My rage forces the blade in fast considering all the bones and tendons in my way. Ransom howls and tries to jerk his hand free, making it worse for himself. My blade's too wide to keep him pinned to the floor, so I slowly drag it out of his hand, smiling while he screams. He cradles his hand against his chest while I wipe my knife on his pants.

"That was the hand," Trinity says. I stand and face her. *Knowing* what I'm capable of and seeing it firsthand are two different things, but she seems unaffected by the violence I inflicted. Hell, she looks ready to grab my knife and give his other hand a matching hole.

Proud as I am of her, she doesn't need to be here for what comes next. "You have to go. Send Teller in." I lash my foot out, my boot landing against Ransom's ribs. He groans. "This fuck belongs to him."

Her lower lip trembles, but she nods. Without another glance at the pile of trash at my feet, she runs out the door.

Ransom moans in pain. "I woulda ripped that bitch's tongue out by now. Who the fuck tries to make a whore into an ol' lady?"

He's trying to bait me so I'll put him out of his misery quick. "I ain't here to give you relationship advice, Ransom," I respond with calm. "Won't do you any good after tonight."

His eyes widen, and I can see his tiny brain trying to come up with another approach. "Which one's Teller? He the one who fell for Mariella's innocent act? Christ, you fuckers are stupid."

I land another solid kick to his ribs. "You really burn down my gym? Or are you so pathetic you have to take credit for someone else's work?"

Bleeding from a couple locations or not, Ransom's dying to brag to someone about all the shit he's done. "Yeah, asshole. I did it. Who else would have the stones—"

The door opens and Rock steps in.

"Hey, prez," Ransom shouts at Rock. "Here to take care of business for your boy?"

One corner of Rock's mouth curls up, but he doesn't respond.

Ransom tries again. "Shoulda known you caved too easy."

Instead of answering, Rock crosses his arms over his chest and stands next to me, silently watching the scene in front of him. The lack of a response seems to unnerve Ransom for a second.

"Your prospect cried like a little bitch when I lit him up," Ransom taunts. "Smelled like a fuckin' pig roast."

My face stays neutral, but inside I'm raging. "He was a kid," I say evenly.

Setting aside the disgusting mental picture Ransom just offered, I lock all my emotions down. No matter how much I hate doubting Twitch, *I* brought him into the club. Before Teller ends this fucker, I need to know if Twitch was voluntarily working with Ransom.

Turns out I don't have to ask, because Ransom's dying to spill how fucking clever he is while his blood leaks out on the floor.

"He was pathetic." He laughs, which turns into a hacking cough. "Tried bribing him with pussy, then money, but he wouldn't budge."

And there's my answer. Another reason Ransom needs to suffer. I grind my boot down on his non-bleeding hand until he screams.

Rock places a hand on my arm, and I back off. "What else you been up to?" Rock asks quietly when Ransom settles down.

Ransom sneers at the question and cranes his neck toward the door. "Tried to hit that fat, red-headed brother you got working for you, but he's such a pussy, his girl had to save him."

Doesn't surprise me at all that Ransom's the one who shot at my gym, narrowly missing putting a bullet through Murphy's skull. "Yeah, takes a real man to shoot at two unarmed people from a thousand yards away."

A small smirk curves Ransom's mouth, and his eyes drift shut. No way am I lettin' this fucker fade. My boot thumps against his side. "Uh-uh. Wake the fuck up. You got a long night ahead of you."

207

Slowly, he peels his lids back and seems to be surprised the two of us are still staring down at him. Tough shit—I'm not done with my questions. "Why'd you want my girl so bad?"

"Figured right before your wedding would be the best way to get at *you*. Knew that night you came to see Eduardo. How fucked up you were over some piece of ass." He snorts and shoots a glare at Rock. "Got your pussy prez there to agree to all sorts of stupid shit."

Rock snorts, not at all insulted by anything Ransom has to say.

Anger boils inside of *me*, though. This prick tried to grab Trinity once before. One of his hangarounds put his filthy hands on my woman because this piece of shit ordered it. I *knew* it. At the time, I'd swallowed down his lies and now it pisses me the fuck off.

"Easy," Rock mutters, as if he knows exactly where my brain went.

I take a breath and dial back my rising fury. "See, I don't get you, Ransom. You got an issue with one of us, come at *us*." I tap my chest and Rock's shoulder for emphasis. "Real men don't go after a woman 'cause he got a beef with her ol' man."

He coughs and struggles to sit up, but Rock presses him back against the floor with a boot to the chest. Ransom slaps his hand against Rock's leg, which does, well, nothing. He glares up at Rock. "I went at *you*. You were supposed to die in Slater county jail. After my guard-buddy broke you."

Jesus Christ.

Rock doesn't flinch at the information. It's not a surprise Ransom was involved in that. We got our payback against the guard. After tonight *all* scores should be settled.

"Thought messin' with your woman would rattle you." Ransom must really be praying for a swift death to bring up Hope. "But the minute Izzard squeezed her tits, your boys put him out of commission." He spits at Rock's feet.

Rock moves his foot from Ransom's chest to his face. One swift kick. Ransom rolls to the side and spits, then grins at us through bloody lips. "See? Best way to get to you since you're all a bunch of pussies who hand your balls over to your women."

I start laughing so hard, Rock glances at me like he's worried I finally came unhinged. "You got a fucking bullet in your leg courtesy of my fiancée and you're flopping around like a dying fish, but we're the pussies. Okay."

"Stupid whore got a lucky shot," he grumbles.

This time I kick him in the leg. "I'd say your luck ran out."

"Fuck you." He gasps and tries to wrap his hands around his injured leg. "Bitches are good for one thing. Only pussies let women get in the way of business."

"Pussy, pussy, pussy." Rock shakes his head. "Don't you have any other insults?"

I glance down at Ransom. "A good woman makes you stronger. Too bad you never figured that out."

A few seconds later, Teller limps in.

"Seems like I fucked your brother up pretty good." Ransom juts his chin in Teller's direction.

I return the smirk. "Maybe for a little while, but he's about to fuck you *permanently.*"

Teller doesn't move—he isn't in a joking mood. Rock steps back and meets him by the door. He places a hand on either side of Teller's head and leans in, whispering something to him that doesn't reach me. When they're finished, Rock takes up a position by the door and nods at Teller. The door opens again, and Murphy steps inside. He remains silent as he finds a spot next to Rock.

"Took you long enough," I say, when Teller finally reaches my side.

His grim expression doesn't change.

At our feet, Ransom squirms at the sight of my determined brother. It seems to finally sink in that his time is up.

No one's coming to save his worthless life.

This battle with the Vipers that we've been locked in for years is about to finally end.

Ransom struggles to sit up, and we let him. There's no escape.

Ignoring Ransom for a second, Teller focuses on me. "Loco's comin' up to deal with Kidd."

"Good."

Crazy laughter spills out of Ransom as he falls back against the floor. "Fuckin' Loco. Christ, you even managed to turn that crazy motherfucker into a goddamn pussy. Treatin' whores like fuckin' supermodels." He spits.

Teller's eyebrows draw down, and he shoots a look at me.

I shrug. "He's got some sort of fascination with the word pussy."

"Fuck you, pussy."

Ignoring Ransom, I place my hand over Teller's shoulder. "He's the one who shot at Murphy and your sister," I explain. "So make it hurt."

"No problem," Teller answers in a voice barely above a whisper.

Each one of my brothers has the ability to lose their grip and do crazy shit in a rage. Over the years I've known Teller, he's rarely let anyone witness the demon who lives inside him.

Tonight's a different story. His anger and anguish cling to him so tight I can almost see it.

He stands over Ransom and pulls out a long knife. Same one he uses during hunting season to gut deer.

While I'd wanted to be the one to make Ransom tremble and writhe from the pain I inflicted, my brother needs this more. He needs to purge his guilt over Mariella's death.

I won't leave his side. But this moment, this kill, belongs to Teller.

CHAPTER TWENTY-TWO

WRATH

WHEN IT'S DONE, I step outside for some much-needed air. Rock's right behind me. "Where's Trin?" I ask Z, who's been outside watching the front of the house and keeping an eye on Kidd.

He tilts his head. "Down the driveway with Sparky."

"Good." Tonight's ugliness is far from over, and I don't want her near what's gonna go down next.

Rock starts barking orders at Z. "Get Hoot and Birch up here." He rattles off a list of supplies he needs the guys to bring.

"Got a shovel in the back of my truck," Z says, taking one thing off the list.

Headlights wash over the driveway, and we all turn to face the new-comer. Rock's phone buzzes and he flips it open. "Loco. Finally."

Yeah, I'd forgotten about Kidd. Mostly because Z did a good job of trussing the fucker to a tree and gagging him. I nudge Z with my elbow. "He even conscious?"

He shrugs. "I may have *accidentally* whacked him into the tree once or twice."

"Rock, what's doin'?" Loco shouts as he steps out of his car. Interesting that he came to meet us in an unknown location by himself. High level of trust right there.

Rock meets him halfway, and they shake hands. "Thanks for coming out here," Rock says.

"Ain't no rest. It's all good. This what we do twenty-four hours a day, seven days a week, right, Rock?" His voice falters and he glances around, clearly confused but not alarmed about why we brought him here and why we're all so silent.

"Hey, big man," he says as he approaches me.

"We found your long-lost cousin."

His eyes widen and his gaze darts around the area before finally landing on Kidd. "What the fuck?"

I place my hands on his shoulders forcing him to face me. Touching him was a bad idea, because he reaches for a weapon immediately. Before I have a chance to snarl "calm the fuck down," Rock and Z draw, aiming at Loco's head. "Easy, bro," Z growls.

When he puts his hands up, I release him and explain. "He jacked my woman tonight."

"What? She okay?"

It takes me a second to answer the unexpected question. "She's fine. He was working with Ransom."

I sense his disbelief. His mistrust of anything I have to say regarding his family, even though he struggles not to show any emotion. "Where's he at?"

"Inside," Teller answers as he comes down the front steps, Murphy right behind him.

Loco's not sure where to look first. Teller's bloody hands. The open door. In my eyes. At Rock. He does a slow sweep of everything, and his shoulders sag. "Fuck," he mutters.

Rock walks him inside the house, and a few minutes later he stumbles out—a little greener than he went in. Teller's quiet. Busy cleaning his hunting knife. Loco makes a point to steer clear of him.

"Where's your girl?" Loco asks me while keeping an eye on Teller.

I narrow my eyes, considering whether I want to answer. "Somewhere safe."

From behind Loco, I catch Rock nodding.

Loco jerks his head toward Kidd. "He hurt her?"

"I don't think so. I haven't had a chance to talk to her yet."

He nods slowly. "Business. Brotherhood first. Yeah." He bobs his head up and down a few more times like now he respects me or whatever.

Fucking asshole.

I glance at Rock and this time he shakes his head, as if he knows I want to put a bullet in Loco's face. Or at least a fist in his throat.

Unfortunately, Loco storms over to Kidd next. "You went behind my back to work with that fuckin' slob. You serious, cuz?"

Kidd, of course, can't answer. Whatever he mumbles at Loco doesn't sound all that respectful, though.

He rips the gag off Kidd's mouth and pistol whips him. Murphy comes up next to me. "This should be entertaining." He chuckles softly, his shoulder bumping against my arm.

"Teller okay?" I ask in a low voice.

Murphy's laughter stops. "He'll be all right. Eventually."

Rock strolls over, shaking his head. "I really don't have all night for this bullshit," he grumbles.

"No kidding." I have a wedding tomorrow.

He gives me a sympathetic nod and returns to Loco's side.

"I been tryin' to teach him how to focus. Lay low. But he gotta be flamboyant all the time, ya know?" Loco shouts to Rock.

"Yeah," Rock agrees.

Murphy and I join Rock. We have some questions for Kidd. Who else was working with Ransom? What else were they planning? I'm so irritated, I'm ready to beat the information out of him and anyone who gets in my way.

"Fuck you," Kidd spits. "You lettin' these fools run your business. It's bullshit."

"So you go behind my back? Outside the family?"

"Loco," Rock says, trying to grab the gangster's attention. I guess he feels the ranting has gone on long enough.

"What?" Loco asks, whipping his head around.

"We need to wrap this up. You takin' him with you?"

"No. Fuck that." Loco pulls out his pistol, and none of us are close enough to stop him from shooting Kidd in the face.

The blast is deafening. The aftermath, gory.

"Jesus Christ," Rock snaps. "What the fuck'd you do that for? We needed more information from him."

Loco stares at his gun as if he just noticed it in his hands. "Shit. Sorry. I'm a little worked up." He glances at his dead cousin again. "Shit. I shoulda found out if anyone else in my crew was helpin' him."

"Ya think?" Rock growls.

Embarrassment's a big thing to a gangster like Loco. Only one thing's worse than being criticized by the people you do business with—having them laugh at you. He takes a step back, smooths his hands over his hair and down his sides, trying to magically erase the hot-headedness we all witnessed.

Rock shoots a look my way. I guess checking to make sure I won't open my mouth and make the situation worse. Behind Rock, Z has his pistol in hand—watching Loco's every move.

"Fuck," Loco says. "I told your boys the other day. He and I were tight. This betrayal—"

"I understand," Rock says, setting aside his irritation for the good of getting this night over with.

"What can I do?" Loco asks.

"Well, now we got another body to bury," I say stepping forward.

Loco's face twists in disgust. "That's a lot of work."

I flick my gaze at Rock, who's rolling his eyes. "You can go. We'll handle it." Then Rock explains in detail *how* exactly we plan to handle it, and I swear Loco sways on his feet—close to passing out.

"No. No. My cuz. My mess. I'll help. Just seems...excessive."

"We're not afraid to get dirty," I say.

"Especially if it keeps us out of jail," Rock adds.

Loco stares at us for a few seconds, like it finally dawned on him this isn't the first time we've disposed of a few bodies. "Good point." Nervous laughter follows his words. "So this is why enemies of Lost Kings go missing. Never seen or heard from again."

The cold smiles we give him instead of an answer wipe the silly grin right off his face.

HOURS PASS WHILE I wait with Sparky in the car. A vehicle I don't recognize passes us, heading down the driveway. Not long after, there's a gunshot that makes Sparky reach for his revolver and a blunt. Before he lights up, I pluck it out of his hands. "You need to drive home eventually."

Ignoring his pleading eyes, I tuck the blunt inside the pocket of my hoodie. "You can have it later."

Nothing happens for so long, anxiety creeps up on me and I wish I'd let Sparky light up. I could've used the contact high.

"I'll text Z," he says, as if he read my mind. A few minutes later he receives an answer. "They're whole."

I recognize LOKI's van drive in next and figure someone brought up something to help bury a body or three.

"This was the perfect wedding present for him, Trin," Sparky blurts out.

A snort flies out of me. "I think a watch would've been easier."

"Yeah, but this means more."

I doze for a while.

A few hours later, the unfamiliar car leaves. Three dark figures come jogging down the road. One's so big it can only be Wrath. I fling open the door and run to him. He catches me, pulling me tight to his body, but not saying a word. While we're holding on to each other, the scents of earth, smoke, and something else much more unpleasant fill my nose. I back away, coughing and his mouth flattens into a grim line.

"You're riding with me," he says when I stop gagging.

I wheeze a relieved breath. God, I hope that means this night is almost over.

The rest of the guys join us. While Wrath talks to Rock and Z, I notice Teller standing by himself at the edge of the group. Sliding up next to him, I nudge his arm.

"You all right?"

He turns his head slowly and glances down at me. He seems off. Fuzzy and unfocused, so I wrap my arms around him for a quick hug. After a second, he returns the embrace. "I'm good, Trin."

Pulling away, I tap his chest. "You're one of the best."

"Did they...hurt you?" he asks.

"Nope." I force a smile for his sake. "You guys got there in time."

Before I'm able to say anything else to Teller, Wrath jogs over. "Let's get out of here."

"Fuck yeah," Teller mumbles.

"T, you're with me," Rock calls out.

Wrath punches his shoulder lightly. "Go have a chat with Dad. It'll do you good."

Teller finally smirks and lets out a quick laugh. "Thanks."

CHAPTER TWENTY-THREE

'VE NEVER BEEN so happy to see the clubhouse.

If I'm this bone-weary, I can't imagine how the guys feel. Z drove us home and barely said a word. Wyatt tossed his stained sweatshirt on the floor, then wrapped himself around me in the back seat of Z's SUV and held me the whole way home.

I'm empty. Can't think about anything that happened. Or what *could* have happened.

Tonight I shot a man, and I don't have a speck of remorse.

One of the guys most likely finished Ransom off. I'm not bothered by that, either.

Ransom made it clear what he planned to do to me. Plus, I know how he treated Mariella and who knows how many other women over the years. I don't feel anything over his death. Except maybe relief that there's one less evil person in the world.

No, I do feel something—gratefulness to be part of this large family who protects its own with everything they have. No matter how fucked up things were tonight, every time fear crept in, my faith that Wyatt would rescue me never wavered.

I let myself be dragged to the edge of hell, because I knew Wyatt and the club were coming for me.

In the living room, Hope's curled up on one of the couches sound asleep. Someone covered her with a blanket, probably Ravage, since he's sitting at the other end of the couch keeping watch over her.

Rock steps in behind me and surveys the scene in front of us. Immediately, Ravage jumps up. "She wouldn't go home, prez."

"It's fine." He strides over and sits next to her, gently running his hand over her arm. "We're back, baby doll," he says softly.

She blinks and sits up, throwing her arms around him. I catch her wrinkled nose when she pulls away and assume Rock's covered in the same dark scents Wrath brought back with him.

"Trin?" She tosses off the blanket and hurries over, throwing her arms around me. We stand there like that for a while, not saying anything. Finally she pulls back and looks me over. Surprised I'm not covered in blood maybe.

Well, not too much blood anyway.

Rock stands and motions Ravage and Dex to the war room. "I need you two…" their voices trail off as Rock closes the door behind them.

Wyatt steps into the clubhouse. "I'll be back in a few," he says, touching my side on his way to the war room.

Hope watches him for a second, then turns back to me. "You're all right?"

"I'm solid."

Her gaze strays to the door. "Is everyone else…okay?"

"Yes."

"Good."

We had planned to have our version of a slumber party the night before my wedding, but now I can't even think of it. "I need to sleep in my own bed."

"I figured. I just…needed to make sure you came home safe." Her voice catches on the last word.

I grab her for another hug then stumble down the hall to my room.

It's not too much later when Wyatt enters our bedroom. I've been drifting in and out of sleep while I waited for him.

"You can turn the light on," I whisper.

"Nah, I'm fine."

The bathroom door closes and the shower starts up. I must drift off again, because what seems like seconds later, Wyatt's warm solid body is behind mine, pulling me against him.

"Got your alarm set?" he whispers.

"Mmmhmm."

His arm flexes, anchoring me to him. Reminding me he'll do anything in his power to keep me safe.

He kisses the side of my head and whispers in my ear, "Big day tomorrow."

WRATH

DESPITE THE GRIZZLY business we took care of tonight, there's a festive atmosphere in the war room.

Sparky lights up as soon as he steps inside.

"Your woman owes me a blunt," he informs me.

"Thanks for sticking around and staying with her."

He drops the goofy smile and pulls me in for a quick embrace. Because I'm feeling celebratory myself, I pick him up, holding him off the ground for a big bear hug.

"Put me down, motherfucker!" he yelps, kicking one of the chairs over.

He laughs as I set him down. Each of my brothers makes a point of coming over to give me a fist bump or back slap.

Everyone except Stash, who's the last one to stumble into the war room. Since we had the situation under control, after the cops let him go, we told him to head home.

"I'm so sorry, brother," he says as soon as he sees me. "I was so focused on not losing sight of her, I wasn't thinking—"

He looks so miserable, I can't even ream him out. "It all worked out."

Rock asks us to sit down at the table for a few minutes.

"Kidd was the one helping Ransom?" Dex asks.

"Yeah. Loco's such a fuckin' hothead, he put a bullet in Kidd before we were able to question him." Rock's clearly still fuckin' pissed. So am I. It would have been nice to know what other shit Ransom might have set in motion.

"That explains how Ransom got away with hiding out in Iron-works," Murphy says. "Kidd musta been feeding Loco bullshit when we asked for their help, too."

"He better pray that's all that was going down," Teller grumbles.

A niggling thought that's been hovering in the back of my mind fully forms. "Rock," I say to get his attention. "Ransom knew stuff Kidd wouldn't have been able to tell him."

Z sits forward, pinning me with a fierce expression. "Like what?"

I try to remember exactly what it was he said, but it won't come to me. Closing my eyes, I go over all the details from the night. "I don't know."

"Sleep on it," Rock says. "It'll come to you when you're not expecting it." He takes in the rest of the guys. "Glad no one was hurt." He nods at Stash. "Or thrown in jail."

Couple of the guys punch Stash's arms. It'll be a long time until he lives tonight down.

Rock finally claps his hands together. "Big day tomorrow." He grins my way. "He's finally crowning his queen." His stare turns more serious as he glances at each one of us. "You all owe Trinity for puttin' herself on the line for this club."

Z reaches across the table and slaps my hand. "She's one badass little bitch. Don't ever piss her off."

I finally shake off the rest of the darkness that followed me home and laugh. "Fuckin' A." That's when it hits me. "The *wedding*. Ransom knew our wedding was this week. That's why he hit the gym."

Rock drops back into his chair. "That's right."

"I don't even think Loco knew."

OUTSIDE THE WAR room, Hope's waiting. Without asking, she wraps her arms around me. After a minute she looks up. "You know I'd be pissed if you got hurt, right?"

"Is that your way of saying you don't think I'm an asshole anymore?"

She chuckles and pulls away from me. "No. You're still a big jerk. Just a kinder, gentler jerk."

I laugh so hard, my eyes water.

"Go," she says, smacking my chest. "You got your way after all. Ruined our slumber party."

"Doubt he'll be able to do much about it," Rock says, slipping an arm around her waist.

"No kidding. Night."

Trinity's asleep, and although I try to be careful not to wake her, she ends up mumbling a few words at me before turning over.

There aren't many emotions I experience with much intensity. Love for Trinity. Love for my brothers, my club family. Those are about the only civil feelings I have.

Before Trinity, violence calmed me. Fighting. Unleashing my anger on others in a semi-controlled place.

Now, she's my peace.

Tomorrow, she's mine forever.

CHAPTER TWENTY-FOUR

Five hours before the wedding...

WRATH

WHAT FEELS LIKE only minutes later, I'm woken up by my phone ringing. Rolling over to grab it, I realize I'm alone. A shot of panic jolts me until I hear the shower running.

"What?" I snarl into the phone.

"Mr. Ramsey? This is Investigator Brand."

"Oh." I crane my neck to check the time. "It's fuckin' early."

"Yeah. I need to meet with you."

"Now?"

"Sometime today."

"It's a busy day for me." Never mind that I'm getting married in five hours, I'm wary of how insistent this prick is. The thug in me is worried it's a set-up so they can arrest me.

"I can come to you." I hear him shuffling through papers in the background. "Except all I got is a p.o. box over in Sterling."

Yeah, he ain't coming here. "You know where Hog Heaven is?" I ask.

"That's way the fuck out in the boonies."

His annoyance makes me chuckle. "Best I can do."

"Fine. I can be there in an hour."

The shower's still running when we hang up. I sneak into the bath-

222

room, prepared to give my bride an early, orgasmic wedding present, but she shuts the water off as I'm pulling my shorts down.

"Hey," I call out.

She yelps and opens the shower door, steam escaping into the bathroom. "What are you doing in here?"

"I want to fuck you."

An innocent smile curves her lips. "No sex before the wedding."

"I need to meet with Investigator Brand in an hour."

She steps out, wrapping her body in one towel and her hair in another. "Now?" She meets my eyes. "I don't like it. Sounds like a set-up."

"I thought so, too."

She stands there chewing on her lip. "What are you going to do?"

"I want to find out what he thinks is so fucking important this early on a Saturday morning."

Her worried honey eyes finally meet mine. "He couldn't...there's no way he knows...about last night, right?"

"Doubt it." I hate upsetting her on our wedding day with this shit. "Hey, it's probably nothing. I'm meeting him down at Hog Heaven. I'll be at the park before you even get there."

"Hog Heaven, huh?" Her lips quirk. "Brand tries to arrest you there, crusty old Frank might shoot him."

I snort at the way she describes Hog Heaven's owner. "Yeah, that's what I was thinking."

ROCK DOESN'T HAVE the same faith in Frank that Trin does.

"No fucking way. You're not going by yourself," he snaps as soon as I explain where I'm headed.

"I gotta go see what he wants. Last thing I need is him puttin' out a warrant."

"Christ," he says, stepping back and opening his front door wider.

"Get in here. Let me make a call before we go."

I don't bother arguing with him. It will take longer, and in the end he'll get his way, so I might as well chill for a few minutes.

Turns out I didn't wake anyone. The whole house is already up. I have a feeling it has more to do with Alexa's unhappy wailing than wedding prep. That's confirmed a few minutes later when Murphy carries a red-faced Alexa into the kitchen. "Hey, she okay?"

He turns as if he hadn't even noticed me there. "No. Can you hold her a sec?" He thrusts her into my arms before I answer, which is fine. She stops screaming in favor of pulling at my beard and drooling on me.

"Aw, I think she likes me better, bro."

Murphy rolls his eyes and grabs a bag from the fridge. "Here, then you can give her this." He hands me a cold plastic ring, which Alexa grabs for almost immediately.

"You like that, kiddo?" I ask while she gnaws on whatever the hell it is.

"Why you over here so early, groom?" Murphy asks after a lengthy yawn.

"Fire investigator wants to meet with me."

"Fuck. Really?" He turns, his gaze sweeping over the living room. "Rock going with you?"

"He wanted to make a call first." I glance down the hall. "Where's Heidi?"

"Sleeping. She's been up the last couple nights with her," he says, running his hand over Alexa's head.

Alexa throws her arms in the air and lunges for Murphy, almost tipping out of my arms. "Whoa—"

"I got her." Murphy swings her into his arms, and she settles down.

"We're clear. Let's go," Rock calls out as he thunders down the stairs. "Morning, baby," he says, stopping to kiss Alexa's forehead and ruffle her hair. "You good?" he asks Murphy.

"Yup. If you're not back by ten-thirty, I'll go to the park and check on things."

Confident we'll be back in time, I follow Rock out to the garage and we head down the mountain to Hog Heaven.

Brand's already at the restaurant. He chose a table with two chairs in the back, which is good because both of us weren't gonna fit in one of the tiny booths this place has. Rock decided to wait outside, but Brand notices him and smirks at me. "You guys ever travel alone?"

"No."

He nods slowly and kicks out the chair across from him. "Sit. I ain't here to arrest you."

I ease the chair out farther and drop into it, casually leaning back and lifting my chin. "I don't have all day."

"What's your hurry?"

"My wedding is in a couple hours."

"Oh." He nods slowly. "Sorry."

Frank stops by and fills my coffee cup but doesn't ask if we need anything else.

Brand and I stare at each other for a few seconds before I sit up. "Listen, you're really not my type. So if you brought me here to stare into each other's eyes all morning, it's a wasted effort."

He snorts and pulls out a folder. "I feel like you're hiding something." When I don't respond, or even blink, he continues. "Yet, I really don't think you had anything to do with the fire."

"Good."

"Arson investigations are complex, expensive, and lengthy." He drums his fingers on the table for a few beats, then pulls an iPad out of his folder and sets it on the table. "Off the record, I'm being told to back off this investigation." He glances out the window at Rock. "I can guess why."

I still keep my mouth shut.

"None of my findings support you or your partners as having any involvement in the fire, so the people *suggesting* I drop this case will get their way. If there was even a hint that it was part of some larger terrorist attack or something, we'd be all over it no matter who was callin' in favors." He pins me with a sharp look. "But a disgruntled employee who tried to vandalize your building and died in the accidental fire that resulted? We can't waste resources on that."

"Okay," I answer carefully.

"Your insurance company is a different matter. They're only interested in my opinion if it supports their theory." He tosses his card on the table. "I'm qualified to testify as an expert witness if it comes to that."

I take the card and stick it in my wallet. "I appreciate that." I mean it, too. As Teller said, this guy's rep is solid. Having him testify on my behalf or even the threat of having him testify might turn things in my favor with the insurance company. "But you didn't drag me down here this early because you need some side work."

"No. I didn't." He flips open the iPad cover and flicks the screen on. After searching for a few minutes, he passes the tablet to me and reaches over to hit play.

A grainy video fills the screen. No sound. Black and White. Taken from an awkward angle above. Gas station. It looks familiar, but because of the shitty lighting, I can't be sure. A car I recognize drives up to one of the pumps.

I recognize it because it's the same black car that took Trinity last night.

Ransom.

My jaw clenches, and I work hard not to show any response. Two figures get out very close together. One pale, tall, and skinny. The other tall, dark, and bulky.

Neither of them turn their faces up toward the camera. They don't have to for me to recognize them.

Twitch and Ransom.

Ransom shoves something against Twitch's side, and I don't need to be a cop to know it's a gun. Twitch shakes his head. Ransom turns and lifts something out of the back seat.

Gas cans.

Brand leans over and pauses the video. "We just received this. All the stations in the area were told to check their footage. The Mobil *right down the fucking street* from your gym found this and handed it over last night."

"Jesus." My heart's hammering so hard. Ransom's dead, but fuck do I want to kill him all over again.

"You recognize either of them?" Brand asks.

"That's Twitch." There's no point in pretending I don't know it's him.

"And the other one?"

I lift my shoulders. "Too hard to tell."

He cocks his head and makes an *are you shitting me?* face. "Let me tell you who *I* think it is." He taps the screen over Twitch's cut. The small Lost Kings MC patch on the front can barely be seen, but that doesn't seem to stop Brand. "After running your prints, your *affiliation* with the Lost Kings MC popped up."

"Club's got nothing to do with Furious." My couldn't-care-less tone doesn't seem to convince him.

"Yeah. Right." He taps the screen again and the video unfreezes. Ransom turns and Brand pauses the screen again. Tapping a tattoo on Ransom's neck. "Now, *this* asshole isn't wearing his cut. Not a surprise, since Gang Taskforce says the Vipers suddenly started *disappearing* about eighteen months ago." He makes this cocky "poof" gesture with his hands that almost makes me snort with laughter. "But when you blow this up on a big screen, the Viper's insignia is pretty clear."

He hits the screen again and lets the video finish.

Twitch shakes his head. Ransom slugs him in the gut. The back door of the car opens. An arm—probably Kidd—reaches out, grabbing Twitch and yanking him into the backseat. Ransom slams the door. He fills two gas cans, puts them in the trunk and the car drives out of the shot.

Rage pours through me. My fist's in my mouth, and I'm biting down on my fingers hard enough to leave marks. I figured it went down something like this. But guessing and seeing it play out before your eyes are two different things.

Twitch fought 'til the end.

Brand observes my reaction with a blank expression. "I'm guessing you know who that is with your prospect."

I tip my head up and glare at him.

He holds up a hand. "I don't want to know. I figure you and your—" he glances out the window at Rock again. "—*brothers* will handle it your way. I just thought you should see this."

What the fuck am I supposed to say—thanks?

He pushes a folder across the table at me. "This is my official report. Yesterday *afternoon*, I ruled the cause as incendiary—juvenile fire-setting. Your insurance *should* cover losses caused by vandalism and malicious mischief. I don't know if the fact that the young man was employed by you will muddy that up, though."

Christ, he determined that Twitch caused the fire and then a few hours later realized the poor kid was a victim himself, and I can tell it's not sitting well with Brand.

He can get in line, because it sure as fuck ain't sitting well with me, either.

I really wish we'd let Ransom suffer longer.

CHAPTER TWENTY-FIVE

Another queen is crowned...

WRATH

I T'S NOT EASY to shake off my meeting with Brand. The sick feeling clings to me as I leave Hog Heaven and meet Rock in the parking lot.

He raises an eyebrow as I approach.

"Not here," I mutter.

Once I'm on my bike, headed back to the clubhouse, some of the ugliness fades.

I'm marrying Trinity in a few hours.

That's all that matters today. The rest of this...stuff I'll deal with later.

Rock's not going to let me off that easy. He pushes me into the war room as soon as we step foot inside the clubhouse.

I explain the video and everything else Brand told me.

"Jesus Christ. Poor kid."

"We let Ransom off too easy."

"No kidding." He pulls out a bottle of Scotch, and we sit at the table and drink to Twitch.

When we're finished, Rock's still wearing a serious expression. It hits me that my best friend looks *tired*. Not I-got-woken-up-at-dawn-by-a-screaming-baby tired. More like a what-did-I-sign-up-for tired. Even before the loss of Furious, the wedding and finishing our house was consuming a lot of my attention, and Rock's been picking up my slack. Something I haven't bothered to thank him for or even acknowledge.

"I know I've been all wrapped up in—"

"Stop right there."

"You don't even know what I'm gonna say."

"I can guess." He stares straight ahead, not speaking for a second. "It's what we do. Help each other out. Right?"

I nod and wait for him to continue.

"I'm so…happy for you two. I love that girl. The two of you…you're two different people now. Better. Good for each other."

"You getting' choked up, prez?"

"Maybe. Deal with it."

Unable to get in touch with any more of my feelings this morning, I stand. "My suit still safe in your closet?"

He follows me out of the war room. "Hope doesn't seem to know what her *own* closet's for, so no reason for her to be in mine."

I burst out laughing. "Now, that's not fair. You knew she was messy when you married her."

The corner of his mouth quirks up. "You sticking up for my girl?"

"Guess so." My gaze strays to the stairway. "The girls upstairs getting ready?"

"Yeah, Murphy sent me a text while I was waiting for you. House is clear."

"Let's suit up."

He rolls his eyes. "Christ, I never thought I'd hear that come out of your mouth."

"I'm full of surprises."

About an hour later, we're at the park and I'm a lot less amused.

"I feel like an asshole," I grumble, tugging at the sleeves of the suit I'm wearing specifically for Trinity. Because it seemed to mean a lot to her. She better fuckin' *love* it.

"You look like one, too," Rock says with a grin. I'm pretty sure I had that coming, so I resist the urge to punch him.

"How can you stand this?" I ask, yanking on the collar that barely fits around my big neck.

"I climb into one like once a decade, brother. Didn't you do enough bitching on our way here? This is an important day."

"Fuck, yeah it is. You're lucky a woman like Trinity would marry you," Ravage says, smacking my arm as he walks by.

"Don't I know it."

"How you feelin'?" Murphy asks. He has one hand on Heidi, who's carrying Alexa. Someone stuck her in a frilly, flowery dress and pulled her hair into two little pony tails. I'll admit, she's adorable.

I nod at Alexa. "Cute dress. You pick it out?" I ask Murphy.

"Fuck you."

"Would you stop saying fuck around her?" Heidi says, then realizes her mistake. "Dammit."

"I think that's a lost cause, Heidi-girl," Rock says.

"Where's your brother?" I ask Heidi.

"Last I saw, he was talking to the Park Ranger. There were some noise complaints because of all the bikes."

"Shit."

Rock slaps my chest. "Stay put. I'll handle it."

"Yeah, I don't want Trin gettin' upset. Make sure she doesn't find out."

As if they knew, Z texts me that he's leaving the clubhouse. "Girls are on their way."

Rock pulls out his own phone. "They'll be here in ten." He glances at Heidi. "If you see Swan, have her meet them over at the stone building."

"I will."

Murphy takes Alexa from her. "Go. I got her."

After she leaves, I bounce up and down on my toes a few times. Adrenaline's roaring through me, and I can't settle down.

"Nervous?" Murphy asks.

"Not exactly."

Alexa baby-babbles at us and tries to grab everything in her reach. Since Murphy's holding her, she mostly pulls on his beard.

I slap his arm. "Think she'd freak out if you shaved it off?"

"Probably." He turns and makes noises back at Alexa. This right here is why I don't want him underground fighting. That's a discussion we're not done having.

"If you were just a lil' bigger, you could've been a flower girl," Murphy tells her.

"Job's still open if *you* want it," I say to Murphy.

He throws me a fuck-off stare. "Where the fuck is everyone?" he asks.

Alexa squeals, then yells out something that sounds an awful lot like *fuuu*.

I can't even pretend to hold in my laughter. "Oh, man. Heidi's gonna kill you."

Z TAKES THE roads to the park at a much slower speed than he's probably ever driven before.

"Best man has your husband waitin' for you. You ready?" he asks, flashing a dimpled smile my way.

"You're not upset, are you?" I ask. "We thought it was easier to have two witnesses, rather than do the big bridal party thing."

"No, Trin. I totally get it." He's quiet, watching the road for a few minutes before speaking up. "It's good you and Hope are so close."

Hearing her name, Hope pops up between our seats. "Hurry up, Z, we're going to be late."

"Look who's lecturing *me* about being on time," he jokes. "Put your seatbelt on. Your man will kill me if you arrive with a single hair out of place."

I close my eyes and enjoy the sound of them bantering back and forth for the rest of the trip.

"Trin, wake up. We're here," Hope says a few minutes later.

"I'm not asleep."

Z opens my door and offers me his hand. "Were you planning your escape?" he asks.

"No. I was having too much fun listening to you two bicker like children."

"We were not," Hope protests as she jumps down from the truck. "Where is everyone?"

"Out front. You told me to park behind the building," Z explains.

Hope glances around. "Right." She leans inside the truck and drags out our bags and assorted other stuff. "Swan and Krystal should be waiting inside for us, and I have a smaller bag for last minute touch-ups."

"Hey, baby doll," Rock says, sneaking up behind Hope. She squeals and turns to kiss him, almost dropping my train case.

"Hey, matron of honor." I snap my fingers a few times to get her attention. "Makeup now. Make-*out* later," I tease.

"Yes, ma'am." She wipes a trace of lipstick off Rock's mouth and steps away. "We won't be long."

Rock runs his gaze over me, then pulls me in for a hug. "You ready for this?"

"Not yet," I say, gesturing to my leggings and sweatshirt. In the interest of not getting my dress wrinkled, or ripped, or dirty, or any of the ten million horrific scenarios I came up with, I'm finishing my wedding prep at the park.

"You still look beautiful, Trinny."

My throat closes up and tears prick my eyes. "Thank you. Where's

Wyatt? Is he okay?"

"He's fine. Even better once he heard you were on your way."

Z taps Rock's arm. "I'll head over and let him know the girls are here." He tugs on my hand. "How long do you think you'll be?"

My gaze strays to Hope who shrugs.

Z shakes his head. "Someone text me when you're ready." He leans over and gives me a quick kiss on the cheek. "Thanks for finally making that big bastard happy. He's damn lucky to have you." Z doesn't do serious often, so when he does, you know he means it.

"Thanks," I whisper.

Hope grabs my hand and drags me to the small stone building where Swan, Dex, and Heidi are waiting outside.

"Oh, Trinity, are you excited!" Heidi gushes, rushing forward to give me a hug.

The four of us stand there chattering about nonsense—makeup, hair, dresses, the weather—before Rock finally interrupts us. "Let's not make him wait any longer, please."

Inside there's a full-length mirror and Swan pushes me in front of it. "Hope, is there any way to get more light in here?" she asks.

Hope and Heidi open the windows they're able to reach, giving us more natural lighting to work with. Swan's quick and efficient. "You don't need much," she murmurs as she dabs concealer under my eyes.

"Please, I need that whole tube. I didn't sleep at all."

She tsks at me. "Not supposed to have nookie before the wedding."

I'm guessing no one informed Swan about what went down yesterday, so I force a smile on my face and pretend sex is the reason I'm so tired.

"Do you need anything else?" Heidi asks. "Murphy has Alexa—"

"Go ahead, honey. We're okay," Hope assures her.

Krystal rushes in and squeals when she sees me. "Hi, bride. Excited?"

"Yes."

Since I'm busy with makeup, Krystal turns Hope's way. "What are we doing with your hair?"

Hope hesitates. "I was going to wear it down."

"Hmm." Krystal tilts her head, eyeing Hope's purple fit-and-flare pin-up dress. "Can I do some Victory Rolls?"

After Krystal gives her a quick explanation, Hope still seems hesitant. "Do it, Hope. Pretty please, it's my wedding, you have to. You'll be adorable."

"Fine," she grouches, plopping down on the bench next to me. She squirms and runs her hands over the bench. "All this stone looks pretty, but it's hard on the ass."

"Stop making her laugh, Hope," Swan complains, sweeping make-up remover over my eyelid and starting over.

The Victory Rolls turn out perfect, but since Swan still isn't finished, Krystal decides Hope needs more dramatic lipstick. After throwing me an I'm-only-doing-this-because-it's-your-wedding-day face, she agrees.

Since her mouth is occupied, I quiz Hope about the food. If the games were set up for the kids. Who organized a hike down to the waterfall after the ceremony.

"Trinity, chill," she says as soon as Krystal's done. Her tone stops me from spiraling into a full-on freak-out. "This is your day. Relax. I know I'm not the most organized person, but I swear it's all handled."

"I'll try. Just tell me everyone's going to be fed. That's the most important thing at a wedding."

An indulgent smile curves her bright red lips. "Grills are going now. Rock went through the checklist with the caterer. No one will go hungry."

"The food needs to be good since there's no alcohol."

"Someone needs some liquor," she grumbles.

Ignoring that, I ask where everyone's going after four when we get kicked out of the park.

"It's all taken care of," Hope answers.

I catch Swan's mouth turning down in the mirror and decide I don't care for Hope's evasive answer. Swan starts poking at me with her makeup brushes again, so I don't have a chance to question Hope further.

The longer we take, the more worried I am about Wyatt. He texted me earlier to say everything went fine with Brand. But if I know him, he's probably tense, and the guys are ragging on him, only annoying him more.

"Hope." Krystal's ready to work on my hair, so it's a good time to ask. "Will you go check on Wrath for me?"

"Me? Why?"

"Because, you'll calm him down, when the guys are probably trying to piss him off."

She snorts then thinks about it. "I think I annoy him more than anyone."

"I doubt that. Please?"

"Okay." She leans in and gives me one last hug. Swan receives a brief embrace, as well, and then Hope leaves.

"Are you really worried about Wrath?" Swan asks, dusting the last bit of powder over my cheeks.

"Trinity, I forgot my light bobby pins, I'll be right back," Krystal says, dashing out the door.

I turn my attention back to Swan. "A little."

Swan squats down in front of me and takes my hands in hers. "Can I tell you something without you thinking I'm weird?" Whatever she wants to say must be making her nervous, because her accent is much more noticeable than usual.

Curious, but unsure, I answer carefully. "It depends."

She lowers her head and blows out a breath, ruffling the ends of her hair. "I'm so happy for you. For both of you. I know it took you…a while to get here." She finally glances up and must interpret the frozen smile on my face as annoyance. "I'm sorry." She drops my hands and straightens up, grabbing the makeup bag off the counter and stuffing items inside. "I didn't mean to bring up bad stuff or make you uncomfortable."

Reaching out, I touch her arm. "Swan. It's okay. I'm not mad."

"I admire you a lot."

I'm not sure what to say to that, so I motion her closer for a hug. "Thank you," I murmur against her hair.

She pulls back. "Thank you for having me here and letting me help you out."

"I should thank *you*. You're probably the first person who pointed out how Wrath felt about me. You know, said it point blank."

Her eyes widen and she laughs. "Really? Well, I'm glad."

My nose twitches, and I refuse to cry after she spent so much time on my makeup. "So," I say, wiggling my eyebrows. "Did Dex drive you up today?"

She rolls her eyes. "Isn't it Hope's job to be nosy?"

"I'm back!" Krystal shouts, bursting into the room. Swan snickers and backs away, giving Krystal room to work.

Krystal grins as she picks my hair up. "Now, I know you said you wanted something simple, but your hair would look so pretty in this big French side braid that we can pin in the back and then have all these long loose curls that show off all the pretty blues in the ends of your hair. What do you think?

I catch myself grinning in the mirror. "Go for it."

WRATH

"OH MY GOSH! Look at you." Hope whistles and wiggles her eyebrows at me as she approaches. Oddly, her reaction lessens some of my annoyance about the stupid suit.

"Wow, I think Trinity's going to have trouble getting through the ceremony without jumping you," she says.

"Maybe I should go visit her now. She still down at the—"

She playfully pushes me back. "Don't you dare. You two have had enough bad luck this week. Besides, she's having her hair done. Shouldn't be too much longer."

My gaze roams over her again, taking in her purple pin-up dress and colorful make-up. "You look pretty."

"Aw. I think that's the first compliment you've ever given me."

"Nah. I've complimented you lots of times. Just nothing I would say to your face."

She snickers and slaps my arm. "Trinity sent me to check on you."

"She did?"

Her shoulders lift. "She was worried you'd be nervous."

"Fuck no. I *would* like to know what her dress looks like, though."

"You'll see soon enough. Now, can I hug you?" she asks as she's wrapping her arms around me and squeezing.

"You're going to mess your cute little wings up," I say, patting the rolly-curly things she has on the top of her head before hugging her back.

She backs away. "Ugh, your wife's friend talked me into this."

"No, it's cute. Like you might fly away at any moment."

"Jerk," she grumbles.

Rock catches my eye as he sneaks up behind her. She takes a step back and he grabs her around the waist, pulling her against him. "You look like my forties-housewife wet dream," he says against her neck. She squeals and laughs, while he continues to molest her in broad daylight.

"Are you two trying to make me throw up before the wedding?"

Reluctantly, Rock lets her go and throws a glare at me.

Hope looks him over, then glances at me. "Will you get mad if I want to take a picture of the two of you together?"

"Of course not," Rock answers quickly. He's wrong if he thinks I can't sit still while Hope snaps a few pictures. After the torture of getting into the suit and wearing it in public, everything else is pretty tame.

Bricks and Winter approach us next, and Hope waves them into the picture. "Looking good," he says giving me a hearty handshake. Winter reaches up to kiss my cheek and offer congratulations.

"When you two gonna start on some babies?" Bricks asks.

I catch Hope mouth the word "babies" at me and roll her eyes, which lucky for Bricks, lessens my urge to punch him in the throat.

"I don't know. Probably the same time you make on honest woman out of this lady," I answer, wrapping my arm around Winter's shoulders and smiling. Nervous laughter tumbles out of Winter, but Bricks's expression says he wants to deck me. I lift my chin at him. "Where's your brood?"

He points to the small children's playground set up near the gazebo. "This was a great spot for the wedding. Family-friendly," he says, giving me another cheeky wink.

"Trin wanted everyone comfortable," I explain.

"Caleb was smitten with Alexa. You should have seen them earlier," Winter says to Hope. Unless there's an actual baby in front of her, I've noticed Hope's not one for babbling on about kids. She smiles though. "Oh, boy. Murphy will be getting his shotgun ready," she teases.

Shrill screams erupt from the direction of the playground. "Oh, shit. Caleb." Winter takes off to pick her son up out of the sand.

"Always something," Bricks says with a smile, taking off after her.

"Why is everyone obsessed with babies?" I ask Hope.

She *pffts* at me. "Welcome to my world."

"Yeah, but you're a chick."

"And you're a good-looking guy in his prime—"

"Hey—" Rock says.

Hope ignores him and finishes her thought. "Women's ovaries start tap-dancing when they see you."

"Don't worry, old man." I slap Rock's shoulder. "You're not too far past your prime."

Rock pokes her in the side. "Are yours tap-dancing, too?"

"Nope." She leans in and whispers something in his ear that makes him start molesting her again. I tilt my head back and stare at the sky. While I enjoy making fun of them, I also appreciate having them as a distraction.

Not that I'm nervous.

Eager.

Impatient as fuck.

"Go hurry her up, Hope. I don't think I can wait much longer."

She pretends to huff about all the running back and forth, but she's smiling as she takes off to grab my wife.

"You're antsy," Rock says after she leaves.

"Can't help it. I just don't want one more thing to delay us, you know?"

His grin falters. "Brother, I will straight-up murder anyone who gets in your way today."

CHAPTER TWENTY-SIX

Teller

THE POWER-TRIPPING PARK ranger's lucky I didn't want to stain the new shirt Heidi insisted I wear to the wedding, or I would have gutted the bastard.

"Rock said you had it covered," Wrath says when I approach him.

"The guy was being an asshole. Bikes ride through here all the time."

"Thanks for handling it. I don't want anything upsetting Trinity today." He doesn't give me any meaningful look to make his point stick. Doesn't have to. After our "chat" last week, things clicked in my thick head. Trinity was never mine, and that's okay. She's not supposed to be.

"No problem." I slip the piece of paper the ranger gave me out of my pocket. "You guys did get fined though."

"What?" he snaps, tearing the paper out of my hands. "Four hundred dollars? Fucker."

I wave the cane my sister demanded I use today because of all the walking and uneven ground. "I tried using the cripple pity card, but he wasn't having it. He's probably going to write another one when we all leave."

For a second, murder shines in his eyes, then he shrugs. "Whatever. As long as he doesn't bother us now. I'll take care of it later."

"I tried paying it, but he wouldn't take cash on the spot."

"Thanks." He stares at me for a few seconds. "How you doin' today?"

I know Wrath well enough to know he's not asking about the cane in my hand, and he's definitely not asking how I feel about him marrying the girl I once thought I was in love with. No. He's asking if I've got my head on straight after murdering Ransom last night. "Brother, it's your wedding day. I don't want to talk about me."

"Magic words there, little brother. My wedding day. So you have to talk about whatever I want to talk about."

"Christ, then every day must be your wedding day."

"Fuck off. I'm serious."

I heave out a breath and force myself to come up with something acceptable to say to Wrath, besides "there's a block of ice in my chest so big I can't feel anything else" because that's how I really feel.

"Honestly?" I finally answer. "I'm fine. Slept like a baby for the first time in months. No pesky remorse." Pure truth.

He snorts and claps me on the shoulder. "Good. Glad to hear it."

One thing has bothered me. "Do you think this is finally the end of it with them?"

"Jersey swore up and down they had nothing to do with him." He lowers his voice. "No one's finding that body. I wouldn't worry about it." For a second he's silent, seems to be searching for someone. "We should keep an eye on Loco, though."

"Yeah, no shit. That was fucked up."

We're interrupted by Damon, the judge marrying Wrath and Trin today.

"How do you feel?" he asks Wrath.

"Good. Want to get started."

"That's a good sign."

I tune them out and search the grounds for Trinity. Every one of my club brothers is here. Almost everyone from Sway's club also came. The guys from Wrath's gym. Whisper and his ol' lady. Merlin, the president of the Wolf Knights MC. Stump and Chaser from the Devil Demons

MC are also here. Chaser's wife and son are with him. I recognize Dylan from the gym, and we nod to each other.

We're a rowdy, festive bunch. There's a lot of excitement in the air today. I'm sure lots of people assumed Wrath would never want any of this.

I glance at him again and have to admit he looks happier than I've ever seen him.

Love for my brother and my club chips away at some of the ice in my chest. I'm happy for him. For both of them.

"Girls are on their way," Z says, clapping Wrath on the back. "Ready? Don't chicken out now."

"Fuck, yeah, I'm ready."

Wrath's getting married. The same guy who years ago counseled me on all the reasons marriage was a raw deal and should be avoided.

I trail behind them over to the patio where the wedding's taking place.

Damon's standing with his back to the view of the surrounding valley and mountains. Everything's crisp and green and new. Perfect day for a wedding.

Hope steps into her place up front.

Rock walks Trinity to the edge of the patio where Wrath meets them. They talk for a few seconds while Rock takes his place across the aisle from his wife.

Trinity's stunning. No surprise there. More importantly, she's a brave woman who risked her life for the club last night.

Wrath's really fucking lucky.

Next to me, Heidi bounces on her toes. "Oh, her dress is so pretty! I love that shade of blue." She leans over to Murphy. "Do you care if I don't wear white?"

He answers my sister with nothing but love in his voice. "Whatever you want."

A suffocating grief fists around my throat making it hard to swallow or concentrate on anything being said.

At Rock and Hope's wedding, I had Mariella to look out for.

Now, she's gone.

She had been looking forward to Trinity's wedding. Spent a lot of time with Trin helping her pick things out.

And she's not here for any of it.

My eyes squeeze shut, and for the millionth time I wish I'd never talked her into going for that ride.

I told Wrath I wasn't bothered by ending Ransom. And that was true. I just don't feel like the fucker's death was enough. It will never be enough.

Heidi's holding her daughter, gently rocking her from side to side. Alexa's not having it. She gurgles and reaches toward me.

Heidi glances over. I have no idea if she suspects how I felt about Trinity at one time, or how much I miss Mariella, but a soft look crosses her face. "I think she wants her uncle," she whispers, handing Alexa over. Murphy reaches behind Heidi's back and gives me a brotherly pat on the shoulder.

Murphy. My best fucking friend for most of my life. Closest I've ever had to a little brother and he's settling down first.

With my sister. Still not sure how I feel about that. Most days I'm happy about it. Other days, I'm not. But I guess my opinion doesn't matter. As Wrath so helpfully pointed out, Heidi's an adult now. No longer my responsibility.

It seems like everyone has found something that keeps evading me.

Alexa yells a bunch of happy noises and wiggles around in my arms. "Shhh," I whisper to her, and she settles down.

She fits her little hand over my mouth, and I pretend to bite at her tiny fingers until she squeals, drawing everyone's attention to us. Alexa gives me the perfect excuse to step away from the wedding.

To watch it from a distance.

CHAPTER TWENTY-SEVEN

I T'S TIME.

Rock's waiting for me outside.

"Trinny, you're beautiful." If I didn't know better, I might think Rock was trying not to cry.

"Is Wrath okay?"

"He's fine. Eager to get this done."

My lips quirk. We finally made it.

Rock takes my hands, and I steel myself. "I knew you were special from the moment I met you."

"That's not true."

"Hey," he says, forcing me to look up at him. "Yes, it is. If I'd had a sister, you're everything I'd want her to be."

"Please don't make me cry, Rock."

His mouth curves into a gentle smile. "Don't cry. I'm just really, really happy he has you. Thank you for putting up with him."

"Dammit." I sniffle and swipe at my eyes at the same time Krystal walks out.

She chuckles and dabs my tears away. "Good to go, hon."

Rock steps back and holds out his arm for me.

There's no music. Just the wind blowing through tall evergreens.

It's perfect.

Wyatt meets me at the end of the aisle.

No matter how many times everyone said I look beautiful, I don't truly feel beautiful until I'm standing before Wyatt and he takes me in with widening eyes.

"I…beautiful isn't enough," he murmurs.

His words, more than anyone else's, warm me from the inside. I'm calm as he takes my hand, and I finally take all of him in.

"Oh my…" I'm so stunned I can't finish. Wrath swore up and down no suit. No tux.

Yet, here he is. In a suit.

"Wyatt." My voice comes out all breathy, but he hears me and grins.

Leaning over, he brushes his lips against my ear. "Only for you."

"Thank you."

My gaze sweeps over him again. So handsome.

With a cobalt-blue tie that somehow matches my dress.

I raise an eyebrow at Hope as Wyatt and I walk up front together.

She reaches out and squeezes my hand as I take my place. I can almost hear the *squee* of joy she's holding back, and her excitement makes me chuckle.

The wedding and words we speak are a beautiful blur.

Before I know it, Damon pronounces us man and wife, and Wyatt's lifting me up in front of everyone for a searing kiss.

There's no mistaking who I belong to.

I wrap my arms around *my husband* and hold on tight.

CHAPTER TWENTY-EIGHT

"WHERE'D TAWNY GO?" I ask Hope later in the afternoon. Instead of answering, she bites her lip. "I'm not supposed to say."

"Are you kidding? Did she and Sway leave? Because I'm totally fine with that."

We're wrapping up the party. Making sure to clean up every last scrap of paper so the park service doesn't level more fines on us.

Not that I think Wyatt cares if they do. He seems happier than ever.

Because of me.

I'm Wyatt's wife!

"Okay, don't be mad," Hope says, touching my arm. "When she heard we had to leave the park at four, she volunteered to set things up at the clubhouse, so the reception could continue up there."

"What? She did that? For me? For us? Does she have a head injury?"

"I think she feels bad."

Feels bad my ass.

But Hope's right. When we arrive at the clubhouse, the parking area and driveway around the clubhouse are blocked off by colorful streamers, forcing everyone to park farther down the driveway. Thousands of tiny white lights are strung up outside for when the sun goes down. There are tables and chairs set up outside. Someone set up a bar with plenty of alcohol and another table full of desserts.

Tawny went all out. Obviously, she and Hope planned this before today.

"Thank you, Hope," I say, touching her shoulder.

She leans over and hugs me. "I wish I could take credit, but Tawny really did arrange all of this."

Tawny approaches me slowly.

"Congratulations." I've never seen Sway's wife look hesitant before, and I'm pretty sure the last time she saw me, she called me a whore. I wasn't thrilled I had to invite the Queen Bee of our downstate charter to my wedding. But seeing this—even though I'm sure there's some ulterior motive behind it—dampens my irritation.

"You did all this? Thank you."

She flips her hair back. "I think it was the least I could do for you, Trinity."

"True." I hold her gaze for a moment, and she nods.

"The wedding was beautiful. That was a real nice spot to have it."

"Thanks. We like it up there." This is weird. And unbearably awkward. This woman's treated me like shit over the years. Now, I'm supposed to what? Be friends with her?

Wyatt stops me from having to figure it out, by slipping his arm around my waist. "Thank you for this, Tawny."

She seems surprised and stammers before disappearing into the crowd.

"Come inside with me?" he asks.

We stop and talk to a lot of people inside the clubhouse before making it into our room.

"Did you lure me back here for sex?"

He grins and tugs at his collar. "No. I love you, but this thing is killing me."

I reach up and help him undo the tie. He drapes it over my shoulders. "I think we can find a better use for it," he says with a raised eyebrow.

Next, he slips his jacket off and tosses it on the bed. Once he rolls his sleeves up, he seems more relaxed.

"Jesus," I mutter. "You're even hotter like that."

His mouth curves up, and he runs his hands over his forearms. "Can't resist these, can you?"

"Nope."

Glass-clinking and horn-blowing from outside reaches us. A lot of noise that doesn't seem to be stopping any time soon.

"I bet that's for us," I say.

"Fuckers," he grumbles. Before leading me out the door, he grabs my *Property of Wrath* vest and slips it over my shoulders. He takes a step back and picks up my left hand, nodding at my shiny new wedding ring. "They look damn good together."

"Yes, they do."

WRATH

SINCE NO ONE spoke up at the park, I thought I'd been spared any wedding speeches. *Wrong.* They were just saving them until we were back at the clubhouse.

Feeling less constricted without the tie and jacket, I tolerate the emotional abuse from my brothers a lot better than I think anyone expects.

"We all know I'd do anything for my brothers," Rock begins his speech, glancing at all of us. "That extends to anyone under the club's protection, but it's especially true about Trinny." He flashes a smile I'd call fatherly if he wouldn't punch me for it. "I wouldn't hesitate to murder anyone who threatened her."

Christ, if everyone knew how true that statement actually was.

"She's dedicated her life to the club and is someone each one of us would take a bullet for. One of the best women in the world as far as I'm concerned." He turns and faces me, a wry smile tugging the corner of his mouth up. "There's only one man worthy of her. A man perfect for her, good for her, and good *to* her."

Rock's speech seems to be designed to embarrass me into blubbering all over myself. *Fucker.*

"It wasn't an easy ride to get here. They're both proud, headstrong knuckleheads." Trinity shakes with laughter and wipes at her cheeks.

I flip Rock off, and he returns the gesture.

"But not even their multiple year-long hostile standoff could keep them apart. They're truly meant for one another."

He raises his cup and I nod at him.

Just as I think the emotional torture is over, Z jumps up. "I'm not as much of a poet as our prez." He slaps Rock on the back a few times. My body tenses. I don't think Z would ever say anything to embarrass Trinity, but he does enjoy being a wiseass. "Usually this is where we'd say 'welcome to the family, Trinity' but we don't have to, because she's already been a part of our family for a long time. Rock wasn't lyin'; we'd all take a bullet for you, Trin."

His words are short but undeniable.

Each one of my brothers shares a few words. Even Teller, who stands and raises his glass.

"Not that I know what I'm talking about, but I think the key to marriage is not to marry someone you can live *with*, but to marry the one you can't live *without*. We all know there's nothing these two wouldn't do for each other. We'd all be lucky to find the same thing." He nods at us before taking his seat. Trinity leans in and kisses my cheek. "Aw, that was sweet." A little more seriously she adds, "It's true. I can't live without you."

I wrap my arm around her shoulders and pull her close. "Same for me."

When the toasts *finally* end, Sparky stops by and wraps his arms around both of us. "I'm so fuckin' happy you guys finally made it!" he shouts into our ears.

"Thanks, brother." I toss his arm off and pull him down into the chair next to me. "Feeling good, bro?"

"The best." He takes off, pulling Willow into the clubhouse with him.

"When did *that* happen?"

Trinity shrugs, then giggles, falling against me. "How much have you had to drink?" I ask her.

"Nothing. I'm drunk on *you*."

I grab her, pulling her into my lap so I can kiss the hell out of her, which earns us a round of whistling catcalls and dirty comments.

A few minutes—or hours, who knows—later, someone slaps my shoulder. "Hey, happy couple." I glance up and find Sway leering down at us.

"'Sup?"

"Trinity, do you mind if I steal your man for a minute?" Sway asks. "I think my woman wants to have a word with you anyway," he says, tipping his head toward the drink table where Tawny's busy handing out bottles of beer and cups of whatever the hell she's mixing up back there.

Trin leans over and gives me another kiss. "Sure thing, Sway."

After she leaves, he jerks his head toward the path through the woods that leads to Rock's house. "Can we walk?"

Curious, I stand and follow him. "No offense, Sway, but you're not really who I planned to spend my wedding night with."

"Don't worry. You know you ain't my type," he jokes back.

After that we don't say much. He finally stops walking. We're far from the party but not enough that I can't hear my brothers still carrying on. Z installed solar lights along the path out to the houses, so there's enough light to see the serious expression on Sway's face.

"How long you been upstate, Wrath?"

It's a stupid question, because he knows the answer. "I'm pretty sure you were at my patch-in party." My way of telling him to cut the bullshit.

He nods and glances down the path. "You and Rock still get along?"

"Like brothers."

He huffs a laugh. "So still want to kill each other half the time?"

"Kill's a little strong." I'm antsy to get back to my bride. Still got big plans for her tonight. "What's on your mind, Sway?"

"You know the bullshit that went down with Bull."

"Yeah." No need to mention that Bull was a rat and rub Sway's nose in it. "You got a new SAA though, right?"

"Yeah, but he's got a sick mother down in Arizona, so he's talking about going nomad since we don't have a charter down there."

"That sucks."

He runs his hand over his chin for a few seconds. "We got a lot of action. Big stuff coming up. I need someone I can trust." Finally, he looks me in the eye. "I'd like to have you watching my back. You interested in moving downstate?"

I barely hold back the *fuck no* on my tongue. "I appreciate the offer, brother. I do, but I'm set here."

"Fuck." He shakes his head. "I figured it was a long shot. You sure? I know our gals haven't always gotten along, but Tawny'll behave herself."

"It's not that." Actually, it's a little bit that. I know right now what Trin's answer will be if I ask her about moving downstate.

"I can help you get set up. Start a new gym down in Orange County."

The reminder that my business is nothing more than ashes and rubble right now doesn't make me more inclined to accept Sway's offer.

"If you change your mind, call me. Rock said you'd probably say no since you just built a house and all, but I'll always have room for you."

He just had to slip in that he already asked Rock. I keep my face neutral as I hold my hand out, and we shake. "Thanks, brother."

"Congratulations. You two seem really happy together."

It's an odd observation coming from Sway since he doesn't seem to have a whole lot of respect for the female population. "We are."

The walk back to the party isn't awkward. He asks where we're going for our honeymoon and surprisingly keeps his dirty comments to himself.

Sway splits for the party, but I hang back at the edge of the woods for a second.

"Have a good chat with Sway?"

Glancing up, I find Rock grinning at me.

"Fuck you. Why didn't you warn me, dick?"

"He sprung it on me after the wedding." The laughter dies on his face. "I don't want to lose you, brother. But I don't ever want to hold you back, either. We both know you'd probably earn more downstate."

"And *you* know some things are more important than money."

He nods once. "It wouldn't be right if I didn't allow him to make the offer."

I don't think he was worried I'd accept Sway's offer, but it's still obvious how much the whole situation bothers him.

Motherfuck. Now, I can't even be pissed at Rock. No, I'm pissed that Sway put my best friend in such an awkward position on my wedding day. "You're lucky I love your ugly mug so much."

"Feeling's mutual, brother." He gives me the same weary smile from earlier, and the laughter dies in my throat. I stop him with a hand on his arm.

"Rock, no bullshit. You're not thinking of stepping down, are you?"

My worst fears beat in my chest as I wait for him to answer.

"Not yet. I'll be at the head of the table as long as you guys need me."

"You realize that's probably forever, right?"

"Feels like it." He grins to let me know he's kidding. "Come on, your beautiful bride needs you."

Trinity

WRATH STILL HASN'T returned from his talk with Sway. I'm not sure how I feel about that.

I *do* know how I feel about Tawny chatting me up again.

"So, is the house finished?" she asks.

"Almost. We'll move the rest of our stuff in when we return from our honeymoon." As much as it kills me I add, "We'll have to have you guys over for dinner when we're all settled."

"You're really okay with living up here? Around everyone else?" she asks as if it's the worst thing in the world.

"I'm used to it."

She nods vigorously, but her helmet of hair doesn't even budge, which is just weird. "You and Hope seem tight."

"We are," I answer. "She's been a friend to me since the first time we met." I'd love to add "unlike you" but I don't.

She jabs a bony elbow into my side. "He really lets her do that?" she asks out of nowhere.

"What?" I glance up, following her line of sight. Hope's standing by Murphy's table, her hand casually resting on his shoulder while she talks to him and Heidi.

"She shouldn't be touching another brother that way."

Oh, this is rich coming from her. And a complete surprise since she's always treated Hope with respect.

Before I get to say anything, Wrath joins them. Relief that he's done with his conversation with Sway washes over me. Now, how the hell do I get away from Tawny without being rude?

Hope smiles up at my husband and gives him a quick hug. Same thing she's done a million times in front of me. She says something that makes him roll his eyes and laugh.

"You really okay with her touching *your* man like that?" Tawny's low voice comes out laced with fake-sisterly concern.

I snort and then laugh out loud. "Yeah, I'm not worried about it."

"Oh." Her eyes widen, and she leans in closer. "Are the four of you, like, a thing?"

It takes a second for me to grasp her meaning. "Ew. God, no." I glance back at my husband. "Trust me, neither of them…and me and Rock? No. Nope. No way."

We're interrupted from this wildly disturbing conversation by Teller heading inside the clubhouse.

I practically yank him over to us. "Thank you for the sweet toast," I say.

His mouth lifts in a tired smile. "I meant every word." His shrewd gaze moves between Tawny and me. "How you been, Tawny?"

"Same as always. How's therapy going, sweetheart?" Tawny coos at him, coming closer to brush a lock of hair off his forehead. "You look great."

I have the sudden urge to fake-cough "hypocrite" but somehow manage to contain myself.

Teller fixes his pleading gaze on me.

I mouth a silent apology to him and back away. Before I can run from this freak show, a big warm body brushes up against me. Strong arms wrap around my waist. "Mrs. Ramsey, you're wanted in the bedroom," Wyatt whispers against my ear.

Heat streaks through me and all I want to do is be alone with my husband. Teller will have to escape Tawny's clutches on his own.

I turn and loop my arms around Wyatt's neck. "I'm all yours, husband."

CHAPTER TWENTY-NINE
WRATH

"IT'S OUR WEDDING night," Trinity purrs as I close our bedroom door.

"Fuck yeah, it is. Get changed."

"What?"

"I want to take you out."

"We just got home."

I take a few steps closer, reach for the large, crystal peacock in the center of her braids and curls and pull it loose. She melts against me, placing both her palms on my chest and staring up at me.

"Hi, husband," she whispers.

I plant a quick kiss on her lips. "Hi, wife. Come on, hurry up."

Her lips push into a pout. "I thought you said you wanted me in the bedroom?"

"Yeah. So you could get changed."

"I need your help with the zipper." She turns and picks up all the hair I just freed.

"What made you decide on this dress?" I ask, tracing the large embroidered peacock feather that stretches from her hip to the opposite shoulder of the dress.

She taps her shoulder, right where the peacock feather tattooed up her back ends. "You know I like peacocks. Some people think they're a

256

symbol of renewal or new beginnings, so I thought that was appropriate."

"It's beautiful." I place a gentle kiss on her shoulder after I work the zipper down, and she sighs.

"What's wrong, angel?" I whisper against her ear. "Need your husband to fuck you?"

"*Yes*," she answers in a frustrated voice. "I want to consummate our marriage."

I pull back, shaking with laughter. "Oh, we're going to consummate like motherfuckin' bunnies. Don't worry."

"Bunnies? Did you really just say that?" she teases, stepping out of her dress.

She bends and arches in the sexiest ways possible, until my control snaps and I tackle her onto the bed.

Triumphant giggles spill out of her, and she presses both palms against my cheeks, pulling me down to her for a kiss. "Gotcha."

"You're ruining my plans."

Her mouth turns down even as her hands go straight to my belt, helping me free my cock. Except, I can't get it in her.

"What the fuck are you wearing?" I ask sitting up and taking in the inches of sheer lace separating us.

"Well, I wanted to show you, but you're being incredibly difficult." She slips her hands over her hips and wriggles the panties down her legs, tossing them to the side.

"That's better," I growl, taking her mouth again. She lets out a breathy gasp as I push inside, throwing her head back and arching her hips up to meet mine. Her hands go to my shirt, unbuttoning it and sliding it down my arms, until I'm trapped. She giggles. "Oooh, this is like having you tied up."

"None of that, angel."

By feel alone, she unrolls my sleeves and helps me take the shirt off. Then she wraps her arms around my neck, pulling herself up for more rough kisses. She strokes one of her hands down over my cheek. "Happy wedding night."

I stop for a second, staring into her eyes. This wasn't quite what I planned, but somehow it's still perfect.

ONCE I'VE SATISFIED my wife, I toss a sweatshirt and pair of jeans at her. "Don't bother with underwear."

She screws her face into a curious pout. "I need a bra."

"Come on, hurry up." I stop and stare at her while she slips into a bra. "I can't wait to get you to Belize. Nothing but you in teeny, tiny bathing suits for an entire week."

"I'm surprised I get a bathing suit."

"Good point."

It takes a few more minutes to get her moving. Her giant braid and all the curls I freed have to be tied back, and I'm practically yanking her out the door before she finishes. We have to stop in the kitchen so I can grab a few things.

She laughs as I lead her out the side door. "Are you trying to avoid our party?"

"Fuck, yeah." I glance down at her. "What were you and Tawny talking about earlier? She give you any shit?"

"Oh, no. She couldn't have been sweeter." I don't have to see Trin's face to know she's rolling her eyes.

I lower my voice as we move down the driveway where I parked my bike earlier. "You want to know why?"

"What? Why she was civil to me? Because we're married now and she has to be?"

"Yeah. And Sway wants me to come down there and be SAA."

She stops moving so abruptly, I'm yanked back. "Ohmygod." She laughs uncontrollably for a few seconds, actually dropping my hand and doubling over.

"Trin?"

Her hands flail in the air a few times before she stands up straight. "It all makes sense now." She snickers again. "She was being all catty about Hope. Then she—" She bursts into giggles. "She asked if the four of us were a "thing.""

"Who? What thing?" A few seconds later, I get it. "Ew. Seriously?"

"That's what I said."

"Christ," I mutter.

"Oh, God, what if she was hoping we'd move down there and swing with them?"

We stop at my bike. "Thanks, Trin. I may never get it up again now."

All laughter fades, and she presses her body up against mine. "Oh, I doubt that," she says in a husky voice. Her hand brushes over my dick and proves me wrong. "See," she teases, giving me a gentle squeeze.

"Fuck. Don't distract me."

She drops her hand and takes a step back. "Where are we going?"

"You'll see."

"What's in the bag?"

"You'll see. Stop asking so many questions and get on the bike."

She grabs my shoulder and throws her leg over, hopping on behind me.

Z waves at us on our way out of the gate.

It's a cool spring evening. Perfect for what I have planned.

Ten years ago, I took her to this exact spot.

I'm pretty sure it's where I realized I was in love with her.

Just like that night so many years ago, I glide my bike into a grove of trees. Trin's quiet as she hops off.

Maybe she won't find this as romantic as I thought.

She watches while I grab the saddle bag, then takes my hand as I lead her through the woods. Fletcher Park is quiet. Empty, except for a few night critters off in the distance.

We reach the low stone wall surrounding the overlook, and I set the bag in the grass on the other side.

"Wyatt," she whispers.

There's enough moonlight for me to catch the tears glittering in her eyes.

"Why're you crying?"

"I'm not." She sniffles and swipes at her cheeks. "You…this. I can't believe…this is perfect."

"It gets better."

I spread a blanket out and drop down, pulling her into my lap. Grabbing the bag, I take out a box and hand it to her. She opens it and laughs. "Wedding cake! Thank God, I barely had any earlier."

"I know. I asked Hope to put this away for us to have later."

"That was sweet."

She's quiet, feeding me cake, and taking bites in between for herself.

"What's next?" she asks when I set the box aside.

I shift and slide her down so she's sitting between my legs. Her back is to my front, and I lean against the wall to hold us both up. "I never get tired of this view," she whispers.

My hand brushes a few strands of hair off her face. "Me either."

"Thank you. This is exactly what we needed."

I squeeze her a little tighter. "You're not having second thoughts already, are you?" I tease.

She shifts. "Never."

"This week's been crazy."

"Yes." She looks back at the view. "I needed the reminder."

"What's that?"

"How strong we are together."

"There's no more you and me. There's just *us*." I rub my cheek against hers and whisper in her ear. "And as long as we're together—we have everything."

Epilogue

A few years later...

WRATH

"GRACE! ALEXA!" TRINITY shouts from the front porch of our cabin. She has a fussy, unhappy Brittany on her hip, so it's up to me to wrangle the others.

"When are the girls going home?" I ask. I've been outnumbered all weekend and am beyond ready to send them home with their parents. "This is supposed to be our vacation cabin, not a summer camp."

"Oh, stop. You know you had fun taking Alexa and Grace fishing."

"Yeah, but it *stopped* being fun after dinner when Grace had a hissy fit and—" I jerk my chin at the squirmy bundle in Trinity's arms, "she screamed all night long."

"Poor Bit-Bit," Trinity coos, looking down at her. "I think she misses her mom. It's her first time away from Heidi." She glances up at me and grins. "You'll get your boys' day out. We're watching Chance next weekend."

Before I can grumble about *that*, the older girls race over the lawn and slam into my legs one after the other. "You two are way too big to be doing that," I teasingly scold, while ruffling their hair.

"Pick me up, Uncle Wrath," Alexa demands. She reminds me so much of Heidi at this age. I swing her up into my arms, and she plants a kiss on my nose.

"You look just like your mom did when she was little."

She beams, showing off the spot where she lost a tooth last night.

"What about me?" Grace asks. "Do I look like my Mommy?"

"Don't know what your mom looked like when she was little, squirt. Probably." She screws her face into her pre-hissy-fit pout. "But you're cute as a button," I add, which puts the brakes on the waterworks.

As soon as I set Alexa down, she races up the porch steps to check on her little sister. Grace throws her arms up in the air, so I lift her up next, and we join Trinity and the girls on the porch.

Grace and Alexa end up pulling out their coloring books. Together they sit at our feet chattering and coloring.

Trinity winks at me over Brittany's head.

"I'm going to fuck you so hard when they go." I silently mouth the words at her and point two fingers at the girls. Trinity laughs and shakes her head. I make an exaggerated hip thrust, which makes Trinity laugh even harder.

Alexa turns and studies us. "What are you doing?"

"Nothing. Whatcha coloring?"

She picks up the coloring book to show me, but we're distracted by Murphy's truck coming down the driveway. The girls jump up, ready to run down the steps, but I grab them by the backs of their shirts. "No. We don't run up to moving vehicles," Trinity scolds.

Once Murphy parks, I let the girls go and they scramble down the stairs. I follow behind them.

"So, did you finally knock her up with a boy?" I ask, nodding at Heidi.

She rolls her eyes and rubs her hand over her stomach. "That's not how biology works, Uncle Wrath. You can't get pregnant when you're already pregnant."

"If anyone could do it, he could," I answer, which makes Heidi roll her eyes again and Murphy laugh.

Brittany—I refuse to call her "Bit-Bit" like everyone else does— struggles and reaches for Heidi as soon as she sees her and lets out a screech when Heidi stops to give Alexa and Grace hugs. "I'm here, baby," she coos, finally freeing Trinity up.

Alexa runs to Murphy and wraps her arms around his legs. "Were you good?" he asks, picking her up.

She entertains him with stories of all the fish we caught but leaves out the part about not touching any worms. At my feet, Grace explodes into tears. "Where's my mommy and daddy?"

"Oh, honey. They're like half an hour behind us. They'll be here soon," Heidi explains.

I pick Grace up, and she wraps her little arms around my neck, crying and snotting all over me.

"I think she's tired," Trinity says softly to Heidi who nods. Grace ignores both of them and holds on to me tighter.

"You ready to go home, Gracie?" I ask.

"No!"

Trinity bursts out laughing.

Later, when everyone's gone home, our cabin is nice and quiet. We're still lying in front of the fireplace—where I attacked Trinity as soon as the last vehicle left our driveway and did exactly what I promised earlier.

"This is nice," she murmurs, snuggling against me.

A low noise of agreement rumbles out of my throat.

"You did have fun, right?" she asks.

"With the girls? Yeah. I always do. Why?" I glance down but can't see her face. "Is this you checking in with me?"

I feel her smile against my skin.

"Maybe."

Notes from Autumn

I feel like White Knuckles was the sweetest, yet somehow dirtiest Lost Kings MC book yet. But I loved every second. I hope you did too.

I fully expected White Knuckles would be a novella. In my brain the book would be: Dirty Sex, Burn Down Gym, Wedding.

Easy-peasy.

However, Wrath decided to punish me for burning his gym down.

I was drained after More Than Miles. After writing it and again after publishing/promoting it. I love Murphy's story so much and I'm so happy that an overwhelming number of people loved it as much as I do.

As it is, I'm already probably more emotionally attached to my books than is healthy, but Murphy's story really gutted me. I panicked and came up with ways to bring Axel back, because I felt so bad. I lamented that Heidi and Murphy weren't given enough time together on the page after they're finally together. I cursed Alexa out for fucking up my timeline.

If you follow me on social media or are part of my Facebook group, you know I've been squirrely about saying exactly what the next few books would be or who they will be about. Mostly, I didn't want to hear disappointment that there was going to be another book about Wrath and Trinity. I have a very clear idea of where the next four or five books are going and they need to happen in the order they're going to happen in. Forcing myself to write about another character won't work. I've been told over and over the reason my books don't sell better is that it's too hard to dive into a series with inter-connected books. I've been advised to write stand-alones dozens of times. Personally, I think people can comfortably come into the series at book #4 or #6 but then I'm told readers don't like to do that—*write stand alones, Autumn*. Well, that sounds fun and all, but I'm apparently not wired to write that way.

Besides, what you, my lovely readers who reach out to me, continually say, is how much you love my characters. You tell me how much you enjoy catching up with them and starting one of my books is like getting together with old friends. THAT is why I write and share my stories. Sales, obviously, are nice, but I love that you love my characters and look forward to hanging out with them.

I keep saying I'll worry about writing stand-alones in my next series. And then I sob because I don't *want* to write anything that isn't Lost Kings. I need to take this series where it wants to go.

And oh the places it's going to go!

I'm so excited about the next four books I have to remember to contain myself, so I don't give anything away.

So, back to *White Knuckles*.

After *More Than Miles*, two months sort of came and went and I hadn't made a lot of progress on *White Knuckles*—because I thought "Hey, it's going to be a simple novella: dirty sex, destruction, wedding." I had a vague outline and a few key scenes. Then I did something I don't do normally, I plotted. Physically sat down and wrote out a scene-by-scene diagram of the book. Oh, I was so proud of myself—like a toddler who just learned to pee in the potty proud. Usually I pants my way through the stories with minimal plotting and certainly nothing so formal. I enjoy allowing the characters to guide me. Now, I had a map of where I needed to go.

Wrath didn't care for that.

Even though this too was a "wedding book" I didn't want you to feel as if I just copied White Heat. Obviously some things were going to be similar, but I tried to keep it to a minimum. And I didn't want to rehash any of Wrath and Trinity's issues from Tattered or White Heat. They've both grown and changed a lot and I loved being able to show that. Much like Hope in White Heat, I knew Trinity would be strong for her man, no matter what happened. I love Trinity. People who define her by her sexual history make me shake my head. If Hope is secretly me (as has been suggested), then Trin is who I secretly want to be—a chick who shoots a guy one minute and kisses the love of her life the next.

This book became complicated because, hey, when you do something serious like burn down a building, there are consequences for that. Let's just say the first draft of White Knuckles was incomplete.

And Twitch. I do feel a little guilty, because I kind of knew back in Tattered that he wouldn't be long for this world. Sorry, Twitch.

Eventually, after some very frustrating weeks of sixteen hour days staring at my computer, the story went where it needed to go. I love Wrath and Trinity. A lot. I feel protective of them and wanted to give them a book that was worthy of their journey and how far they've come.

There's something you can't do with stand-alones.

If *Tattered on My Sleeve* was a stand-alone, you'd be left wondering "hmm, did those two ever get married?"

See what I mean about emotionally attached to my books?

Maybe you don't give a rat's ass if Wrath and Trinity ever got married, but I suspect if you're still reading this, you care a little.

I wanted to tie up loose ends with White Knuckles and as I am always fond of doing, leave some things open for future books, like "WTF is Murphy doing fighting now? Did Loco double-cross the Lost Kings? Will Teller find some peace? Did Whisper have a hand in the destruction of Furious? Is Rock thinking of stepping down? What's Sway up to? Where the hell is Lilly? WHO THE FUCK ARE GRACE AND CHANCE!?"

You know, stuff like that.

By the way, I'm not giving anything away up there. Those are questions my beta readers sent me after reading *White Knuckles*.

In case anyone is wondering, that whole pot-farm-on-a-Christmas-tree-farm is actually based on a true story. Hopefully the owners of the farm never read my books.

Never mind, I totally made the pot farm up.

2016 sucked in some ways, but was also pretty damn good in other ways. I "met" and connected with so many of you through Facebook, Twitter, Instagram and plain old email. I was lucky enough to hug readers at a few signings. In 2017, I'll be in Atlanta, Chicago, Charlotte, N.C., and Huntington, WV, I can't wait to meet you!

As some of you know, I'm usually working on about ten different projects at once. But the two I'm most committed to at the moment are, Beyond Reckless (Lost Kings MC #8) and (gasp!) a stand-alone set in the Lost Kings MC realm. Not Mara and Damon's story—those fuckers are more complicated than I thought.

We'll see which story wins. My money is on Teller, but we'll see. His story is turning out to be more complicated than I expected. Imagine that.

Thank you so much for buying my books and loving my words. I've received so many heartfelt messages telling me how my books have gotten you through a difficult time or that the struggles Rock, Hope, Wrath, Trinity, Heidi, Murphy, and the rest of the crew have been through helped you feel less alone in some way. I'm usually stunned silent when that happens and want to weep with gratitude. I'm honored. Your words humble and inspire me and I thank you for that.

Love,
Autumn

Also by Autumn

THE LOST KINGS MC SERIES
Slow Burn (Lost Kings MC #1)
Corrupting Cinderella (Lost Kings MC #2)
Three Kings, One Night (Lost Kings MC #2.5)
Strength From Loyalty (Lost Kings MC, #3)
Tattered on My Sleeve (Lost Kings MC #4)
White Heat (Lost Kings MC #5)
Between Embers (Lost Kings MC #5.5)
More Than Miles (Lost Kings MC #6)
White Knuckles (Lost Kings MC #7)

THE CATNIP & CAULDRONS SERIES
Onyx Night
Onyx Shadows
Feral Escape

Wrath's Girl

THE LOST KINGS MC SERIES

www.ingramcontent.com/pod-product-compliance
Lightning Source LLC
Chambersburg PA
CBHW070852260626
47170CB00007B/2588